VACUUM PRESSURE

The Quantum War: Book Two

Jonathan Paul Isaacs

This is a work of fiction. All of the characters, organizations, and events portrayed in this novel are either products of the author's imagination or are used fictitiously.

VACUUM PRESSURE

To Garrett, Karys, and Hudson:
May you always dream

VACUUM PRESSURE

1

"*Let go of me!*"

Chris grimaced as Annika tried to pry his arm away from her waist. Her nails scratched at the green ink of his tattoos and slipped needles of pain past the adrenaline coursing through his body. It hurt. But he had a job to do, and it didn't matter whether one of the principals was a willing participant.

"Anni, we have to leave," he said, trying to placate her anyway.

"I don't want to go!"

"There's no time."

He hauled her bodily toward the door. Annika kicked and screamed, contorted in his grasp, sobbing incoherently as her arms clawed back toward her parents' bed. It broke Chris's heart to see her in such hysteria. She was eight years old, and any child that age deserved to hold on to their innocence just a bit longer. But he didn't have a choice. He led the security detail, and he had a job to do.

"Please!" she sobbed.

Chris activated his comm as he marched toward the bedroom door. "Acid Three, Acid One. I have Daisy. Repeat, I have Daisy."

"Copy, Acid One," Finn replied. "We are moving down the south hallway—" A burst of static filled the transmission.

Somewhere in the distance, a muffled explosion rumbled through the governor's mansion. The light fixtures on the ceiling dimmed in response.

"Say again, Acid Three?" Chris said.

Intermittent words stabbed through the white noise. "… we have contact … front foyer."

"All elements, fall back to extraction two," Chris said. "Get the other principals out—"

Annika bit Chris's forearm.

He jerked in surprise and dropped her to the floor. Annika scrambled on all fours back into the room.

On the king-size bed, a figure was sitting upright and looking at them. The person who was once Jessica Hewitt, the governor's wife, Annika's mother, now turned an expressionless gaze toward the child desperately trying to reach her.

"No!" Chris yelled.

He dove for Annika, flattening her body on the ground just before she reached the bed. She let out a little grunt.

The mother didn't speak. She didn't react. But Chris could feel her presence, the cold in the air, the little golden sparks that nipped at his peripheral vision. He knew they had only a few seconds to get out. Otherwise it would be too late.

"Mommy!" Annika croaked, using what little air Chris's body weight had left in her lungs.

Desperation drove him. Barely cognizant of what he was doing, Chris scooped Governor Hewitt's little girl into his arms and rolled away from the bed. He managed to come up into a crouch with her between his arms. But when he tried to stand, his legs buckled as the golden sparks stung him from beyond the edge of sight.

Annika's body went stiff as a board. She was staring over his shoulder, her pupils constricted to tiny pinpoints.

"Don't look at her, Anni!"

The bedroom door was only a few meters away, but it might as well have been kilometers. Chris became dimly aware of his body crawling toward it. He couldn't focus on what was happening. His mind flooded with confused thoughts. Years of training and deployments moved his arms and legs toward a vague notion of cover from enemy fire.

Stay with us, a voice echoed somewhere in his skull.

Annika remained motionless in his arms, her eyes fixated on her mother.

"No. Not you. Not ... *you*," Chris grunted. He would not let this happen. Not to this little girl.

They reached the door. Despite the muffled explosions and laser fire from somewhere on the other side, Chris grabbed the latch and tugged it open. The golden sparks began to roar at him in such a torrent that their noise completely overwhelmed the fray of combat just down the corridor. The voice in his skull dropped its beckoning invitation and transformed into a cascade of fury. Chris's stomach churned. It was all he could do not to vomit.

Chris tossed Annika into the hall and she collapsed on the floor. Then, with his last shred of control, he lifted his hand through the hurricane of sparks. It felt like they were shredding him to pieces. His consciousness began to slide away, delaminating like a piece of plastic left too long in the sun. Such was the price for refusing capitulation.

His fingers closed on the latch. The last thing he saw was the unearthly shape of Annika's mother, standing in front of the bed, her pinprick eyes boring into him.

2

Chris's eyes snapped open.

Gone were the memories of the governor's mansion. The distant gunfire and harsh voices faded even more quickly than the coup. Now all Chris saw was the cold and gray underside of the bunk above him. The tinge of plastic from a spacecraft's atmospheric processor replaced the ozone scent of laser blasts.

Something pulled his foot. Chris lifted his head and saw a small silhouette standing at the end of his bunk.

"Annika?"

He propped himself up on his elbows. He was covered in sweat and wiped some of it from his eyes. The grogginess of waking up still enveloped him, and the dim lighting in the berth made it difficult to see. But the figure standing at the end of his bunk had to be the girl he'd fought so dearly to keep safe.

Two small hands tugged on his foot again.

"How did you get in here? Why aren't you in your quarters?"

She shook her head and pulled some more.

Chris frowned. *Chalk up the nightmares to the painkillers.* The ship's physician, Dr. Kenta, had given him a boatload for the arm he had broken weeks ago on Juliet. Without them, the cellular stimulants repairing the bone were making him battier than a rat chewing through a supply bin. So much for being a tough guy. A career in the Marines hadn't made him impervious to modern medicine.

Looking at Anni, he knew he didn't have a monopoly on bad dreams. To lose both parents in a single day, one to constriction, the other to murder? Such trauma would be a lot for anyone to bear, let alone a little girl. He also didn't need to understand the psychological mechanisms behind someone turning mute. Chris just accepted it. In fact, he almost envied her. What he would give to have a full night's sleep, not consumed by his own screams.

But now they were aboard a troop carrier belonging to RESIT, the Remote Environment Search and Interdiction Teams, charged with patrolling deep space shipping lanes and filled to the brim with troopers and rescue equipment. Chris couldn't think of a more secure place in the Alpha Centauri A.

He leaned toward the little silhouette hovering at the foot of his bunk. "Go back to bed."

She slapped his foot in frustration.

Chris sighed. She wasn't going to go away, was she? He swung his legs out and stood up. The deck felt cold against his bare feet. The three other bunks in his berth lay empty, their folding curtains secured against the constant acceleration of *Vigorous*.

Annika moved quickly to the oblong hatch and waved her hand for him to follow.

"Seriously?" Chris asked.

The look she gave him was impressive for a preteen.

"Fine, fine." His voice sounded groggy even to his own ears. Anxious seconds ticked away while Chris located his borrowed RESIT utilities. He was thickly built, and the spacer clothing had proven to be too tight around his chest. Leaving the upper part unzipped wasn't regulation, but at least he wouldn't be wandering the corridors in his underwear. "Now what?"

Annika didn't wait. She darted down the corridor, and Chris found himself hard-pressed to match the pace. He turned a corner and immediately kicked an environmental technician squatting in front of a disassembled maintenance panel.

Chris fell face-forward over the man's back. As he went down, he clutched at the blue uniform and pulled them both to the deck. A splayed hand sent a ventilation cover skittering down the corridor.

The technician didn't say a word. Instead, his gaze followed the piece of molded metal with the intensity of someone who knew what it meant to lose parts on a spacecraft.

"Sorry," Chris said.

Chris pushed up and gave the tech a pat on the shoulder before continuing his jog down the corridor. Annika was up ahead, rushing past the closed hatches of the trooper berths. She seemed to know where she was going. Chris had to hurry to keep up. It took him a moment to remember that the trooper platoons didn't keep a 24-7 rotation like the ship's crew. They were asleep, just like he had been.

Annika slipped down a wide staircase that emptied into a sizeable landing outside two powered blast doors. The trooper armory.

"You aren't allowed in there," Chris said.

She turned around, seemingly annoyed at the challenge.

Chris felt the dampness on his back. He was breathing hard from the exertion. This wasn't funny anymore. He pointed at the orange border around the armory entry, the heavy door sitting open in its track.

"That's the armory. They keep guns and spacesuits in there. Not a place for little kids."

Annika pointed at the blast door, insistent.

Chris thought back to when they had ridden the catapult into orbit. That look on Annika's face when they slipped into zero gee? Priceless. And in truth, he was happy that their journey into space had been so much of a novelty for her. Not being hunted as fugitives had been rehabilitating, to say the least. But an after-hours scavenger hunt right now wasn't something he cared to fit into an exhausting schedule, especially since he'd been forcibly attached to Wyatt's RESIT platoon.

"I'm sorry, Anni, no tours tonight. This isn't the time." He stifled another yawn. "Let's get you back to bed."

She glanced over her shoulder at the armory. Chris saw tears running down her cheeks.

Is she crying? What the hell?

"Come on, girl," he said, sounding like an exhausted parent. "Tomorrow. If you really want to see all the gear that badly, I'll ask Wyatt for clearance. But *tomorrow*."

Chris blinked at a sudden insight from his own words.

You needed clearance to go into a secure area.

The armory was secure, which meant access remained closed and under guard.

Where was the guard?

His senses struggled to shift into high gear through the fog of the newly awake. An armed trooper should be on duty at each entrance. Yet no one stood by to cover this one, and the heavy motorized hatch sat in a quarter-open position. Had the guard gone inside?

Annika was trembling.

Something was wrong.

Part of him thought about sounding an alert. He could just dash back to the troop quarters and wake up Laramie, or maybe Kenny and Rash. But was that really necessary? To whip everybody up when he had no idea what it might all be about?

Military operations needed attentiveness, but they didn't need drama. If the guard just made a bad judgment call to go take a leak, there were other, more appropriate avenues for correction.

He'd go look first.

"Wait here," he said.

Chris slipped past heavy doors that seemed as if they could crush a Javelin into a frisbee. A heavy bulkhead ran parallel to the entrance and formed a lateral corridor that obscured the personnel staging bay beyond. He moved to the right. A motion sensor tripped a nearby light into full brightness and forced him to shield his eyes as if standing in a windstorm of jet wash.

The air betrayed no sign of activity save the ambient noise of the environmental system. Chris reached the end of the bulkhead and peeked around the corner. Another floodlight clicked on and illuminated rows of personal lockers the troopers used to trade shipboard attire for their operational gear.

A guard was lying on the deck near the lockers. He was on his knees, his forehead pressed against the deck as if praying. It was a pose Chris knew all too well from the pandemic on Juliet.

The blood drained from his face.

His eyes drifted to the Vector that lay on the deck next to the trooper.

Chris took careful steps along the wall until he was within arm's length of the prone guard. The tether that kept the weapon from inadvertently floating away in microgravity stretched out from the trooper's ARC vest. The trooper must have fallen quickly for his Vector to sprawl away from his body.

He bent over. The hair on his neck stood on end as he reached forward. Then, in one delicate motion, Chris squeezed the sides of the small buckle and released it from the strap. The *click* echoed hollowly against the hull.

No response from the guard.

Chris slid the Vector away and picked it up from the deck. The prone trooper didn't seem to notice. He just lay there, inert, the process of constriction eating away at his mind. Chris wondered what his name was, whether he had any family, where was home. All that would be gone, now and forever.

With a start, he realized he was already pointing the Vector at the trooper's head.

No, no. There was time before this guy became hostile. Chris would need to alert security. But first he had to find who did this to him. If another constricted was onboard, hunting, he had to eliminate the threat. *Now.*

The lockers in the personnel staging bay stretched in a long row perpendicular to the entry bulkhead, with a bench on either side. Everything looked closed and secured. Chris stepped with care along the compartment, past the Closed Oxygen Rebreather or CORE helmets in their recharging stations, past hardsuit lockers, until he was pressed against a row of storage compartments mounted on the far bulkhead. At his feet, a wide ship's ladder descended through the hatch to the adjoining vehicle hangar.

He glanced over his shoulder, checking his six. Annika stood in the corner back near the entry. Her face reflected the fear that Chris felt inside.

"Get Wyatt," he whispered.

Annika nodded and disappeared.

Vector up, safety off, Chris swung through the hatch.

The hangar was far larger than the berth for the troopers to gear up, and provided space for everything from simulated virtual reality rehearsals to the obvious servicing of the heavy equipment. Behind him, small arms lockers and the armorer's workstation lined the walls behind black-and-yellow floor tape. The Javelins themselves occupied most of the floorspace as they sat clamped to the deck and waited patiently for the next operation. In between were the powered equipment stations. A row of cubbies held the BHEASTs, the half-drone, half-hardsuit heavy assault suits used for storming prepared defensive positions.

Three of the Belkin suits were popped open and waiting for their troopers to crawl inside. One was missing.

A metal clatter echoed from the other side of the bay.

Chris scanned the area over a wobbling Vector that his healing forearm struggled to hold steady. He had already spent way too many hours crawling around this space, usually while wearing a CORE helmet that fed fictitious, computer-created rehearsals of close quarters battle. This was just another one of those, he told himself. He had this.

He moved around the recharging cubbies. In the center of the hangar, equidistant from the four Javelins, he spied a stout, bulky shape huddled in the middle of the floor. It looked to be crouching over something, with a flickering white light silhouetting it against the enveloping darkness. Welding. Or maybe cutting.

What the hell? Does this guy have any clue of the danger he's in?

Chris approached the figure, relaxing his Vector slightly. "Hey, pal."

The white flickering stopped. Only an amorphous afterglow remained in his vision as darkness enveloped the figure.

A slight panic filled him at being suddenly blind. Chris fumbled along the side of the Vector until his thumb found the switch to the tactical flashlight mounted along the body. He switched it on.

The figure reappeared, closing on him inside a narrow beam of light. A BHEAST suit with no helmet, holding a heavy laser cutter.

"Izzy, what are you—?"

Too late, Chris saw the pinprick pupils. Then a beam of searing heat touched his shoulder and he went flying through the darkness.

3

Laramie McCoy jumped when the alarm system blared. *"General quarters, general quarters. All hands, man your duty stations. This is not a drill. I repeat, this is not a drill."*

Again? she thought. They'd been calling the crew to GQ a lot, but each time had proven to be nothing.

She tapped save on her tablet and stood from the small couch that served as the squad's common area. She felt tired and irritable. The last time she had looked in the mirror, she still had the same blue eyes, the same dirty blonde hair down to her chin, but the rest of her face had been barely recognizable. Haggard. Too many nights of staying up late, worrying, pacing, and fighting unwanted runaway thoughts. Sleep wasn't coming to her as easily as it once had. Before Juliet. Before Firebreak.

Drafting mail packets had allowed her a small mental reprieve. With a comms blackout, there was no way she could reach out to her family, but the simple act of composing mundane correspondence, even if one-sided, seemed to force everything back into some kind of normalcy. *Where are you, Mom and Dad? Have you heard from Jessamy? The boys? Is anyone acting strangely?* She had channeled her flood of questions into a series of letters that would never see the light of day. In a weird way, they didn't need to. It helped get the noise out of her head and free her to focus on leading her team. It compartmentalized.

But now her bubble was gone, invaded by a klaxon that screamed urgency across the interior. All around her, the enlisted berth came alive, tearing away her privacy, collapsing her solitude, as troopers stirred from slumber like wasps defending their nest. Laramie stomped toward her bunk, trying in desperation to tie off the last thoughts left half-finished on her tablet.

Mom and Dad are fine. They live in the middle of the country. My brothers still work the range. And if any community can fend for itself, it's West Hadensville.

The memory of another independent ranch called Parrell intruded on her mantra. Bile rose in her throat.

She wanted so badly to know what was going on down there.

Are you safe, Mom?

Anger became the salve against fear. Laramie yanked open the drawer underneath her bunk and shoved her tablet inside. Her pressure sleeve felt no mercy as she jerked it from the equipment locker and pulled it over a muscular frame that was the byproduct of growing up in the heavy gravity of Juliet. The hustling troopers that made up her squad—veterans and boots, replacements and old friends—she would make each of them toe the line to the letter. Sloppiness cost lives. There would be no lives lost today.

"Battle Squad, let's go, people!" she barked. "Sleeves on, ARC vests on, helmets at the ready. Thirty seconds!"

She saw Carlos emerge from the head. The trooper ambled awkwardly toward his bunk, wincing as he reached for the pressure suit that would protect him from hard vacuum.

"Your mama need to get you dressed, Carlos?" Laramie growled, her voice sharp.

"No, ma'am. I got it."

She immediately regretted her tone. The pain in her friend's face betrayed the broken ribs he'd received in Venice. Reconstructive drugs might stimulate new bone growth, but the psychological effects from such a beating would be with him far longer.

She had to keep things moving. Now was not the time to show compassion.

"Twenty seconds," she yelled to the room. "Come on, guys, you're too slow!"

Laramie pulled on the rest of her primary equipment set. Over her pressure sleeve went her Ablative Resin Carrier, her ARC vest, that held an array of gel pucks that would protect her from laser fire. Her Closed Oxygen Rebreather helmet would let her breathe in vacuum and stay in communication with her platoon. Both were mandatory for general quarters, where potential combat might place *Vigorous* in danger of a hull breach, or worse.

The last buckle snapped closed on her vest before Laramie had enough of watching Carlos's valiant failure. She looped her arm under his armpit to support his weight so that he could wrestle with his boots.

More troopers formed up on the white line that ran down the middle of the berth. At thirty seconds, Laramie realized that Corporal Isi Watanabe was missing. Fury boiled over with such force that she struggled to make words come out of her mouth.

"Where is Izzy?"

Various don't knows and not sures batted about.

Apoplectic, Laramie forced herself to breathe. Izzy wasn't authorized to be *anywhere* but the enlisted berth during sleep shift. This was a major breach of protocol. When she found him, she was going to kick his ass so hard he'd have to lie prone in order to sit down. She was going to make him terrified to get in his bunk without someone to spoon with. She would PT him so hard that he'd be vomiting dinner in zero gee for a week. She would ...

Forty seconds. Wyatt would be waiting for them in the staging bay, wondering where the hell his team was. Laramie had to focus on the rest of the squad. She forcibly relaxed her fists and felt the fingernails extract from her palms.

At the fifty-second mark, deathly too long for anything Laramie had ever run, she ordered the squad to follow her into the corridor.

They marched double time, quickly but with the discipline required to prevent pandemonium, past flashing red lights and intermittent audio alerts until they descended the crew stairs leading to the armory on the next deck. But instead of finding a wide-open hatch, Laramie saw the blast door sealed tight. Troopers from Chemo Squad crowded together on the landing and prevented Battle from proceeding forward.

Laramie didn't break stride. She elbowed troopers out of the way until she reached the hatch. Once there, she saw that two maintenance techs had removed a panel next to the controls and were attaching some kind of diagnostic device to the exposed wires.

"Open the door," she said.

The older tech didn't even give her a glance. "That's what we're working on, ma'am."

"Do it faster."

"I'll take a note of that, ma'am." The tech's eyes stared into space, his pupils vibrating as the diagnostic reader sent its findings directly to his neural stub.

With no access to the armory, the crush of troopers behind them pressed forward. Laramie shouted at everyone to step back. At least the weight of gravity remained constant as they stood in the landing. If *Vigorous* was about to perform combat maneuvers, the changes in orientation would slosh them all over the place while they waited here, helpless.

Staff Sergeant Charles Washington, her counterpart in Chemo Squad, brushed past the trooper between them and grabbed her elbow. He had his CORE helmet on and stared at her through an eyeless faceplate.

"Laramie, you been on the platoon channel?"

"No—not yet. What's the news?"

The noncom dropped his head for a moment as he listened to something. Then he jerked his head toward the armory. "The problem's in there."

"Huh?"

"They called GQ because of something in there," Charles said. His words were slow, careful. "Something about gunfire and structural damage."

She did a double take. "What?"

"That's what they're saying."

"The armory and the bridge are the two most secure locations onboard," she said.

"I know."

This didn't make any sense. Laramie pulled on her own helmet and activated the comm. She needed to listen firsthand to whatever it was that Charles thought he heard. His conclusion simply couldn't be correct.

The next few moments left her head spinning to the point that she didn't even notice the crush of troopers around her.

Captain Chappelle, her platoon leader, was having a terse conversation with someone on the bridge about security cameras. The armory guards on duty were unconscious or dead. Corporal Watanabe had donned a BHEAST suit and was cutting up the deck. And two of the evacuees from Juliet were lying motionless between the arms lockers.

A Marine and a little girl.

What the hell was going on?

Laramie ripped her helmet back off and grabbed the maintenance tech by the collar. "We've got to get in there *now*," she said.

The technician forced off her grip and threw her a look that made it clear he didn't appreciate an intrusion into his zone of responsibility. "The power's cut to the hatch. We have to override the lock so we can manually slide it open."

"How long will that take?"

"Maybe ten minutes."

"What?" Laramie felt her hands balling into fists again. "Why so long?"

"We've got to wire up a different way to control the latch. The person inside went out of their way to damage the primary circuit." His eyes narrowed. "The *trooper* inside."

She wanted to kick him. Troopers and crew didn't always get along, but that was a hell of a thing to say.

Charles moved next to them with a more impartial attitude. "Can we cut it open?"

"No. It's a hardened door. It would take longer than what we're doing."

"We can breach it with a charge?" Laramie asked.

"*No*. It's a hardened door."

It took all Laramie had to control herself. She wanted to smash someone's face. Anyone. The idea of one of *her* troopers going off the rails? Assaulting others, possibly murder? She couldn't even find the words for the retribution she would deliver. Izzy wouldn't even make it to the brig.

And he might have killed Chris.

Charles grabbed her elbow again. "Laramie."

"What?" she snapped.

His dark eyes had a look that made her afraid.

"They're going to vent the compartment."

4

First Lieutenant Wyatt Wills tried to ignore the intermittent blast of the alarm as he hurried through the corridors. He had to focus on where he was going before he got lost.

In his six years of active duty, he had never actually been to the bridge before. There had never been reason to. A platoon trooper spent most of his time boarding spacecraft—performing inspections, making repairs, or even managing evacuations. And when they were groundside, it usually meant direct action against insurgent groups that had risen from the flotsam of off-world expansion. Wyatt's role as a squad leader didn't really provide him much opportunity to mix with the crew that drove the spacecraft.

But he'd received the order to report to the command deck immediately after general quarters sounded. God only knew how those two things might be related. Maybe they'd finally reacquired *Razor's* location in the inky blackness. He would love a front-row seat for that show.

Wyatt shook off his fantasy and climbed up a ship's ladder toward the bow. One of the steps sent an errant nerve pulse through his artificial leg, a zinger through a funny bone that didn't actually exist.

Jeez, not again. Ever since that crash so many months ago, his embedded prosthetic just hadn't worked right. He'd have to get Dr. Kenta to adjust the electrical feeds yet again.

A fake leg at twenty-eight. Wyatt let out a mirthless chuckle. He would never forget the night of that raid on Tiamat. Anti-air had taken down their Javelin and killed everyone else aboard. It had almost killed him, too. But Laramie, tough as nails, had hauled him out of the wreckage under fire and gotten them to safety. And all it had cost him was one leg.

He reached the top of the ladder and saw a bold red stripe painted on the access corridor wall. The stripe soon led him to a powered hatch flanked by two guards. Wyatt noted each of them had a Vector at low ready.

"Lieutenant Wills reporting to the bridge," he said. "I have orders to see Major Beck."

One of the guards stared at him through his CORE helmet camera. A moment later he nodded. "He's cleared."

The second trooper gave him a quick pat-down. When he confirmed Wyatt didn't have any weapons, he used an access card to open the hatch and jerked his head to motion him through.

He stepped over the threshold into a short, narrow corridor. The yellow pulse of the alert strobe faded behind him as the first hatch motored shut. A moment later, the other end of the corridor opened into the tight quarters of the command deck of the troop carrier.

"Over here, Lieutenant," a voice said.

Major Beck waved him over to the side. To his left, a young woman huddled over a control console in front of a holo monitor. Another woman in a plain, steel-blue tunic with bright orange piping stood next to the major. She had her back to Wyatt.

"Sir, Lieutenant Wills reporting as ordered," Wyatt said, stopping next to the huddle.

The woman with the orange piping turned toward him. She had brown hair pulled into a regulation bun that framed a thin face filled with sharp features. A pair of blue eyes nailed him with their intensity. "What the hell did you bring on my ship, Lieutenant?"

Wyatt blinked. "Ma'am? I don't understand—"

It took a moment to realize this was the skipper of *Vigorous*. Beck might lead the RESIT troopers, but Captain Kate Kazimira held overall responsibility for the missions themselves. Wyatt felt himself withering under the gaze of the most senior crew officer on the bridge.

Beck seemed not to notice Wyatt's discomfort. The major just turned his eyes back to the monitor and spoke to the young woman between them. "Marley, replay the feed from frame three-six-six for the lieutenant."

Wyatt moved over to Beck to satisfy a sudden spontaneous need for protection. On the holo monitor, security camera footage showed a downward-looking view of a row of personal lockers and some benches. He recognized it as the staging area of the troop carrier's armory. Two RESIT troopers were standing near a corner, facing each other as if in quiet conversation.

"Do you recognize that trooper on the right?" Beck asked.

Wyatt squinted, then frowned. "Is that Corpsman Watanabe?"

"Yes. Keep watching."

Something wasn't right. Based on the timestamp at the top of the screen, this happened about fifteen minutes ago. Izzy should have been asleep in the enlisted berth. The docs had cleared him for active duty, and that meant adherence to the tight schedule maintained by all RESIT platoons. What was he doing in the armory?

Izzy took several steps back from the other man. Wyatt's curiosity turned to horror as the trooper slowly knelt down and placed his forehead on the deck.

"Oh my God."

Beck didn't turn from the monitor. "You know what this is?"

"Yes, sir." Wyatt's voice sounded detached to his own ears. "Constriction."

"Recommendations on how to respond?"

His thoughts were already running away from him. *Izzy. How?* Jack Bell said constriction took weeks to infect its host. Elton had even showed him video footage of one of his staffers during the incubation phase of the strange, debilitating disease. None of that had happened to Izzy. True, he'd been in a coma after they were attacked, but he'd seemed fine afterward. Well, not exactly fine. Shell-shocked. But functional, and more importantly, without any of the symptoms or patterns Wyatt had been led to believe would indicate the presence of an infection that seemingly turned people into zombies.

Yet here he was, watching it in the security footage from the armory. Izzy had stared at another trooper and sent him to his knees.

"Recommendations?" Beck prodded again.

God help me.

"Shoot him," Wyatt said.

Beck turned his head and gave him a hard look. "Those are our troopers in there, Lieutenant. You better start providing acceptable input."

"Let me clarify, sir. You've got two constricted in there. The corpsman is active. The other trooper ... well, if he's face-down like that, he's likely infected, too. According to Doctor Bell, they're goners. We can't save them. And if we try to subdue them, whoever we send in could get infected themselves, or have their brains burned to a crisp." He fought a shudder as he recalled fleeing through the streets of Parrell, the infected colonists watching him from the windows, the visions of ghostly sparks bringing waves of debilitating suffering, "There's no other alternative, Major. Someone needs to shoot them from as far away as possible. Both of them."

A tense silence hung over the holo monitor's audience. Wyatt felt a trickle of sweat drip underneath his shirt.

"Marley," Beck said, "replay the segment we were watching right before the lieutenant joined us."

Wyatt glanced over the technician's shoulder. The holo image momentarily danced forward until it reached a new point in the timeline. It took a moment before he realized he was looking at a view from a different camera.

Izzy appeared to have donned a heavy power suit and was hunched down in the middle of the staging bay. The dark shapes of open Javelin cargo ramps jutted from the blackness just ten meters beyond. To Izzy's sides, loose deck plates lay strewn about, exposing the rounded edges of pipes and conduit underneath. A white light flashed sporadically in front of him.

Now a third person holding a Vector edged his way around a corner. Chris.

"Jesus."

The Marine held his Vector ready. But a noise must have betrayed his approach, because Izzy stood up and turned around. A barely visible laser wavered behind a jet of compressed air from the laser cutter in the BHEAST suit's hands.

Time seemed to slow to a crawl. Wyatt's eyes remained glued to the holo monitor as Chris fell backward and scrambled around the corner. Izzy followed, waving lethal light around as if spraying a water hose. The corpsman released the trigger and lumbered forward in pursuit.

"That's impossible," Wyatt whispered.

Beck's voice broke through the silence, a distant breaker crashing against the shore. "What's impossible?"

"He's using a weapon. Constricted don't use weapons."

He didn't understand how this could be happening. He had seen constricted up close, their eyes blazing into him. You could *feel* their intent. They wanted to spread the disease. They wanted you to succumb. He had been there, in Parrell and at the spaceport. There was no point in an infected person picking up a weapon. It just didn't fit.

But that was small consolation as the corpsman moved up to blast a lethal hole into Wyatt's friend.

Chris looked injured. The Marine crawled on his elbows and left the destroyed remnants of his weapon wallowing in a cloud of smoke. The laser cutter beam must have hit the weapon as well as flesh. But Wyatt could still see the determination in Chris's face, the supreme effort that came with discipline and the will to survive. He was dragging himself toward the bays holding the power suits.

Izzy crossed the threshold behind him. The RESIT trooper raised the laser cutter and pointed it at the man desperately trying to get away.

Wyatt wanted to yell at the monitor. He wanted to grab a weapon. He wanted to rush in and punch that constricted son of a bitch corpsman right in the face. Anything, *anything* to help. Then the cold realization gripped him that all of this had already happened, and his body shivered with chills as if he were fighting the flu.

A small shape darted into the scene. A little girl was throwing herself in front of Chris's prone body.

What?

The next few moments didn't make sense. Wyatt's anger shifted to puzzlement as he realized it was Annika who was covering the Marine. She rolled over at the last second to face the corpsman aiming at her, a cub protecting its lion.

The girl and the Izzy stared at each other as the laser cutter locked on her.

Then nothing happened.

"What's going on?" Wyatt asked, confused. "Did you pause the recording?"

Beck cleared his throat. "No. It's still rolling. This is why I called for you. Can you explain what's going on here?"

Wyatt studied the bizarre standoff. Annika was having some kind of stare-down with Izzy. But instead of staring back, Izzy's eyes swept back and forth over the compartment. It was as if he was searching for something he couldn't find.

The lingering moment seemed to last forever. Then Izzy turned around and staggered awkwardly in his BHEAST suit back toward the hangar.

"Well?" Beck repeated.

All Wyatt could do was shake his head. "I—I don't know, sir. I don't understand this at all."

"Do you still recommend I shoot everyone inside?"

Wyatt swallowed hard. He couldn't think of a more horrible situation. In his head, the hard edge of a RESIT trooper complained that it didn't matter who Annika was, or whether Chris was a good person who deserved better. *Vigorous* had an entire company aboard. They couldn't risk spreading the infection.

In the monitor, Chris stared at Annika. He seemed just as confused as the rest of them. Then he tried to move, and his face contorted in agony.

There was only one course of action that Wyatt could come up with.

"Sir, the master sergeant and the girl need help. Send me in. I volunteer to get them out."

"Admirable," Beck said. "Unfortunately, that's not going to happen."

"Sir, I know what I just said before. I understand the danger. That's why I should be the one to go in—"

"Corpsman Watanabe locked down the armory right after this altercation. We don't have access."

Wyatt blinked. "He locked the armory?"

The view of the holo monitor changed again. Izzy was once again hunched over open deck plates, and the flickering white flash illuminated the area in front of him.

"What's he doing?" Wyatt said, barely aware of the words leaving his lips.

"He's exposed the main power conduit that feeds the Javelins," Captain Kazimira said. She stepped next to Wyatt and stared at the holo monitor with him. "It runs straight to the reactor room."

"Why would he do that?"

Kazimira turned her head. She was a good deal shorter than Wyatt, but the look she threw his way made him shiver again.

"Sabotage. That would be my guess."

5

Chris sat in the hyper-awareness of someone about to die.

He remembered the bluish gleam in the laser cutter nozzle. The hiss of the compressed air leaking from the hose regulator. Normally both converged to melt a hole and blow the metal slag free. Izzy held the tool just a meter away from Chris's head.

That should have been the end. The universe was ready to roll forward as it always did, only it would be short one Marine.

And then Annika was there.

Izzy didn't pull the trigger. The infected trooper stared right at them but somehow his gaze was wrong, his focal point set on something far over Chris's shoulder. Then his pinprick eyes wandered across the rows of lockers nearby, and he abruptly left as if he'd suddenly forgotten what he was looking for.

Chris allowed a shallow sip of oxygen to replace his lack of breathing.

His attention tracked down to the little girl with her back to his chest. Whatever had just happened, he needed to get Anni to safety. Understanding could come later. He clutched her arm to push her up, and as he met her gaze, he saw how her irises had swelled over almost the entirety of pupils.

Pinpricks.

Horror flooded his entire being. *No. Please, not you.* Not after everything they had just been through. He had tried so hard to bring her to safety. They had come such a long way. An eruption of emotion overtook him, his mind screaming profanity at a God he didn't believe in.

Annika began to pull away, her constricted pupils remaining locked with his. Chris waited for the flood of sparks to dig into his vision. This time, there was no point in resisting. He would just slip into nothingness as unseen voices carried him to rapture.

But they didn't come. And instead of the blank expression of the infected, Anni's face held the revulsion of someone coming to grips with what had just happened. She shrank further away until her back came up against an ordnance elevator housing protruding from the deck.

A loud *clank* echoed from the other side of the BHEAST suit bays. A metal panel falling to the deck?

Chris was shaking uncontrollably. He forced himself to take a series of steadying breaths, his eyes locked all the while on Annika just a couple meters away. Maybe he could get to her if he tried to sit up. He started to shift his bodyweight and an avalanche of fire swept over him. His hip and torso throbbed with an unnatural rhythm his brain knew meant a traumatic injury. Very carefully, he slid his hand down his side until it brushed against something furry and shredded.

Then there was some kind of crust. His fingertips inadvertently dipped into the wet gash on the other side and the world was spinning...

The hangar ceiling came into focus. Had he passed out? Shallow gasps of air filled his ears as he fought to breathe.

Another *clank*.

The noise. Izzy was up to something. Back to cutting up the deck?

No, wait. That couldn't be.

Izzy was constricted. Constricted people didn't use tools. They didn't wear equipment. Their only weapon was a stare that sent you into oblivion.

Chris turned his head and saw Anni huddled in the shadows. She clutched her knees and stared blankly at the deck in front of another bay holding a powered suit.

How did you stop him, Anni?

But Izzy wasn't stopped. He was acting with purpose, cutting holes in the armory deck. And something told Chris they were running out of time.

More carefully this time, he prodded the wound in his side. He wasn't sure he could stand, let alone walk or run or rush Izzy from behind. His Vector lay strewn about in pieces, so he wasn't going to shoot him. And all the other personal weapons were stowed securely in the small arms lockers.

Chris glanced again at Annika and his eyes slid toward the powered suit next to her. It sat in its recharging bay, the front access panel popped open as it waited for its operator.

Maybe.

Teeth clenching, arms buckling, Chris tried to get up on his hands and knees. A searing pain exploded inside of him. He collapsed in an ungraceful heap and his face planted hard against the deck. When he looked up through the pool of black specks, the assault suit might as well have been a kilometer away.

He took a moment to compose himself. Chris pulled up just enough to lift his elbow and extend it forward. The wave of fire came back, but he found that this time he could take the pain. He dragged himself forward maybe a quarter of a meter. That seemed to work. Chris repeated the motion, taking his time, moving his good arm and dragging his lower body behind him like some kind of maimed walrus. Sweat stung his eyes as unbidden groans came from somewhere inside his body. With all the hurt, it seemed odd to think that he was lucky. He wasn't trying to do this on the arm that he had broken just a couple weeks ago.

Somewhere in the distance, the scrape of metal on metal dragged through the hangar. Izzy seemed to be done cutting. He was moving things now.

Get to the suit.

Elbow and drag. Elbow and drag.

The Belkin Heavy Assault Suit loomed over him, impassive and resolute. It had been ages since Chris had seen one up close. Two massive and powerful legs supported an imposing torso covered in ceramic armor. More plating covered the arms and shoulders. An odd, rusty-red camouflage pattern used on the exterior paint reminded Chris of time spent on Mars, although presumably this suit was configured for somewhere in the Proxima system. The entire rig stood nestled in a recessed bulkhead, held in place by recharging couplings and maintenance clamps.

The barrel-shaped plate on the front lay open, hinged downward at the waist. Chris dragged himself toward the base and grabbed at the belt line. This was going to be the part that hurt like a mother.

Agony.

His body seemed to weigh a ton. His arms wobbled. It took everything he could to pull his knees forward and get them under him. He thought he might be able to stand if he just worked a little more. But the suit shifted, and in a momentary panic Chris eased off lest it pull free of its power coupling and topple over him.

His body slid downward against the access plate. Chris held on, shaking, fighting to regain his breath. A pang of fear washed through him. He thought he might be able to stand, but there was no freaking way he would be able to board this suit.

Even if he could, what if it wasn't enough?

All he knew was he had to try. For Anni.

***

Annika had never felt so tired in her life.

She slumped against a locker and fought to keep her eyelids open. Every couple of seconds, she would jerk her head upward and realize she'd been dozing. Her arms and legs seemed like they were weighted down against her body. It was all she could do to not give in and just go to sleep, right then and there, against the grippy, rubbery squares that covered the floor all around her.

A horrendous crash nearby jostled her back to wakefulness. Then a big shape was marching toward her from the big open area. She watched it move, wondering what it was, not comprehending. For a moment Annika thought it might be Chris. But it was too big, and it seemed mean. It held some kind of tool with a long orange hose trailing behind it.

The shape stopped at the threshold of the little area where Annika sat. She saw a person's little head sticking out the top and thought it looked funny on such a large body. The little head turned slowly. It seemed to be interested in something to her right.

Annika followed the little head's gaze until she saw another large shape, identical to the first. But this one wasn't standing. It was face-forward on the floor, like it had become unbalanced and tipped over. That must have been the crash.

The shape with the little head raised its tool and started walking toward the other shape on the ground.

Even through her grogginess, Annika could tell it meant to do harm. She knew she should care. But she was so tired. All she could manage was a vague sadness that things weren't working out differently.

The shapes converged, and Annika saw a flash of light from the tool. A sharp hiss echoed through the air. The flash sent sparks flying from the big suit on the ground.

Then a smaller figure stepped from the shadows. It was stooped over, clutching its side, but it managed to hobble quickly behind the big shape slicing chunks off the thing on the ground. She couldn't quite focus on what the figure was doing, but she caught a metallic glint held close to its body.

The glint moved. Then she heard another sound, this one meaty and solid, as the figure swung a wrench into the back of the little head.

6

Wyatt stepped across the threshold of the med bay and instantly felt the tension. He tried to ignore it as he took stock of the aftermath.

Annika lay on one of the surgery tables, a fixed platform far stouter than the foldable zero-gee observation beds. She stared numbly at the wall while robotic sensor arms assessed her body with radiation and physical probes. Dr. Kenta, a middle-aged Asian woman with perceptive eyes and bad posture, stood next to her without expression. The doctor was studying a holo monitor that displayed a multicolor, three-dimensional model of the little girl's brain that twinkled with occasional highlights. Occasionally she pressed her hand against Annika's skin as if checking for fever.

Other people stood around the perimeter of the room. Jack Bell, the former chief analyst of the Juliet Department of Health and now RESIT refugee, watched in silence. Laramie and their platoon leader, Captain Chappelle, stood next to each other with matching dark expressions. Only the nurse, a young woman with jet-black hair, seemed unperturbed as she glided from task to task.

"No, Epione, go back." Dr. Kenta slid her fingers to Annika's face, lifting her eyelids. "I want a longer read on that brain activity."

The sensor arms of the MedSurg robot rerouted into an orbit around Annika's head, abruptly starting and stopping in a staccato pattern as the stepper motors paused for their readings. Trend lines and other vitals blinked on the side of the holo monitor in ways that Wyatt couldn't understand.

He did, however, notice an obvious absentee at this gathering.

"Where's Chris?"

His platoon leader pointed at the adjacent berth behind Wyatt. Laramie just stood a little straighter, the way people did when they had unwelcome news.

Wyatt ducked through the hatch. On one side of the compartment, a cylindrical decompression chamber dominated the area against the interior bulkhead. Three foldable beds extended from the other. Chris was lying in the middle one, a white sheet over him, a mess of tubes and wires snaking from underneath the covers. His brown hair now conformed to a shorter regulation haircut, but the stubble on his chin seemed to be ever-present whether he shaved or not.

An armed RESIT trooper wearing a helmet and vest stood to the side, his hands resting on his Vector.

"You mind giving us some privacy, trooper?" Wyatt said.

The faceless front of a CORE helmet swept toward him. "Sorry, Lieutenant," came a muffled voice. "Orders."

Wyatt sighed. Whatever. *His* orders from Beck were to interview the Marine as soon as possible. He supposed it didn't have to be a private conversation.

Chris's brown eyes flicked toward him as he approached.

"Hey," Wyatt said. "You okay?"

"No."

A stifling silence hung over them. Chris looked terrible. Scrapes covered one side of his face so extensively that his skin looked like a piece of fabric. His right eye could have been made of ketchup, with a burst of shattered blood vessels wiping away any traces of white. Underneath his sheet, the profile of some kind of medical device encircled his torso. He realized with a start that Chris had already been through surgery.

Wyatt didn't know what to say. Normally he didn't have problems delivering encouragement. People got hurt or saw horrible things all the time in RESIT. But this wasn't some depressed trooper in the aftermath of recovering freeze-dried corpses. This was Chris. Cynical. Resolute. Wyatt couldn't even offer him the comfort of his faith.

He rested his hand on Chris's arm with a pat. It felt immediately lame.

"They think she has it," Chris croaked.

The Marine's face said it all. Wyatt could see the anguish, the heartbreak. He thought back to the deal he'd negotiated at the safe house, of how important it was to Chris to get this eight-year-old child, Governor Hewitt's daughter, away from the runaway outbreak. To see that all that effort may have been for nothing would be a bitter pill for anyone.

"I'm sorry."

A few empty moments passed. Wyatt steeled himself for what was next, for the conversation Beck had ordered him to have.

"Chris, there are some questions I have to ask you." He leaned over him so that he stood directly in front of Chris's line of sight. "Can you tell me what happened in the armory? Izzy was going to kill you. What did Annika do?"

"I don't know. I don't ... remember." The response came out flat and dull. Painkillers.

"Think, Chris. You were lying on the deck. Izzy was charging you. Then Annika dove between you and stared him down. What did she do?"

"They think she has it," he repeated.

"Maybe she does."

That got a response. Chris's eyes focused on Wyatt with a newly found edge. "No."

"Why do you believe that?"

"Because I was there."

"Security cams recorded everything, Chris. We studied close-ups of her face from the bridge. When Izzy moved in, her pupils shrunk down to almost nothing."

"No ... no ..." His face took on a confused quality as he searched for some word just beyond his grasp.

"What?"

"... no sparks."

The shower of sparks. Wyatt could never forget what he had seen and felt on Juliet, the dancing flecks of gold that nipped from just beyond out of sight. Jack Bell theorized it had something to do with the optic nerve overloading, that constriction affected those faculties first. Before overwhelming the rest of the brain. Before nothing remained. Just the thought made Wyatt's stomach turn.

"You never saw any sparks when Annika was with you?

"No."

"What about when Izzy attacked?"

"No."

Wyatt rubbed his chin. He didn't quite know what to do with that.

"Chris, have you ever seen someone with constriction use tools before?"

The Marine narrowed his eyes, his mind swimming through a sea of pain meds. Finally he shook his head. "No."

"Izzy was doing something very deliberate with the power conduits, Chris. They think he was trying to blow up the ship. Why would a constricted do that?"

He shook his head again.

A voice carried over from the other compartment. It sounded like Dr. Bell was arguing with Dr. Kenta over something.

"Is there anything, Chris, anything you can tell me that might help me understand what Annika did in there? I need to know how she saved you."

The Marine furrowed his brow. But a moment later he drifted off to sleep.

Wyatt stood empty-handed at his bedside, with only the RESIT guard for company. A *guard*, standing over a wounded man, a good man. He deserved better. God should have given him better.

And where is God right now? a small voice asked in the back of his head.

Good question. Was Chris forsaken? What about a corpsman who spent his career healing others, or an eight-year-old child just caught up in the maelstrom? Was this the sort of mercy good people could expect? Was this their reward on Earth?

Of course not. He knew the theology, the platitudes. Bad things happened to good people. It didn't mean God didn't love you. If you believed, you would still be saved.

Is this what 'saved' looks like?

The frustration hit quickly enough to surprise him. Wyatt clenched his teeth at the unfairness of it all. He'd always sought a deeper relationship with the Almighty. He prayed each night. He wanted it to be there. But at times like this, he doubted. He questioned. Wyatt could see his father standing over him as a child, disapproving at his lack of faith, holding his bible and drilling dogma into him with relentless repetition.

Perhaps his father had drilled a little too hard, leaving stress fractures in the foundation of Wyatt's belief.

Anger suddenly welled up inside him. He turned to the trooper and jabbed his finger accusingly at the Vector. "Do you really need that? This Marine isn't going anywhere, and he singlehandedly may have saved all our lives. I think he deserves a little more respect."

"I'm not watching him, sir. I'm watching *them*."

"What?"

The guard motioned with his head toward the decompression chamber.

Wyatt stepped cautiously toward the viewing plate in the side of the pressure vessel. He saw two figures lying end-to-end inside. The first appeared to be the armory guard, the one whom Izzy infected and had been found face-down. Shackles bound his hands and feet even though he was unconscious. Wyatt thought he recognized him from some of the joint training exercises. Corporal Dean, maybe.

The other form lay wrapped in a white sheet. Wyatt thought the contour of the head seemed wrong. Indented.

Were they so afraid that they were guarding corpses and the comatose?

Perhaps. But these were people, too. Someone's brother, someone's son. His comrades.

They deserved better, too.

God, if you're there, give me strength.

Wyatt bowed his head. He closed his eyes, let the words of a silent prayer come to his lips. He let himself fall back into the hope that there was in fact a supreme being, one who created the universe, almighty but unknowable, reachable only through faith. He needed that hope right now, more than anyone.

7

By the time he left the med bay with Laramie and Chappelle, Wyatt didn't feel like he had gained any insight whatsoever. The MedSurg AI had scanned Annika ten times over but had no answers to share. Kenta and Bell argued over which tests to run next while their other witness was stapled up in an unconscious stupor. And neither the dead trooper nor the infected one lying next to him were giving up any secrets.

"I don't know what to think about all this," Wyatt confessed. They walked down the corridor in single file. "I don't know what to tell Beck."

Chappelle craned his head around and fixed a pair of intense brown eyes on Wyatt. Sometimes Wyatt wondered if their platoon leader had missed his calling as a litigator.

"Run through what the Marine told you," Chappelle said, continuing down the corridor.

"Chris wasn't really in a clear state of mind. Very preoccupied with Annika. Very insistent that she isn't infected."

"Did he say anything about Watanabe? He was the one trying to cut into the power trunk."

"Nothing, other than we both agreed that constricted don't act like that."

"What do you mean?"

"According to Dr. Bell, constriction is very debilitating," Wyatt explained. "People who get it become lethargic. Their pupils shrink and they stare at the wall. Izzy's been pretty normal by comparison. Maybe a little withdrawn, but that's it."

Chappelle glanced back again, his sharp features giving him a hawkish look. "But the security cameras showed the corpsman doing that ... thing to the guard on duty. Right?"

Wyatt sighed. "Yes, sir."

"So maybe this guy Bell doesn't know what he's talking about."

"I think he does, sir. He was one of the lead planners for this Operation Firebreak thing, looking for patterns in the disease transmission. So the government could head it off."

"Head if off? Explain that."

Wyatt hesitated. "To kill citizens about to be infected, before constriction could spread to them." He glanced at Laramie, who scowled and stared at the deck.

Chappelle slowed for a few steps. "Your team went through quarantine procedures, right?"

"Yes, sir. Twice."

"Don't be surprised if they have you do it again."

Wyatt traded a glance with Laramie. More tests and bad-tasting medications, all for the sake of checking a box. He felt fine.

"Anything else you want me to do with Chris or Annika, Captain?" he asked.

Chappelle dodged around a pair of maintenance troopers headed the other way. "Go back in a couple hours and see if either of them is lucid. I want you to ask the questions. The major seems to think you've got insight into how this whole thing works." Chappelle glanced over his shoulder at Wyatt. "I hope that faith isn't misplaced."

"I'm confident in my judgement here, sir."

Their platoon leader stopped abruptly in the middle of the corridor.

"Be careful, Lieutenant. We don't have a lot of margin for error here. This task force is bare bones."

"He's got a destroyer and a Fast Attack," Laramie said.

"Like I said, bare bones." Chappelle glanced around as if to make sure they were alone. "Alpha A has ten times the population of Proxima. The only reason we came at all was because we saw *Mozambique* get blasted before the gate closed. Consider yourself lucky that Caustic had jurisdiction to intervene. But make no mistake— there should be a ton of RESIT assets from Dagger Team patrolling this area, and we haven't seen any. We're just three ships. Whatever happened to them, they outnumbered us by a lot."

"Aye, sir."

Chappelle stared hard at his two subordinates. After a long moment, he took a deep breath. "Look. Just realize there aren't any troop carriers to spare. So if Beck wants to know what the hell is going on, we don't have room for mistakes. That includes letting one of your troopers blow us up."

Wyatt straightened up at the barb.

This wasn't a new dynamic. Chappelle was calculating and deliberate, Wyatt far more intuitive. It had been the source of plenty of friction across their deployments. And lately, every time Chappelle looked at him, it almost seemed like he was privately thinking *that's why I have two legs and you only have one.*

Regardless, Wyatt knew when to shut up and take it. "Yes, sir."

"Aye, aye," Laramie said in a show of solidarity.

Their platoon leader didn't seem convinced. His eyes found the chronometer on his wrist. "It's almost oh ten hundred. I'm sure your squad is going apeshit wondering what's going on. Get them squared away, help them process it. It's not going to be easy to lose another trooper so soon after Maya."

"Yes, sir."

"Dismissed."

A few moments later, Wyatt and Laramie walked side by side down the wide ship ladder that led back to the crew berths. Troop carriers like *Vigorous* arranged their decks one atop another so that "down" pointed aft, and the constant acceleration would keep a nominal level of gravity. Two cargo lifts spanned the length of the vessel for deploying large groups in urgent situations. Since this wasn't one of those times, it meant a lot of stairs.

They stepped onto a lonely landing absent of other troopers. Laramie tugged at Wyatt's elbow to pull him aside.

"What is it?"

"Tell me what you saw on the bridge, LT."

"Between Beck and Kazimira?"

"No." She widened her eyes slightly, as if she couldn't quite believe he was so dense. "On the security feed."

Oh. That. He rattled off the list of events with what was becoming a practiced delivery. "I saw Izzy stare at the armory guard and send him face down to the deck. Then I saw him go after Chris with a laser cutter." He thought back, still trying to get the next event right in his memory. "Then Annika dove in front of Chris and stared at Izzy, and Izzy left."

"She drove him off?"

"Yeah."

"How?"

"I don't know."

Laramie watched him intently, waiting for more.

"So, she does have it," she said finally.

Wyatt shook his head. "I'm not convinced. Think back to Parrell. What's the number-one thing you remember when we engaged with those people in the rec center?"

"Sparks," Laramie said, not hesitating.

Wyatt scowled at the memory. The intense stare of the constricted had been like a flood of static electricity stabbing inward from just out of view. Muscles seized, thoughts burned away. Even thinking back to the experience brought Wyatt to a visceral wave of nausea.

"Yeah. Sparks." He cleared his throat as if it would make the displeasure go away. "Maya and I saw the same thing at the spaceport. It wasn't painful. It was sort of euphoric. But the sparks were still there."

"Okay. So?"

"Chris said there weren't any sparks. Not with Izzy, and not with Annika."

Laramie raised her hands in triumph. "Then Izzy doesn't have the disease, right? I mean, we passed quarantine. The symptoms are wrong. And there are no sparks, and sparks are a symptom too. Right?"

"I'm pretty sure Corporal Dean saw sparks before he went into that kneeling pose."

"Oh. Right." Laramie's eyes drifted to the bulkhead as if it might hold some hidden answer.

"Look, either way, something's not adding up," he said. "We just have to keep at it. Maybe Elton has some ideas. I'll see what I can get between now and when Chris's sedatives wear off."

"And I guess I'll get our team ready for another quarantine protocol."

"I think that's a waste of time." He gave her a look. "You should get on it immediately."

Wyatt had meant to lighten the mood. It didn't matter if they were under fire or eating chow, RESIT life had stress woven through it like reeds into a basket. Levity had been helping grunts cope since time began.

The comment flew past Laramie without the slightest reaction. Instead, she just nodded and started walking down the corridor.

8

"*General quarters, general quarters. All hands, man your duty stations. This is not a drill.*"

Another one. At least this time, Wyatt didn't have to deal with side excursions to the bridge or anything beyond standard operating procedure. He left the officers' mess and trotted down the stairs with two other squad leaders toward the armory. Laramie happened to link up with him as they merged into the same corridor.

"Getting tired of these," she said.

"Yeah. It's going to be The Boy Who Cried Wolf before too long."

"What's a wolf?"

"Come on. I know you know what a wolf is." He could tell this was about to be another deadpan exchange about the differences between their home planets.

"No idea what you're talking about."

"It's like a wild dog."

"Oh." Laramie thought for a moment. "So why did the boy cry? Did he lose his dog?"

Wyatt sighed. "I'll explain later."

The armory blast door stood wide open this time as Wyatt and Laramie hurried to their lockers. Troopers milled all about in the controlled chaos of donning gear. Wyatt unrolled his pressure sleeve and quickly pulled it over his legs and torso. When he drew his ARC vest from its compartment, he noticed one of the ablative pucks was still missing from the back. When had that happened? From the drone?

A pair of troopers on the other side of the compartment were conjecturing about this new alert. Wyatt could just make out part of the exchange. "Korbett said we're tailing a RESIT spacecraft."

"Dagger?"

"Yeah. Maybe we'll finally get some answers."

Uninvited anger surged inside Wyatt again as he thought back to the Fast Attack that had dogged them since his arrival in Alpha A. The drone strike on the freighter. The drone strike on *Kumano Lily*. Maya, her chest exploded from laser fire, a lifeless body in the microgravity. A heaping of murder wherever that spacecraft went.

Had they really found another spacecraft? *Please, God, let it be* Razor.

His helmet came after the sleeve and vest. He pulled it over his face and a momentary flash evaporated the darkness as the neural stub pressed into his temple. Gone were the normal impulses from the synapses leading to his orbital lobe. Instead the neural stub took over, hijacking the biological pathway used to send visual information to the brain, replacing what would normally come from Wyatt's eye with a kaleidoscope of telemetry and video from the sensors mounted in his faceplate.

Wyatt looked left and right. His squad mates were preparing to move to their assigned muster point on the ship. Distributed manpower meant troopers could deliver faster damage control. It also meant higher survivability if part of *Vigorous* was destroyed.

He finished his video calibration and switched audio to the platoon channel. "Acid One, Battle One Actual, check."

"I read you, Battle One," Chappelle replied.

"Any word yet on the GQ?"

"Maybe. I'll patch you in. Wait one."

A moment later, the bone-induction speakers in Wyatt's helmet started feeding him audio from the bridge. At least Chappelle was good about not holding much back from his squad leaders.

"*—range from* Vigorous *is thirty-six thousand klicks, two-hundred kps negative closure.*"

"*Any new contacts?*" said a female voice.

"*Negative, ma'am.*"

A few moments passed with no dialogue.

"*No response to hails.*"

"*Understood.*"

Wyatt waited, listened.

"Sawtooth *is coming up behind them, now in range yellow.*"

"*Are they in aft position?*"

"*Aye, ma'am.*"

"Okay, that's good enough," the woman said. *"Tell Otto to offset a few degrees so they know he's there. Then hail again and order them to cut thrust."*

"Aye, ma'am."

Wyatt sorted through the comments to mentally arrange the pieces on the chess board. Beck and Kazimira had taken all three spacecraft of Havoc Company through the quantum gate. *Vigorous*, their troop carrier, formed the nucleus of the detachment. It had its destroyer escort *Piranha* typically pulling security not far away. *Sawtooth* was their own Fast Attack. Just like *Razor*, it was an inceptor used to hunt down and reel in anyone trying to be somewhere else.

The Fast Attacks could pull more gees than almost any other spacecraft ever designed. And *Sawtooth* was closing in on someone who might be learning that for the first time.

Laramie's voice boomed from several lockers over. "Battle Squad, line up on the double! Let's *move!*"

Troopers moved in a hurried shuffle away from their personal lockers. Wyatt listened with half an ear as he managed a slow drift toward Chappelle in the other direction. His platoon leader possessed a far better grasp of spacecraft engagement tactics, and hopefully could explain what was happening nearly three Earth diameters away across the frigid expanse of space.

"Is it *Razor*?" Wyatt asked him.

"I don't think so." Chappelle listened some more. "Kazimira's using *Sawtooth* to press them, make them run away at an angle where *Vigorous* can overtake them. She wouldn't be so aggressive against another FA."

"Are you sure? Maybe this is just the first time two Fast Attacks have ever engaged each other."

Chappelle grunted. "No. Range yellow is pretty damn close—they can fire with one-meter accuracy. If it were *Razor*, don't you think they'd be shooting back already?"

"Good point."

"Yes, it is. Now get to your squad."

Wyatt peeled off to take his place at the front of his team. Now they had to get to their assigned damage-control stations. Battle's assignment took them toward the stern, which meant a ride on one of the dual cargo lifts that stretched the length of the entire ship. They trotted to one end of the hangar and waited for half a minute until the safety doors parted. Then the squad shuffled onto the hexagonal platform normally used for storage containers and cargo pods, and after a thirty-second ride, they were disgorged into a corridor full of storage lockers and cargo netting. A blue navigation stripe stenciled with the word *Propulsion* extended along the walls.

"Battle One, come in," Chappelle's voice said on the comm.

"Battle is almost in position," Wyatt replied.

"Understood, but it doesn't look like we'll need it. It's not *Razor*."

Wyatt felt the disappointment course through his body. No payback this time. "Who is it, then?"

"Search and Rescue vessel. RESIT, Fast Scout class, unarmed and apparently undamaged. The bridge is in contact with them." A momentary pause filled the channel. "Sorry, Lieutenant."

"Yes, sir."

Wyatt frowned inside his helmet. Even his platoon leader knew how badly he wanted revenge. Where the hell was *Razor*?

Perhaps this scout ship would be able to shed some light.

Laramie sauntered up just as *Vigorous* made a course correction that nearly threw off her balance. She grabbed a pipe to save herself from stumbling. "What's the deal, LT?"

"False alarm. The rabbit we found is different than the one we were hoping for."

A pause. "What's a rabbit?"

"Oh, come on. Juliet has rabbits." Here they went again.

"Is it a type of wolf?" Laramie asked.

"*No*. They're rabbits. Bunnies. Cute little furry animals with big front teeth."

Laramie cocked her head. "You sort of described a hopper, except for the cute part. Do rabbits eat people, too?"

Wyatt let out an inadvertent snort. "No. But you have me thinking now that maybe hoppers are why you don't have rabbits."

"Maybe." She paused again before going back on topic. "So, this Fast Scout. Do we know anything else?"

"Not yet. They're built to hide and observe, so I'd assume he was doing that to *Vigorous* before we picked him up."

"And now he's trying to get away."

"He's not getting anywhere. *Sawtooth* has that big powerplant that can push close to five gees."

"No, thanks," Laramie said. "I like my ribs."

"Truth."

Wyatt found he also had to reach for a nearby handle as their course correction continued. His legs felt heavier, too. "Wow, we're really bending our trajectory."

"Maybe we're going to play with our rabbit?" Laramie suggested.

The comm's platoon channel switched on and Chappelle's voice crackled in Wyatt's ear. "Battle One, Acid One."

"Copy, Acid One."

"The skipper has us moving to rendezvous and dock with the Fast Scout, officially FS-22 *Needle*. ETA in fifty minutes. I'm giving you the welcome-committee honors. There's only a crew of four. Get your Javelin together and board their vessel once they move into formation. Secure the ship, collect the crew, and bring them aboard for debriefing. Questions?"

Wyatt had a million of them but knew better than to bring them up now. "No, sir. Wilco."

"Out." He turned to see Laramie slipping her helmet off. "Catch that, Staff Sergeant?"

"Aye, sir, grab and go." Her face soured. "Our squad's understrength by two troopers. Why is he sending us?"

Wyatt shrugged. "Because he is."

"Aye, sir. I'll get 'em moving."

As Laramie turned to go, Wyatt had to admit she had a good question. Their squad had been through a lot over the past couple weeks. He supposed Chappelle might be trying to get them back in the saddle, to stay busy enough that they wouldn't lose focus. Inattentiveness in space cost lives. Even more so when they were dealing with an outbreak of a strange disease and armed spacecraft gone rogue.

His squad hauled ass back to the armory while *Vigorous* pulled at them with unexpected accelerations. By the time they arrived, their newly prepped Javelin had been repositioned over one of the hangar airlocks by the overhead crane. They boarded and strapped into their couches while the crew chief closed the rear cargo ramp.

Wyatt sat in the squad-leader seat near the cockpit and tapped his keyboard. When the tactical display pulled up on his holo monitor, he saw his pilot's call sign and couldn't help but smile.

"We must be getting the royal treatment today," he said. "How are we doing, Teo?"

"Just fine, Lieutenant." The pilot who had kept them alive on Juliet flashed a thumbs up through the open cockpit hatch. "Seems like you're getting all the good missions."

"No rest for the weary."

"Roger that. Stand by for launch."

"Are you taking us through the chute?"

The pilot sniffed. "Of course. Nothing but high speed today."

Wyatt cinched up his harness. Muffled thuds shook the fuselage as the Javelin moved through the airlock system, followed by a faint hiss as pumps evacuated the atmosphere. He felt another shudder as the docking clamp opened. Then, suddenly free of the constant acceleration of their troop carrier, he felt weightlessness.

"We are clear of *Vigorous*, stand by for maneuvers," Teo said.

Now the Javelin banked and twirled. Wyatt cycled his display to tactical mode and watched the minutes click down as a yellow chevron slowly glided from the edge of the screen toward their position. Eventually the chevrons converged, and Teo used more thruster burns to match velocity and orientation with the Fast Scout.

Wyatt switched back to the nose camera. A new spacecraft filled the screen, long and slender, with two sensor array spheres protruding from the bow like blunted tusks. Four drive nacelles graced the aft end at ninety-degree spacing. A vessel built for search and rescue, with speed determining success or failure.

"Stand by to dock," Teo said. "Thirty seconds."

The troopers grunted brief, functional exchanges to each other as they unstrapped and coordinated their move into place. Wyatt felt thankful that his remaining team knew how to work together. Gavin and Carlos, his veterans. Kenny and Rahsaan, proven in the crucible of the previous mission. Laramie, always.

Carlos swung himself across the interior grab bars until he hovered near the ceiling airlock. Laramie flanked him. Soon a metallic scraping reverberated through the hull, and the barest hint of downward acceleration suggested that the two vessels had connected.

"We're docked," Teo said.

Wyatt moved toward the edge of their stack and scanned the other troopers in the bay. Everyone wore their helmets, with ARC vests snapped over the pressure sleeves that protected their bodies from hard vacuum. They lined up in the microgravity, ready to board and render aid.

Carlos was watching a digital readout next to the hatch. "Pressure's equalized."

"Okay, everybody keep your eyes open," Wyatt said. He focused his attention on Laramie. "Ready, Staff Sergeant?"

"Aye, sir. Let's go."

"Open it, Carlos."

The trooper pulled a lever. The pop of a pressure seal breaking came from the hatch. Wyatt looked up just as Carlos swung the door open.

He saw four people in ARC vests crowding the tiny airlock. Each held a Vector with the aiming laser pointed directly at him.

9

Laramie saw the lines of green light sweep over Wyatt's face in her CORE helmet's camera. She vaguely felt her own Vector coming to her shoulder, her fingers brushing against the safety, her mind screaming warnings mixed with a hundred thoughts of inadequacy and failure. *Hostiles. You're too slow. You should have been prepared. Your friend is about to die.*

A harsh voice shouted from the airlock. "Nobody moves!"

To his credit, Wyatt retained an icy calm. Laramie watched as he opened his hands and moved them away from the pistol at his hip. Everything was slow and steady, his movements coordinated so that he didn't send himself into an unwanted spin.

"Take your helmet off!" the voice warbled.

Both Carlos and Wyatt floated in front of the airlock hatch, two frozen statues in the garden. But Gavin was moving carefully on the far side of the airlock, unseen by the shooters. Laramie wondered if she could tell him over the comm to slam the hatch closed.

"I said, helmets off!" the shooter repeated, now in near hysteria. "All of you. Now!"

Wyatt spoke in a flat voice over the comm. "CORE helmets off, everyone. No sudden movements."

Laramie hesitated. With her safety off, the integrated targeting computer in her helmet had updated positions of everyone around her. She would be able to draw a bead on everyone in the airlock if a firefight started. Yet they weren't yelling at her squad to throw down weapons. *Why helmets?*

Wyatt pulled off his helmet. He cradled it in his arm and stared at whoever was in the airlock. Then Laramie saw him flinch as a bare-headed man with a dark crewcut flew out the hatch.

They crashed together and went sailing across the Javelin interior. Laramie's Vector tracked them as if it had a mind of its own. A shout from the other side of the hatch signaled that Gavin was doing the same thing.

The dark-haired man held his own Vector muzzle jammed underneath Wyatt's jaw. Their faces were close. He was shouting.

"Your eyes! Let me see your eyes!"

Laramie's finger increased its pressure against the trigger.

Time seemed to stop. The dark-haired man stared at Wyatt with blazing intensity. Then, inexplicably, he exhaled a slow stream of air as if he had been holding his breath for a hundred years.

"They're not infected, boys. Stand down."

The aiming lasers drifted off target. The Vector slid away from Wyatt's chin.

Wyatt didn't miss a beat. He wrenched the muzzle sideways in the man's grip, throwing their bodies into a spin that sent them careening into the far bulkhead. Carlos pinwheeled away from the open hatch. In a span of seconds, Gavin, Kenny, and Rash all took up firing positions away from the direct line of sight of the airlock.

Laramie shouted her own commands this time. "Hands off your weapons. Float them through the airlock or we will open fire!"

Dead silence. A Vector drifted through the microgravity. Then two more.

"Gav," she directed.

Gavin plucked the weapons from the air with one hand and flipped them toward the flight deck. One of them almost hit Wyatt, who was now wrapped around his attacker with the man's neck in a submission hold.

"Okay," Laramie continued, "one at a time, nice and steady, come out of the airlock. Any sudden moves and you're dead. *Slow.*"

Another young man floated through the hatch wearing a pressure sleeve and ARC vest with the RESIT Dagger Team logo on the chest. To Laramie's approval, Kenny grabbed him by the collar and slammed him face-first into the hull.

Two more came out, and in thirty seconds her team had them zip-tied and secured. Laramie could tell from their slight build that they were spacecraft crew rather than troopers. None of them wore helmets or even rebreather masks.

One who had close-cropped blond hair stole distrustful glances in her direction.

She glanced at Wyatt. "You okay, LT?"

"Fine," he replied, his tone saying anything but. He still had the commander in a headlock. "You. What was the meaning of that attack?"

"I ..." the man grunted. "Had ... to be sure."

"Sure of what?"

"You ... your eyes ... constrict ..." His face turned colors in the crook of Wyatt's arm.

Laramie thought the spacer was about to pass out. "LT," she said.

Wyatt maintained his hold a couple more seconds before finally releasing him. His expression looked like he would have rather popped the guy's head off. The spacer floated free and clutched his neck.

"Identify yourself," Wyatt ordered.

"Lieutenant ... Klarion ... Echols. RESIT Dagger. Captain ... of the *Needle*." He blinked hard, still trying to regain his air.

"You knew who we were. You spoke with our commanding officer before we even came out here. You had no cause to draw your weapons."

"I apologize. A lot ... can change ... between one conversation ... and the next." He took a couple deep breaths before continuing. "You don't know what's happened here in Alpha A."

"Constriction," Wyatt said.

Echols gave him a curious look. "How ...?"

"We had a recon team land on Juliet," Wyatt said. "We know what happened on the surface."

A dark pall washed over the lieutenant's face like an approaching storm.

"Not just ... on the surface. Everywhere."

10

Chris Thompson blinked again. His mind wasn't processing where he was.

Strange smells and sounds permeated the air. Bleating noises from a computer alarm. The crisp odor of disinfectant. He glanced upward and saw an odd metal track traced a pattern at regular intervals on the wall. No, not the wall. The ceiling.

Gradually he realized he was lying in bed. He turned his head to see the figure of a woman standing in a nearby hatch, reading something in her hand.

"Hey," he croaked.

The figure glanced at him. A moment later it materialized into Dr. Kenta with her tablet computer tucked under her arm. She reached out and felt his forehead.

"I see you've decided to join us again," she said.

"Where am I?"

"*My* house." Kenta's tone had an odd inflection to it. "Do you remember anything?"

All that came to mind was a whole lot of empty. "Like what?"

"What's the last thing you do remember?"

Chris closed his eyes.   Emotions swirled through his mind more than distinct images. He had trouble keying in on anything specific.   But there was one thing that came through very clear. "Being scared."

"No cursing?   Or throwing my instrument tray across the room?   How about arm-wrestling Epione?"

He stole a glance at the sensor arm stowed in the metal track above him.

"Huh. No." A second later he added, "Ma'am."

The doctor arched an eyebrow at him, giving her Asian features a particularly disapproving look. Chris felt a pang of embarrassment. But he didn't have any recollection of why he should.

"Well, then," Kenta said. "We'll just chalk it up to the pain meds. But you need to promise me you're going to behave from now on. Okay, Mister Difficult?"

"Okay."

She reached over and fumbled with something near his wrist. A moment later a restraining cuff dropped away. Chris grimaced, wondering what the hell had happened during his apparent blackout.

"Why am I here?" he asked.

"Apparently you stopped a saboteur on the hangar deck. You received a good-sized hole in your abdomen for the privilege."

He closed his eyes and tried to remember. Nothing came at first. Then a flood of sounds and images hit him all at once. Stumbling through corridors in the middle of the night. A missing guard face down on the deck. A trooper in a heavy assault suit, turning, pinpoint eyes.

The eyes. Here on the carrier. Oh my God, it's onboard, we've got to get out, where's Annika, I've got to find Anni no not her not her not her...

Someone was shouting his name. He had to get up. He had to get away ...

"Hey! Sergeant Thompson!" a voice said loudly. Chris blinked.

"Hey," Kenta said. "It's okay."

She had both hands pressed firmly against Chris's chest. He looked down at them through watery eyes, watching his chest rise and fall in rapid succession, his ears filled with the freight train sounds of panicked breathing. His hands hurt. Each fist held a death grip on the rails lining his bed.

"It's okay," Kenta repeated. She reached off to the side and pressed something.

"I have to see Anni."

"You will."

The room was getting dark. Chris stared up at Kenta but had trouble finding her in the fog.

***

Pounding echoed through the compartment from the nearby open hatch. Chris's eyes shot open. It sounded like someone was beating a nail with a hammer in preparation to hang a picture.

He looked around. He was in Med Bay.

"Hello?" he said loudly.

The pounding stopped.

Chris looked down at his body. He was lying in the same bed as earlier. Amazingly, he felt stronger and more energetic. His thoughts seemed clearer, too. He tried to sit up. Instead of searing pain, a wave of dullness rubbed his side from a million klicks away.

Doctor Kenta emerged through the hatch. Sure enough, she held a hammer. "You're back."

"I'm back." He glanced at her hand. "Is that in case I get out of line?"

"No, this is for Bell."

Chris laughed. The dullness tickled at him again.

"How are you feeling?" Kenta asked. She stepped next to the bed and pulled a tablet from her coat pocket.

"I need to see Anni."

"Let's worry about you first."

"Doc. Please."

He found Kenta's eyes. He could see the analysis, a physician silently weighing the pros and cons of what potential treatments might speed up recovery. It only lasted for a moment. The doctor gave him a nod and carefully retracted one of the bed rails. Her other hand still held the hammer. Chris somehow found it strangely calming.

"Be careful sitting up. I don't want you tearing your sutures."

Slowly, Chris managed to position himself upright. His torso had something stiff around it, a plastic sleeve that stretched from his chest to his hips. He could hardly bend at all. But with Kenta's help, he swung his legs off the bed and managed to rise into a wobbly stance. All the while his pulse kept the beat to an internal soundtrack of confused feelings and sensations.

"Hold on to me. We're going into the next room."

"Okay."

They moved slowly into the adjoining berth. The lights shone brighter here and caused Chris to squint. He noticed Jack Bell seated behind a holo monitor. On the far side of the room was another open hatch to the pharmacy, and then a row of stowable patient beds. Only one of them was folded out from the hull. A small girl lay unmoving on top.

Annika.

"How is she?" Chris asked.

Bell looked up and gave him a wary look. "Sleeping," he said.

Chris withdrew his arm from Dr. Kenta's grasp and staggered one foot at a time over to the patient bed. Annika was tucked under a thin sheet, her face peaceful if not exactly content. She lay undisturbed except for the whir of the sensor arm from the AI bot that continually hovered nearby.

He placed his hand on her forehead. Her skin felt cold. He unfolded the thermal blanket at her feet and pulled it up to her shoulders.

"Is she going to be okay?"

Silence hung in the air. When he didn't get an answer, Chris pivoted around to find Kenta and Bell staring at each other.

"According to all the tests, there's nothing wrong with her," Bell said. "Physiologically. But that doesn't explain much. So, for now, let's be content with the fact that she's just sleeping."

Sleep. Chris felt like he had slept for a year. His arm moved to tuck the blanket around Annika's body. It was the same arm he had broken on Juliet. The splint was gone.

"What happened to my splint?"

Kenta watched him closely. "It got bloodied up in the hangar. When you confronted the corpsman."

"I don't ..." He studied the skin on his arm, the green ink of his tattoo. The image of a fiery eagle stared back at him with its talons extended. "My arm itches."

"Side effect of the cell-growth medication. Be thankful it's healing as well as it is. Just don't break it again before it's done."

"Okay."

"You really should lie down, Master Sergeant." Kenta stepped up next to him and put her hand through his elbow. She had a strong grip. "You need your rest."

"I'm fine. I need to know what happened with my girl."

"She's under observation. It's all we can do for now."

He felt his face contort. "How can you regrow chunks of flesh on me, but not tell me what's wrong with her?"

"Modern medicine is more than sufficient to resolve *your* injuries, Mister Thompson," Kenta said. "I can cut you, medicate you, or radiate you. But that's not what we're dealing with regarding Miss Hewitt."

He turned toward the health director sitting at his workstation. "Bell, you must know something. Your freaking Firebreak slaughtered thousands. God knows what you dissected out of those bodies at the Health Department."

"I can't even begin to respond to that," Bell said dryly.

Kenta grasped his elbow. "You really should lie back down."

"No ..." Chris's attention remained fixed on Annika. "Please."

He could feel Kenta and Bell sharing another look.

Bell finally cleared his throat. "Do you know anything about how the human brain works, Thompson?" he asked.

"I'm a Marine, Bell, not a scientist."

"Then I'll use small words."

It took a moment to catch the insult. But Bell had already plowed ahead, a hint of something vindictive in his voice as he tilted his head toward the ceiling. "A demonstration. Epione, give me a health summary for patient Christopher Thompson, standing here in the med bay."

"What?" Chris said.

A long, multi-jointed robotic arm unfolded itself from the wall near Annika's bed. The next thing Chris knew, it had traveled along the ceiling track until it hovered next to him and extended a thin wand next to his face. A violet light flashed back and forth in a staccato pattern.

"Mister Thompson, how are you feeling?" an ethereal woman's voice asked. A sensor wand rotated just centimeters away and made the hair on his skin stand up.

"A little freaked out."

"I'm sorry to hear that. I'll try not to startle you with my instruments next time. Is your arm still hurting?"

"A little."

The sensor wand whirred quickly down to his side, where the violet light pulsed again.

"It appears you've traumatized the soft tissue around the newly fused bone. The good news is the fracture is still mended. I can give you a neural blocker for the pain if it would make you more comfortable?"

"I'm fine." Chris drew his arm away from the wand.

"Very good." The wand on the robotic arm slid through the air around him. "I noticed from your last bloodwork that your cholesterol readings continue to be high. Based on your historical records, your genetic pattern has a history of heart disease. I can prescribe a medication regiment to lessen your chance of a heart attack or stroke. Would that be acceptable?"

Chris felt his heart beating faster. He scanned the med bay for an exit and found Dr. Kenta instead. "Is this why I wrestled the robot?"

"Epione, that will be all for the moment," Kenta replied. Her face remained bland, but her eyes registered disapproval at Bell's little stunt. Lots of people didn't like MedSurg bots. That's why there were still human doctors.

"Very well." The robotic arm folded up and whirred along its track back toward the wall.

There was a trace of a smirk on Bell's lips. "You may not realize it, Master Sergeant, but Epione just spent an exceptional amount of thought on you."

"I know. She undressed me with her eyes. Uh, wand."

"Do you know how she works?"

His heart was still going a hundred klicks an hour. He wanted to throttle the man. "Lights blink and shit happens? Why are you asking me all this?"

"Doctor Bell," Kenta said.

"Humph." Bell leaned back and folded his arms. "I'm sure there are probably blinky lights in the AI core, if that makes you happy. There are also a hundred billion neural circuits. Epione can *think*. Even Marines have a little ball of gray matter up there that for the sake of discussion we'll call a brain. Billions of little logic gates that handle all your memory and processing power, from whether you like ice cream to how fast you pull your hand back from a hot stove."

"What does this have to do with Annika?"

"Everything." He tilted his head and gave Chris a long look. "Tell me, Thompson, are you self-aware?"

"I'm aware of my blood pressure rising."

"Have you ever worn a CORE helmet?"

"All the time."

"Those helmets have targeting computers inside of them," Bell said. "More memory, storage, circuits. But is your helmet aware of itself?"

"Of course not. That's a stupid question."

"No, I'm making a point. Physical computers don't know they exist. They just do whatever the software says. But you're different. You have awareness. You have consciousness. Your thinking, *your* software, your what-makes-you-you, that's something that is very difficult to measure."

Kenta raised her hand. "Doctor *Bell*, my patient isn't cleared for *combat*. You can do this later."

"Does this have anything to do with Anni?" Chris insisted.

"Indeed it may." Bell glanced at Kenta, then continued in a softer, less aggressive tone. "If something were wrong with Epione, we could run diagnostics on her physical processing unit, right?"

"I suppose."

"Yes, we could. On the physical side. But her software, her thinking, that's a neural network. We don't get to see that. Not only is the original code compiled to a level we can't read, it's also self-adapting. Epione isn't programmed so much as she is trained. She writes herself new code that her original developers won't ever see. She develops proficiencies just as any organic entity does. In fact, she must pass a test in order to make quals and go into service. Some of her peers don't. It's all because of natural variations in the development of her thinking processes."

Bell stood from his desk and walked over to Annika. Chris felt uncomfortable as he watched the ex-Health Director put his hand on her forehead.

"Humans aren't any different," Bell continued. "Medicine is very good at testing for physical abnormalities, even in the brain. Localized hemorrhages. Reduced electrical activity. Across those measures, Annika looks fine. But that doesn't mean the system is well. Because just like with Epione, there is another layer that's very hard to assess, the layer of thought. And I suspect that's where we've got to keep digging if we're to understand how to help her."

Chris frowned. He thought he got the gist of what Bell was rambling about. He walked toward the other side of Annika's bed, opposite Bell. She seemed comfortable, and her face was relaxed. But in his mind's eye, he saw her sitting on the deck next to the power suit cubbies, her expression filled with horror behind a pair of pinprick pupils.

He saw her staring at Izzy and making him turn away.

How was that possible?

"I shouldn't be alive," Chris said.

"Yet you are."

"I don't understand what happened in the hangar."

"I suspect Miss Hewitt saved your life somehow."

"How?"

The air hung heavy with silence. Chris sensed Bell and Kenta were sharing a look again.

"Obviously, some sort of communication took place," Bell said. "It's possible Annika gave Corpsman Watanabe a cue to stop his attack."

"A cue to stop his attack," Chris repeated.

"Yes."

Chris suddenly felt very tired. As a professional warrior, he understood nonverbal communication very well. He had spent years working with highly trained personnel who ate, slept, and fought together. That common experience resulted in a high-functioning unit that could think and act as one.

But Izzy was a RESIT corpsman. He came from a Japanese family on Earth.

Annika was an eight-year-old girl from Juliet and the daughter of a politician.

They had nothing in common whatsoever that might suggest the viability of a shared cue.

Nothing except pinprick eyes and an obvious answer that he desperately hoped wasn't true.

11

USIC *Needle*
Alpha Centauri A
26 March 2272

Wyatt ordered the Fast Scout crew secured inside the Javelin while Gavin and Rahsaan searched their vessel. They didn't find much. Low on food and fuel, the cramped quarters of the search-and-rescue spacecraft must have felt like a prison ship. With Lieutenant Echols refusing to talk more until he saw Major Beck, there wasn't much more Wyatt could do but return to *Vigorous*. Teo sent their copilot aboard the Fast Scout to pilot it back.

Three hours later, Wyatt was standing in the armory once again. He felt beyond exhausted. A deep throbbing pulsed in a steady rhythm behind his eye sockets. It occurred to him he hadn't slept in nearly thirty-six hours. The incident with Izzy, general quarters, and the go-fetch mission were a lot to handle. RESIT had a way of whittling down even the toughest to the barest shreds of what a human being could be.

He had just opened his locker when the call came over his personal comm. *"Lieutenant Wills, report to Ready Room B immediately. Orders of Major Beck."*

"You have got to be kidding me."

Laramie had stripped down to her underclothes and walked up next to him. Her expression mirrored similar feelings. "Report to the Ready Room?"

"Yeah."

"I got the call, too." She toweled off her arms and the back of her neck. "Wish Beck would give us a few. I don't exactly smell fresh."

"Me neither. Won't be the first time we bag it up."

Laramie shook her head and pulled on her utilities. Wyatt did the same, frowning at the idea of stinking up an otherwise fresh uniform. Ninety seconds later they were hurrying through the corridors, trying not to keep their commanding officer waiting.

The ready room had a gaggle of people crowded around the small briefing table near the front. All four of the Fast Scout crew sat on one side. Beck and his adjutant faced them. More RESIT troopers occupied the walls and some of the chairs. Captain Chappelle stood near the wall and waved Wyatt over to him.

"They're just getting started. Beck wanted you to listen in—make sure their story matches what you saw planetside. He'll debrief with you after." Chappelle spoke in a low voice so as to not disturb the meeting.

"Aye, sir."

Lieutenant Echols and his team wore borrowed utilities bearing the *Vigorous* insignia. Wyatt noted how all of them seemed young, almost too young for a spacecraft crew. One of them, a lanky man with bright eyes and dark stubble, barely looked twenty.

Beck maintained a neutral expression as he led the interrogation. "Take me through your last orders, Lieutenant."

"Yes, sir," Echols began. He took a deep breath. "Standard operating procedure for Dagger Command is for the troop carriers to monitor everything moving between Juliet and the quantum gates. As a Fast Scout, we were assigned the secondary shipping lanes inside the system. We would inspect for proper permits, check cargoes, the typical patrol objectives, but we see fewer spacecraft and a lot of dead time. We were assigned a sixty-day rotation and then back to Gateway Station.

"The first two or three weeks were pretty normal. We boarded a Manta-class cargo carrier and wrote them up for missing safety equipment. We boarded another freighter and everything checked out. Then, after about a month, all the traffic just disappeared. All we could pick up on long-range radar was empty space. Optical scans couldn't find any vessel, period, let alone ones that matched the shipping schedules."

"You went from normal shipment volumes one day to nothing the next?" Beck said.

"Yes, sir."

"And you didn't receive any bulletins from Dagger about their involvement?"

"No, sir. Frankly, we couldn't reach *anybody*. We radioed Gateway Station and received no reply. We reached out to Command aboard the USIC *Alexander*. Again, no reply." Echols motioned toward the crewmember with the bright eyes. "I actually ordered Petty Officer Zum to perform an EVA and inspect our communication array. Everything checked out. It was literally like we were the last spacecraft in the universe. We were patrolling by ourselves, totally alone."

"I just want to be clear," Beck said. "You were unable to contact *any* other RESIT vessel?"

"That's correct, sir."

Beck traded a glance with his adjutant. "What did you do next?"

"We continued our patrol route. For twenty days we searched for other vessels, scheduled or otherwise. We had zero contact. Then, we received a priority-one broadcast from Gateway to stay away from Juliet. We radioed for verification but were unsuccessful—all we picked up was the automated beacon. We were nearing the end of our patrol duration, and we hadn't seen any spacecraft, so I decided to abort our patrol and reconnoiter for other RESIT ships. We set course to Macbeth, which is where the *Alexander* was supposed to be on station."

Wyatt leaned toward Laramie. "Macbeth?"

"Fourth planet from Alpha A," she whispered.

"We arrived in orbit," Echols continued. "No command carrier. No response from Fort King on the surface. But we did pick up a faint signal at Macbeth Lagrange Four. Usually, there's nothing there but space junk collecting there around Bering Gate. Bering goes to Alpha B, there's nothing in Alpha B, therefore no one goes to Bering. But we beat it over there anyway."

Wyatt didn't have the familiarity with RESIT assets around Juliet like he did with Earth and Tiamat. He glanced sideways again.

Laramie picked up on his confusion. She tilted her head and spoke low into his ear. "You know Bering Gate?"

"Vaguely. Still used?"

"No. As in, zero."

"Seems like a waste for a trillion-dollar asset."

Laramie shrugged. "I'm sure it'll get redeployed at some point. But it only takes two weeks at one gee to get to Alpha B."

"I thought I remembered a shipyard or something being over there."

The furrows on Laramie's forehead telegraphed the answer before the words came. "Not for like a hundred years, LT."

"Really?"

"Really. I mean, there *was* a shipyard, because of asteroids with metals and stuff, but not now."

Echols made a noise that sounded like a little sob. Wyatt's attention snapped out of his sidebar and back onto the lieutenant.

"And that's when we found her," Echols was saying.

Beck's face seemed very dark. "Found what?"

"USIC *Alexander*. Adrift and on emergency power."

Wyatt stiffened in his chair. Had he heard that correctly? Command carriers were movable space stations. He'd never heard of one having an emergency. Ever.

"Explain," Beck said.

"The bridge tried to wave us off. Said there'd been an accident, that the rest of the spacecraft hadn't been secured. But at this point we're almost out of food, so I insisted we had to resupply and had no other options. They finally let us dock and we came aboard to an armed escort waiting for us. They took us immediately to a secure berth and brought us some supplies and dinner. But we were under guard, and not allowed around the ship. And then the power went out."

"You lost power?"

"Yes, sir. Emergency lights clicked on, and a call must have gone out for all hands to report to stations, because the two guards who were watching us took off without so much as a word. But my crew and I, we're not a bunch to sit passively. We followed them, even though only had our sidearms. Then the alert system switched to general quarters. And that's when we—"

Echols clipped off his words, lowering his chin as if he'd suddenly dropped something. Wyatt wasn't sure what had happened. It took a moment to realize the lieutenant was struggling to keep his composure.

"Lieutenant," Beck prodded after a moment.

Echols's voice wavered. "We saw other troopers. They were ... wrong. Their eyes were wrong. As soon as we saw them, I remember feeling lightheaded. It was the strangest sensation. Euphoric. Then one of the guards fired his weapon, and it all changed.

"Our minds felt like they were catching fire."

An odd noise caught Wyatt's attention.

Petty Officer Zum was hyperventilating. Wyatt watched as the Fast Scout crewman tried to stand, glancing around with bright, desperate eyes. Alarm filled his crewmates' faces. Two of them stood and clamped their arms around their fellow. Chappelle moved to shield Major Beck. But Zum was looking for exits, his expression morphing into one of abject terror.

Wyatt's own stomach turned sour. He could still feel the sparks from Parrell. He remembered how the constricted chased his team from the rec center, how the golden flecks tore at his mind. This, Jack Bell had explained, was how the constricted defended themselves. The gentle, seductive call to oblivion cranked up to the max, transforming the warmth of gentle sparks into a sea of fire. Even the memory made Wyatt fight a wave of nausea.

The situation at the table died down. Someone gave Zum a squeeze bulb of water. The petty officer took intermittent sips from his chair while his crewmates comforted him.

Beck traded whispered comments with his adjutant before clearing his throat. "Just a few more questions, Lieutenant."

"Yes, sir. I'm sorry, sir, I know much of this probably doesn't make sense."

"It's fine."

Echols nodded.

"You mentioned gunfire, a firefight. What happened then?" Beck asked.

"We ran. It was all we could do. The pain was debilitating and we were just trying to get away. Then we rounded a corner. I managed to look back and saw that the guards had stopped shooting. The troopers with the strange eyes were just standing over them, glaring at their bodies on the deck."

Beck listened, his face expressionless.

Echols took the silence as judgement. "We didn't have a choice, Major. We fled back to *Needle*. All hell was breaking loose. We couldn't connect our comms to the main channel. We couldn't coordinate with the security response, and that response was failing. It ... it just turned into desperation. Into survival."

Dropping his eyes, Echols let his words trail off.

Beck conversed softly with his adjutant. Wyatt couldn't hear their words, but he caught the major raising an eyebrow. Then he turned back to the lieutenant. "So, at this point, Lieutenant, you returned to *Needle* and undocked?"

"Yes, sir. That was almost a month ago. We've been searching for rescue ever since."

"Did *Alexander* transmit any sort of distress signal?"

Echols furrowed his brow. "I don't know, sir. We were hell-bent on getting out of there."

Beck studied the Fast Scout captain for a long minute. "Very well, Lieutenant. This has been helpful. I want your mission logs and a written report so I can review this in more detail. In the meantime, get some rest. You've been through a lot. Captain Sims will arrange separate quarters for you and your crew." He motioned to his adjutant.

"Thank you, sir," Echols said. "That is much appreciated."

The debrief ended and Beck dismissed the crew of the *Needle*. Echols rose onto stiff legs and wobbled toward the hatch. The petty officer who had had the panic attack, Zum, kept glancing around the room but seemed to be holding it together. One of the other petty officers held a firm grip on his elbow.

Once they were gone, Beck motioned for Wyatt and Laramie to sit at the table.

"Thoughts, please."

Wyatt went first. "Sounds like they were in a tough spot, sir. If constriction somehow spread to the *Alexander*, to RESIT Dagger ... well, it might explain why all their assets seem to be missing."

"Possibly." Beck rubbed his fingers together. "You said you encountered a normal crew on Gateway Station, didn't you? When you extracted from Juliet on that freighter."

"Yes, sir."

"Echols said they'd been unable to hail Gateway."

"He did, sir," Wyatt agreed.

"He seems to be implying that constriction broke out on the station. Wouldn't that be contradictory with your report?"

Wyatt frowned. "Yes, sir. That is not what we saw."

The major turned his attention to Laramie. "What do you think of their story, Staff Sergeant?"

Laramie seemed reluctant to talk.

"Speak," Beck ordered.

"I think he's full of it, sir."

Beck raised another eyebrow. So did Wyatt.

"Have you ever been hungry, Major?" Laramie continued. Her tone lacked any of its usual sarcasm. "I don't mean like how your stomach growls before dinner, sir. I mean the kind where you haven't eaten for a week, and you're not sure if you ever will."

"I can't say I have, no."

"I've seen it, sir. Up close. You grow up on the frontier on Juliet, sooner or later you're going to come across hunger. You're going to see ranchers who lost all their stock to hoppers. You're going to meet a drifter who would slit your throat for a bite to eat. There's a lot of hardship outside the big city, sir. It can get real basic, real fast.

"These guys don't have that look. They said they were on day ninety of a sixty-day mission? Bullshit. They would have been half-starved crazy. But they don't have that look. They actually seem pretty well fed to me."

Beck turned to his adjutant. "What did they say about resupply with *Alexander*?"

Captain Sims scrolled his fingers along his tablet computer, his eyes glazed over from his neural stub. "He said they received supplies and dinner once aboard, but then immediately pivoted into the firefight. No mention of significant provisioning."

"And then they got the hell out of town."

"Yes, sir."

Beck's gaze swiveled over to Wyatt, his expression that of a professor looking upon his protégé. "It appears we have conflicting information, Lieutenant. The Fast Scout captain claims an outbreak of constriction has overrun RESIT Dagger Command. Your staff sergeant thinks he's lying. What would you do in this situation?"

Wyatt stole a glance at Chappelle. His platoon leader stared back like an enigma, but he felt the weight of the warning from earlier just the same. *I hope the major's faith in you isn't misplaced.*

"Well?" Beck prompted.

"Sir." Wyatt chose his words with care. "If I couldn't prove one story, I'd try to disprove the other. Sir."

Beck steepled his fingers in thought for a long moment. Then he cleared his throat.

"Sims, please ask Captain Kazimira to plot a course for Macbeth Lagrange Four. Let's see if we can find *Alexander*."

12

Part headquarters, part motor pool, a RESIT command carrier acted as a home to the top brass and lowliest mechanic alike. They would deploy around the system to be close to hotspots and support troop carriers like *Vigorous* in monitoring shipping and protecting commerce. But they also typically stayed back from any action, parking instead in nice, stable orbits or Lagrange points as a nearby operating base for troops and supplies. Without steady acceleration, the massive spacecraft relied on spinning centrifugal rings to provide artificial gravity to its crew. Those same rings limited each vessel to the star system in which it had been built; their circumference made them far too large to transit through the quantum gate system.

Command carriers like *Alexander* were the largest spacecraft ever built.

Laramie couldn't get her head around the idea of one of them being destroyed.

Gossip spread from crew to trooper and back again as *Vigorous* closed in on Lagrange Point Four. Constricted had taken over the crew. No, the crew had abandoned ship. A mutiny had killed everyone onboard. Troopers had held their ground, fled like cowards, pushed the constricted back and flushed them out the airlock.

Now Laramie sat in the crowded belly of a Javelin, dressed in full hardsuit while they closed in. Beck had ordered up every squad for boarding. Laramie didn't disagree with that direction. But part of her was terrified at what they would find.

Wyatt was sitting across from Captain Chappelle near the flight deck hatch. She switched on a private channel and called him up. "LT?"

"What is it?" he said.

"Any updates on that ETA? I gotta pee."

Wyatt laughed. "Twenty minutes. Can't help you on the second part."

"Why aren't we in pressure sleeves? We're just boarding a spacecraft."

"Chappelle said the whole ship is dark, so no EM field means full gear."

"Cosmic rays. Meh."

He chuckled again. "You really don't like hardsuits, do you?"

"Do you?"

"Not really."

"Okay then."

The truth was every trooper hated hardsuits. Thick and unwieldy on a good day, the additional covering of plastic mesh to stop meteorites or radiation hazards had earned them the nickname Spread Eagle. More importantly, they made everyone slow. For troopers working around

Proxima, that felt a bit too much like being a target for Oscars.

She cleared her throat for another salvo. "Do you think if we get the power back on, we can switch into—"

"Wait one."

Laramie saw Wyatt lean toward the flight deck, engaged in some conversation she couldn't hear. She could read the tension in his body language even through the bulk of the hardsuit.

"LT? What is it?"

He tapped the tablet on his forearm. "I'm sending you the nose camera feed."

A moment later, the neural stub pressed against Laramie's eye socket hijacked her optic nerve. Her vision filled with the deep black of space. Stars littered the expanse, an audience of little pinpricks waiting to see what performance the Javelin crew would provide. Directly below them, a powerful floodlight washed over a shape that blotted out half the sky.

The Javelin cruised at a slow pace. Laramie watched intently. She had to blink several times before she understood what she was looking at.

Alexander looked like it had been raked by a monster trying to take down its kill. Long gashes sliced through every sensor pod that would have fed signs of danger to the bridge crew. Along the hull, strips of metal twisted away from deep gouges exposing glimpses of the interior. In other places, neat holes anchored scorch marks that radiated across the black, puckered paint. It reminded Laramie of pictures she had seen of the black plague on Earth, victims with skin covered in pustules and sores begging to be concealed.

"My God," she gasped.

Wyatt's voice remained flat. "Those are from energy weapons. *Alexander* took hostile fire. A lot of it."

"Who?" Her throat was feeling tight.

"Do you know anyone besides RESIT who has that sort of firepower?"

Laramie had no words. Even a Fast Attack like *Razor* couldn't inflict this sort of damage. This would have been done by a destroyer. More than one.

The Javelin banked and moved gracefully over the hull. Laramie caught a glimpse of the two centrifugal rings near the middle of the ship, the giant spoked wheels that provided artificial gravity while floating in space. Now they had large sections missing, cut away by a megawatt laser like a surgeon's scalpel.

Chappelle's voice came over the command channel. "Lieutenant Wills. See past the rings?"

It was hard to imagine things getting worse, but worse was exactly what Laramie saw. A massive hole gouged through the hull into the command carrier's hangar bay. Here the edges of metal bent inward, but the surrounding exterior bulged as if buckled from within.

"I see it, sir," Wyatt said.

"That's what a torpedo strike looks like."

Laramie had never seen a Pilum impact. Torpedoes were designed to penetrate even armored hulls and abolish a spacecraft's existence from within—not something RESIT typically employed in their role of preserving life and property. Now she saw how one had been fired into *Alexander*. Her hand went to her mouth, except that her fingers could only press against the outer visor of her hardsuit.

A transmission in the background caught her attention. *Piranha*, their own destroyer, was patrolling the perimeter. A voice advised no hostiles detected. Somehow that didn't seem very reassuring.

The nose camera video abruptly shut off and returned Laramie's vision to the trooper sitting across from her.

"Battle, listen up," Wyatt said. "New orders. We're going to board the carrier through one of the hull breaches. The Javelin will maneuver in close, but it will still be twenty meters of freefall between each spacecraft. We'll use a tow line and assemble inside the hangar bay." He paused. "Have weapons ready."

Weapons ready? What did he think they would find inside a dead hulk?

A series of aye, ayes filled the comm. Wyatt nodded to Laramie. "Let's get it moving."

Time for work. She swiveled the bulk of her hardsuit around so she could see to whom she was issuing orders.   "Gavin, ready up with the harpoon."

"Yes, ma'am."

The Javelin began to reorient itself, twisting in the microgravity as it lined up against a nearby hull breach. The interior light switched to red as Teo called out the warning for depressurization. Laramie listened through her helmet as a hiss matured into a roar and then faded smoothly into nothing more than a faint vibration.

Teo's voice returned on the comm. "Opening the rear door in three ... two ... one."

Another barely discernible hum. The aft of the Javelin spread apart and revealed the silver-white hull of *Alexander* shining brightly under the floods. Smooth metal gave way to a jagged gash that twisted inward from the torpedo strike.

Laramie's hands gripped the Vector tightly in her hands. She thought of her teammates, her squad, her platoon. These were more than friends. RESIT was her family. Her brothers and sisters risked their lives every day in an extremely dangerous job. So how could another RESIT vessel turn its weapons on its own? How many people died from that torpedo strike? Anger swelled within her. If she ever got hold of one of those bastards, she would lock both hands around his neck until his neck popped off.

But another emotion kept trying to break through the fury. She remembered the golden sparks burning her mind in Parrell. She felt her stomach turning inside out from the hundreds of constricted at the spaceport. She knew she had to keep the fires of her anger stoked. She couldn't give the fear a chance to escape.

"Harpoon ready, Staff Sergeant," Gavin said on the comm.

She blinked back to it. Her humanity would have to wait.

"Weapons free," she said.

The burly trooper swiveled the harpoon launcher on its mount and pressed the trigger. The projectile leaped from the barrel in absolute silence. A few seconds later the tow line slackened, carried only by the momentum of its own mass.

Gavin read the status panel mounted to the harpoon gun. "Solid hit."

"Tighten up the line," she told him.

"Aye, aye."

"Battle Squad, latch up."

Laramie opened the carabiner at the end of her suit's tether and clipped herself to the tow line. The others followed suit, one by one, until all eight of her squad were secured against the risk of drifting away. As she floated in the middle of the cargo bay, her feet bumped against a trooper from Chemo Squad who would no doubt be deployed through a different breach in the hull after her own team cleared out of the way.

Wyatt gave her a thumbs up from the other end of the stack.

"On me," she said, and launched herself into the void.

The corpse of *Alexander* stretched left to right in front of her. Her eyes noted the smooth arcs of the hull and how it was interrupted by the ragged cuts of hostile fire. Little eddies of debris floated near some of the wounds. She couldn't help but feel the violation. This was the result of a human act. Not a disease. Not chance. People had done this. It felt like someone had broken into her home and murdered her family.

Approaching the threshold of the torpedo impact, Laramie abruptly plunged into the darkness of the interior. She tapped on her suit's helmet light and saw a large storage rack blare into existence in front of her. Next to it, the end of a harpoon projectile toward which she was rapidly approaching.

Then, contact.

Her legs caught her momentum. She grabbed the tow line to keep from rebounding and unclipped the carabiner. Slowly, Laramie reoriented her body until her mag boots could find purchase against the metal decking.

"I'm clear of the tow line."

"Ten seconds behind you," Carlos said.

Laramie walked carefully so her footing didn't slip. Around her stretched the carrier's hangar bay, a massive open cavity where vehicles and equipment could be serviced in a shirt-sleeves environment. A few storage crates had broken free and now floated silently in the vacuum. On the adjacent wall, the clamp of a zero-gee crane embraced a Javelin engine with several missing panels. Otherwise, most of the hangar lay empty.

"I'm clear," Carlos said.

"I've got the left," Laramie said. "Take the right."

She continued her scan of the area with her Vector raised. Her neural stub fed her only the grainy black and white of infrared.

Carlos's voice crackled in a disapproving tone. "I don't see no bodies, Staff Sergeant."

"Not much debris, either. I wonder if the hangar was pressurized when the torpedo hit?"

"You think they got jumped."

"Maybe."

The rest of the troopers formed up a perimeter and scanned for threats. Even though they were floating in an empty hangar bay of a dead spacecraft, Laramie knew ambushes took place through surprise. She wasn't about to let her squad fall into a trap like whatever caught the crew of the *Alexander*. So far, though, nothing.

Wyatt ordered them to form up near a large powered door that stood four meters square, with black-and-yellow safety tape around the threshold. The indicators on the control pad remained dark. Carlos stood in front of the small viewing port and scanned the other side with his helmet camera.

"Temperature is the same beyond the door. No atmosphere."

Wyatt motioned for Gavin to move up. "Pop it open."

The big trooper removed an access panel to expose a lever and a yellow handwheel. As he braced his feet on a nearby handhold, Gavin gripped the lever with two massive hands and pulled it to the side. Laramie couldn't hear the clutch disengaging from the motor, but it was obvious that was the case when Gavin started turning the handwheel, cranking the hatch door ever so slowly.

"Acid One, this is Battle," Wyatt said on the comm.

"I read you, Battle."

"Be advised, we are entering the port-side access corridor. Area appears to be depressurized."

"Copy. Other squads are seeing the same thing. Be careful."

Wyatt turned to Laramie. She saw the faint traces of his helmet camera array through the heavy faceplate. "Take the squad up."

"Affirmative, LT."

She took a deep breath and ordered her troopers to follow her into the destruction.

13

USIC *Alexander*
Lagrange Point 4, Alpha Centauri A
30 March 2272

They searched with care through the access corridor. Destruction and disarray lay everywhere. Many of the smaller rooms did not have airtight doors, and the ones that did had no pressure behind them. One berth contained a constellation of testing and calibration tools that had burst forth from a poorly secured locker. Another hatch led to a maintenance compartment that harbored a strange knocking noise. After spending fifteen minutes forcing the door open, it turned out to be a broken water line that pulsed intermittent spray into the vacuum.

Laramie found herself struggling to stay focused. Half a decade in RESIT had given her plenty of opportunity to do recovery missions, but this one felt far different that anything she'd seen before. This was a RESIT vessel. She knew intimately how crowded and alive *Cromwell* felt whenever she was aboard. Walking through the corridors meant having to dodge crew headed the other way. Announcements on the comm sent squads of troopers to duty stations or recreational events. Now she was surrounded by an empty shell. Not even the faint whisper of the ventilation system thrummed behind the walls. If a command carrier could slip into the afterlife, what chance did *Vigorous* have against whoever had done this?

Wyatt gave periodic updates to Chappelle as they moved forward. "Acid, be advised, we are approaching Elevator Two on A-ring. Still no power in this section of the ship."

"Copy. Any bodies?"

"No, sir."

"Okay. Be careful. Echo squad is reporting dead troopers near the server room. Signs of small arms fire on the nearby bulkheads."

That caught Laramie's attention. A firefight? Near one of the most secure locations on the spacecraft?

Wyatt apparently had the same thought. He froze dead in the microgravity. "Who were they shooting at, sir?" he asked.

"Unknown. There are five troopers, all with Dagger insignias. Two have holes in their ARC vests. None are wearing pressure sleeves."

"Did laser fire get them, or explosive decompression?"

"Unknown. Just be careful."

"Understood."

Laramie frowned as she listened in. She hailed Wyatt on a private channel. "LT, this is crazy. You think there was a hostile boarding?"

"Or a mutiny. I don't know."

"On a *command carrier*?" she said, disbelieving.

He remained silent for a few moments. "It could make sense if someone was trying to get access to sensitive data. RESIT logs, encryption protocols. Or maybe they were shooting at constricted crew, like Echols suggested."

"I told you I don't believe him."

"Well, if you're wrong, we'd better be ready for an ambush."

Laramie gulped.

"Let's move," Wyatt said.

As expected, the elevator system also had no power. They had to use the emergency access tube. Carlos took point and swung through the hatch as Laramie followed. In the broad beam of her helmet light she saw a long, yellow ladder that extended up to a landing some twenty meters away. Another offset ladder would continue from that landing through the great spoke that connected the centrifugal ring. She started floating up, using the ladder rungs to guide herself in the microgravity.

"See anything, Carlos?" she called.

The reply came back with the labored breathing of broken ribs not quite healed. "Clear so far. I don't see no hull breaches."

"The hull must be compromised at the other end."

"Yes, Staff Sergeant."

A minute later she reached the first landing. She pushed herself through the opening and turned to grasp the next ladder. A quick look back "down" showed the rest of her squad following up the shaft.

"There are holes up here, Staff Sergeant," Carlos said from ten meters ahead of her. "A bunch of them."

Laramie caught the location of one of them. She could see stars through it.

"Jesus. Did they target every compartment?"

"Say again, Staff Sergeant?" Carlos called. "You cut out."

"Talking to myself. Just keep moving up."

"I'm already at the end, at the crew deck," he said. "The hatch is busted open. Looks like it might have buckled."

"From decompression?" Laramie asked.

"I don't think so. There's big damage around it. From big weapons."

"Well, laser fire ripped the hell out of everything else. Not a surprise the rings aren't turning anymore."

"Yes, Staff Sergeant."

Laramie glided in freefall as she closed in on Carlos. At the crew deck level above her, she could see the trooper peering through an open hatch.

"Hold up, Carlos. Let me catch up with you before moving on."

"You got it—oh, *Dios mío.*"

"What is it?"

Laramie reached the top of the shaft. The hatch that should have kept the living quarters safe sat cocked at an angle inside a track that was no longer straight. Wires and buckled pipes poked through bulkheads above and below. Beyond the edge of the heavy door, an emergency light flickered, its staccato pulses revealing a corridor filled with horror.

Bodies dressed in work utilities floated in a motionless ballet around the length of C-berth. Exposed faces gazed into nothing, their skin drawn and desiccated like the pictures of Egyptian mummies Laramie had seen in grade school. One male trooper had dark blotches around his eyes and forehead. The blonde hair of another young woman encircled her face like the halo of a dead angel.

Laramie counted seven of them. Seven lives extinguished so quickly, they probably hadn't even had time to realize they had died.

"LT, we have bodies in the corridor," she said. "All fatalities."

"Understood."

She had to force some extra calm into her voice. "Carlos, check 'em."

They exited the access shaft and reoriented themselves so that they wouldn't be walking on the ceiling. The A-ring corridor curved away with a gentle angle that swept along the circumference of the structure. Without any rotation, the inside of the corridor proved vaguely disorienting.

Laramie worked her way past buckled deck plates to look for signs of life. It quickly proved to be a waste of time. She saw a corpse floating in the hatch of a wardroom, a male, with graying black hair and sunken eyes rolled back into his head. An insignia on his utilities marked him as bridge crew. The pressure sleeve pulled over his legs indicated he had been attempting to suit up for emergency decompression. Obviously, he didn't make it.

Is this what it means to die? Laramie thought. A desperate bid for survival, only to fade into nothing? She wondered if this crewman even knew what was happening to him as he expired, if his consciousness had a chance to record its own end. And if it did, where did the memory go? Did that last memory float away into the ether, evaporating, like the afterburn of a bright light when a room suddenly went dark?

A flashlight beam swept the corridor from behind her. She turned to see the rest of her squad exiting the access shaft, with the lieutenant at the rear.

"Split into two teams and check for survivors," Wyatt said.

There aren't going to be any, Laramie thought. "Aye, aye, LT."

"Laramie, take Kenny and Carlos. Gav and Rash are with me."

"Wilco."

They moved along the sweep of corridor. More officer berths and storage rooms. More bodies. The latrine held two corpses without any clothes, literally caught with their pants down.

Then came the galley. The airless void held a mixture of troopers and their food suspended haphazardly around the tables. Dining trays reflected the searchlights from the hardsuit helmets to create an eerie pall around the compartment. None of the bodies wore any survival gear. One woman's leg twisted around a seating bench, clearly broken in several places.

"Report in," Wyatt said on the comm.

"Battle Two," she replied. "We're in the enlisted mess. LT, whoever attacked *Alexander* must have had complete surprise. The people here didn't have a chance at emergency procedures."

"Copy that. Every squad is seeing the same thing. Keep searching."

"Aye, aye."

They checked the kitchen, sifting through blobs of food that had been frozen, cooked, then freeze-dried again in the cold vacuum. One bulkhead was splattered in grease from the busted seals of a zero-gee pressure cooker. More dead bodies floated in strange poses in some awful menagerie. Laramie didn't have to check for vitals. The gaunt remains gave their owners' condition away, with leathery flesh having long boiled away all its moisture.

They came to one of the airlocks that partitioned off the next section of A-ring. It appeared to be intact. But when Carlos scanned the porthole, it became clear the trace atmosphere on the other side was insufficient for life. He popped the hatch and a gentle wind of decompression blew the nearby debris past them.

"Whoever shot this ship up took care to aim at every section," Carlos said.

Laramie frowned. "Just keep moving,"

Her team moved forward through the darkness. She took the left with Kenny as they entered F berth. A nearby wardroom had a jammed door that had only partially closed, another casualty to explosive decompression. She struggled to force the door open to get inside. Her heart fell as she thought about all the safeguards, all the emergency procedures that were supposed to help troopers survive if a spacecraft lost atmosphere. They'd all failed. And if a RESIT ship couldn't withstand a catastrophic attack, what chance did anyone else really have?

The thoughts refused to leave as she scanned the darkened wardroom, buzzing around her like pesky insects. Another inert body floated here. How long had this crewman lasted when they lost atmosphere? Did he ignore his instincts and exhale everything so that his lungs didn't rupture against the vacuum? Or did he hold his breath, bursting himself from the inside? It looked like he'd been in a desperate race to get his pressure sleeve on, remarkable given he probably only had fifteen seconds before he passed out. It didn't matter. This pour soul would just be another casualty in a long list of names for Beck to file in his report.

She grasped his shoulder to get a better view of his rank insignia.

Two gloved hands snatched back at her.

14

Adrenaline flooded Laramie's senses. She had been so lost in her thoughts that she hadn't been paying attention.

This trooper had managed to seal his pressure sleeve. He had a CORE helmet over his head, recirculating and scrubbing whatever paltry oxygen remained in the closed system. His hands were holding on to her like a drowning man slipping under the waves.

"Carlos! Help!"

The strength left the trooper's grip and his hands slackened. Laramie thought he must be losing consciousness. How long had he been here, holding on to a thread of life? Days? Longer? Had he found a little bubble of air somewhere to lift his helmet and choke down bits of food? It didn't matter. Laramie knew the carbon dioxide scrubber in his helmet had to be on the verge of failing. They needed to act. Now.

A dull reverberation through her magnetic boots told Laramie that something was moving behind her. Carlos stumbled through the zero gee until he was standing next to her.

"Holy shit. Did he get his gear on?"

Laramie was already unhooking the emergency oxygen hose on her hardsuit. A moment later, she snapped the connector to the port under the chin of the trooper's CORE helmet. That would help. But air supply would only be part of the solution.

This guy couldn't be in good shape. According to Echols's story, the attack had been weeks ago. Laramie sure didn't want him to survive long enough just to die later.

"Battle One, Battle Two," she said on the squad channel. "We've found a survivor."

"Say again?"

"We found a live trooper. He's got a sleeve and helmet on but is in bad shape, in and out of consciousness. I'm taking him to the Javelin."

"Copy that, Two." Wyatt's voice took on an extra spark. "I'll rendezvous with you. Get him back ASAP. Have Carlos continue the search pattern."

"Roger."

While Wyatt radioed Chappelle, Laramie pulled the trooper's arm over her shoulder. Even though the microgravity neutralized the extra weight, the last thing she needed was for a floppy appendage to get caught on every single obstacle. She jostled the trooper past the jammed door and started hauling him back the way she came.

It wasn't until they reached the first landing in the emergency shaft that the difficulty started. The trooper was coming to. Uncomprehending of his new development, he tried to break free from the oxygen hose connecting the two of them together. Laramie told him to calm down through the comm, but couldn't tell if he could hear her. Then her hand signals to explain their extraction just made him panic more. She would just have to go for speed, she decided. She clamped her fingers around his wrist and hauled him the rest of the way down the shaft.

"Coming up behind you," Wyatt said.

The trooper was trying to twist out of her grasp. "He's panicked, LT. Help me."

Wyatt took the trooper's other elbow. Using their mag boots, they frog-marched him back to the empty void of the breached hangar and tethered themselves to the tow line. A coordinated push off the bulkhead propelled them back to the Javelin.

The trooper's body went limp again. Laramie wondered again how long he must have struggled to survive, surrounded by corpses in a dead spacecraft, with nothing to pass the time but the knowledge of betrayal by a RESIT attack ship. She couldn't imagine the despair of knowing that treachery. Or maybe he hadn't known. Judging from the other bodies, the attack had happened quickly. Perhaps this trooper had managed to hang on so long by clinging to the vain hope of rescue. Laramie was sure he was probably expecting his own team.

Ahead of them, the Javelin's position lights beckoned at them from across the inky blackness. She could see the crew chief waving at them from the edge of the rear cargo ramp. They were almost there now. Laramie tried to control her own breathing as they crossed the threshold of the interior. Then they were inside. She released the trooper and he ricocheted limply against the harpoon gun.

"LT, we can't medically assess this guy with the bay open," she said.

Wyatt was already grappling with the tow line release when his voice came over the comm. "Acid One, Battle One, priority comm."

"Acid One Actual, go ahead."

"We have the survivor aboard Savage Echo. Request to release tow line and medevac to *Vigorous?*"

"Affirmative on that request, Battle One. We'll hitch a ride back with another platoon. Survivor takes priority."

Wyatt pulled the release lever, and the tow line snaked away through the microgravity.

"Close the door, Teo."

Laramie hauled the Dagger trooper to the side of the hull and looped his arm through a cargo strap. He was coming back around again, his head jerking left and right. They were going to have trouble keeping him calm enough for the MedSurg. Lack of oxygen, malnourishment, extended exposure to cosmic rays—she couldn't imagine it would be good. But maybe he still had a chance, and that was all she needed to fight for him.

The hissing from beyond her helmet turned into a dull roar as Teo finished repressurizing the cargo bay. Laramie broke the seal on her suit and slid her helmet visor up. The crew chief was already pulling an IV bag out for the peristaltic pump. Wyatt swung the MedSurg sensor arm free of its mounting so that they could start getting vitals. She reached toward his CORE helmet and turned the ring collar along the bottom edge.

"It's okay, Dagger," she said. She tried to make her voice sound reassuring. "We're here to help. It's going to be okay."

Two hands went up to her wrists. They started to push her arms away.

"We're RESIT. It's okay."

One of the trooper's hands closed around her arm. She noted how weak his grip felt. He was still in a panic but didn't have the strength to defend himself.

"Hey. I'm Laramie. You've been in there a long time. We just need to stabilize your vitals, and then we'll talk. Okay?"

"IV's ready," the crew chief said.

"It's okay," Laramie repeated.

She pulled his CORE helmet off. The trooper had close-cropped hair. Gaunt cheeks with weeks of a scraggly beard—

Eyes—

"*Get away from me!*" Laramie screamed.

Time skipped.

It felt like a movie vid that was bouncing past corrupted frames, breaking continuity by slipping into the next scene without a smooth transition. Laramie was looking down the sights of her pistol, her hands shaking. She was pointing it at the Dagger trooper staring back at her.

Pinprick pupils.

Her index finger tightened on the trigger.

Suddenly she was flying sideways through the microgravity. Something shoved her arms upward. Then she saw stars as her body slammed into the unforgiving metal of a rigid bulkhead. She fought to bring her pistol back down and get off as many shots as she could before the sparks came back ...

"Staff Sergeant! Look at me!"

Someone shook her with a violent edge. Her body rotated and then the trooper was gone, his face replaced by that of her squad leader.

"LT?"

"Release your pistol! That's an order!"

She realized Wyatt had his hand over the barrel and was twisting it out of her grip. Laramie blinked. What just happened?

Then it came flooding back to her—the threat, the urgency, the precious few seconds she had to shoot. She struggled to win her pistol back. Wyatt wouldn't let go, and their bodies rotated violently in freefall. Out of the corner of her eye, she saw the Dagger trooper slackening in his chair.

Her voice found its way out. "Jesus Christ, LT, shoot him! Before the sparks!"

"Laramie," Wyatt said. His voice held the forced calm of command. "Look at *me*. Give me your pistol. Now."

Their eyes met. She could see the lucidity in them. She forced her grip to relax, and Wyatt bent the weapon from her fingers.

"He's ... this trooper is—"

"We don't know what he is," Wyatt replied. "But burning a hole in him won't answer anything."

"He's dangerous!"

Wyatt glanced over his shoulder. "Not for the time being."

She followed his gaze to see the crew chief velcroing a used syringe against a nearby medical kit. He must have added a sedative to the IV bulb. Now, with his upper body secured in a seat harness, the rest of the constricted Dagger trooper drifted into a full neutral position. The crew chief glanced over at them with a slightly panicked expression before he finished strapping him against the hull.

Wyatt loosened his grasp on Laramie's wrists. "We'll keep him out cold until the medical can take a look. He won't be able to attack anybody."

"Why take that risk?" Laramie wanted her Beretta back.

He gave her a stern look, as if the answer was obvious. "Because we need to find out what happened here if we're going to save your home."

15

This time, waking up wasn't a gentle ascent to consciousness. Chris came to with a jolt of pain in his side that sent his arms flailing. He jerked upright in his patient bed, halfway between yelping for painkillers and ready to defend himself with hand-to-hand, only to find Finn standing over him and grinning ear to ear across a sea of freckles. The finger his friend had jammed into his bandage stood out like a gangster's tommy gun.

"What the hell?" Chris grumbled.

"I said your name five times. I had to wake you up somehow."

"By jacking with my injury?"

Finn made a series of kissing noises in reply.

In reality, he was overjoyed to see his friend. They had known each other since the early days of Governor Hewitt's security team. Both shared that unbreakable bond of brotherhood that came with being Marines. And the same caustic sense of humor.

The flare of fire around his wound began to subside. Chris managed to sit upright and rolled his head around his shoulders. Popping noises called out his age.

"So, give it up," Finn said, scratching the reddish stubble on his chin. "How much longer till you're out? I'm getting tired of showing all these troopers how to fight."

"Up to the doc. Any answer isn't fast enough."

"Copy that. Hey—easy, don't reinjure yourself. You trying to get up?"

Moving was proving more difficult than when he'd last been awake. Who knew healing could hurt so much? Maybe Kenta had changed his medication levels. Chris pivoted on the bed with clenched teeth until he had one leg off the side. As usual, his concerns were not about himself. "Did you see Annika?"

"Yeah, Calista's talking to her right now."

"She's awake?" It took all his concentration not to hurt himself.

Finn grabbed his arms. "I'm not sure you should be getting up."

"I need to see her."

The two men swayed back and forth for a moment. But determination and wide stances won the day as Chris managed to keep his balance. The Marines hobbled together into the main med bay area.

Doctor Bell was sitting in his usual spot at the physician workstation, ringed by a bank of holo monitors like some defensive embankment. On the other side of the berth, Annika sat propped upright against a pillow on her bed. Finn's daughter knelt next to her, her thin and wiry body pressed close, continually sweeping away the black hair drooping in front of her face. They were taking turns writing on a tablet to each other.

"Hey," Chris said, his voice suddenly thick with emotion.

Two sets of eyes swiveled toward him. Calista jumped to her feet and rushed Chris, cinching her arms around his waist more tightly than he would have thought possible by a thirteen-year-old. It would have knocked him over if Finn hadn't been next to him.

"Uncle Chris, you're okay!" the girl squealed.

"Hey, kiddo. You know me. Almost as tough as your dad."

"Definitely almost," Finn added.

Chris felt his eyes moisten as he hugged her back. Her hair obscured her face, but he could feel her sobbing. This past year had been a hard one. He had watched his friend's daughter grow up far too much during that time.

Calista's voice came out muffled from the side of his patient gown. "We were so worried about you. Are you okay?"

"Still kicking and screaming." He looked over at Annika and found her staring back with a broad smile on her face. She lifted her arms, waiting expectantly for a hug of her own.

He shuffled to her bed, Finn on one side, Calista still attached to the other. The next thing he knew he had a third human being somehow wrapped around his body. Annika's embrace felt gentler but no less intense. He smelled her hair, felt the coolness of her arms against his neck. Chris closed his eyes and let the sensation of the moment settle into him, the press of humanity that reminded him he was alive.

After a long embrace, Chris leaned back to assess her. She seemed, for lack of a better word, normal. No pinprick pupils, good skin color, a broad smile that displayed pearly white teeth. She watched him with affection, not with any predatory, otherworldly intensity.

A rush of relief flowed through him faster than water rushing out of an overturned tub. This was still the same girl. She didn't have it, no way.

"Good to see you awake, Anni."

The smiles kept coming, and that was enough.

The med bay hatch slid open and Dr. Kenta walked in, her arms clutching an array of supplies against the blue piping of her gray medical uniform. She placed several zero-gee drink bulbs on the desk and shot a disapproving look at Chris. "You're not supposed to be up, Master Sergeant."

Chris glanced at her while he kept his hand on Annika's shoulder. "I had a hasty family reunion I couldn't miss."

For the briefest of moments, the trace of a smile almost graced Kenta's lips. Then the professional façade of a physician returned. She set down the jumble of supplies she had brought. "Okay, we've got milk, juice, and hot chocolate. Who wants what?"

"Hot chocolate!" Calista said brightly, releasing her prey. Annika's eyebrows went up as she craned her neck past Chris's shoulder. She raised her hand.

"I thought so." Kenta sorted through the bulbs and selected two for the girls. "And for you, Doctor Bell, we have coffee."

"Oh, that's beautiful," Bell said. "Thank you."

Kenta kept one bulb in her hand and looked over at Chris. "And how about you, Mr. Difficult?"

"Whiskey?"

"No," she said.

"What if we dilute it in coffee?"

"Still no."

Chris threw her a grin, but his charms failed to break the barrier. He noted how tall Kenta was, and older, with Asian features and thick, black hair pulled back into a bun. If medicine hadn't been her calling, he could have easily seen her as a schoolteacher.

She held out a drink bulb.

"Coffee it is," Chris said.

"How's your arm? You're still favoring your left."

"It's okay. Aches a little bit. Don't miss the splint, though."

"Give it another week. Simple fractures are easy. The wound in your side is the tricky one because of the organ damage."

"I can fix that with whiskey."

Kenta narrowed her eyes at him. A twinkle of amusement almost slipped through the cracks again. "How about your other pain? You're about due for another dose of terranol."

"Let me try without. I'm not liking the side effects so much."

Kenta nodded. "Epione can give you a stool softener with it if you need it."

"Copy that."

Chris didn't really care about the constipation. He just didn't want the fog. The narcotic pain meds clouded his mind in a way that made him feel dull and slow—not a good feeling for someone embroiled in guerrilla warfare for the better part of a year. And if that meant he had to tough out some discomfort for a week or two, he'd gladly do it through gritted teeth and balled fists.

He turned the valve on the drink bulb and took a swig. He spit it back almost as quickly. "Oh my God. I thought you said this was coffee?"

Jack Bell chuckled. "Tiamat's finest, Thompson."

"Do they grow the beans in shit?"

Bell laughed again and drank another long pull, as if spiting him would somehow cross off a couple more items on his to-do list.

Kenta wasn't listening to the banter. She had faced the bulkhead and her hand was pressed against her comm earpiece. When she turned back, her eyes flitted with urgent efficiency across the med bay's current inhabitants. "Okay, I need all of you to clear the med bay. Master Sergeant, you can continue your reunion with Annika in the other room. Doctor Bell, I'd appreciate your help. The rest—out. We've got incoming injured."

Chris could tell from the doctor's tone that this wasn't some ensign slipping down a ladder. "From where?" he asked

Kenta pointed her finger at the hatch.

"Going," Chris said.

With Finn's help, he shuffled back to the bed from which he had only just won his freedom. Annika waited patiently for him to swing his legs back under the covers before she climbed up near his feet. A last few hugs from Calista. Then Finn patted Chris on the shoulder and escorted his daughter out, with a last glance clearly telegraphing that he still expected a full debrief on the events in the hangar. Then they were gone.

Annika smiled at Chris, eyes shining. She clutched a personal tablet computer to her chest.

"Isn't that Calista's?" he asked, pointing to the tablet.

A mischievous smile flashed across Annika's lips.

"I see," he said. "So, what were you two monkeys chatting about while I was asleep?"

The tablet lowered and a few quick finger taps allowed Annika to type a message. She showed the screen to Chris.

SCHOOLWORK.

"Huh. No wonder you were so happy for me to interrupt."

Tap-tap-tap. THAT'S NOT WHY!

"I'm just saying." Chris glanced through the hatch and saw Doctor Kenta and Jack Bell prepping a new patient bed. Terse snippets flew between them as they hurried about the cabin. He turned away and tried to stay focused on Anni. "So, you're keeping Calista's schoolwork for her. Uh-huh. What could possibly be so interesting that she's letting you do that for her?"

She showed the tablet again. HISTORY.

"Oh, okay. You always did like that stuff. What's she studying? Egyptians? The American Revolution?"

She frowned and tapped some more.

THAT'S NOT OUR PLANET.

"But it's mine. Doesn't that count?"

Annika made a face somewhere between frowning and smiling.

WE'RE LEARNING HOW DUNCAN PIPER DISCOVERED JULIET.

"Pretty sure a satellite telescope did that."

BUT CAPTAIN PIPER FLEW HERE.

Chris had to remember he was talking to a third grader. "Long way to travel from Earth, huh? It took Longshot like fifty or sixty years."

HE MUST HAVE BEEN OLD.

"He was by the time he got here." Chris was getting into this; it seemed like ages since he had held any sort of conversation with the young Miss

Hewitt. "But he got that quantum gate up and running, didn't he? That way it wouldn't take as long for other people to travel to Earth."

WOW.

"What does your lesson say about the *first* mission, the one before Piper's?"

I CAN'T REMEMBER.

A computerized voice sounded from the other room. Chris glimpsed one of Epione's arms prepping IV bags. He tried to blot it out. He had craved this moment, a sliver of normalcy with Annika, free of gunfire and constriction and death. "It was called Scattershot. You see, the scientists who discovered Juliet still didn't know much about it because it was so far away. No one wanted to travel that far and find just an uninhabitable rock. So, they had this idea to do something before. Know what it was?"

Tap-tap. WHAT DID THEY DO BEFORE?

"They sent probes first. They shot a dozen little probes through space toward Alpha A. It took them over a hundred years to get to Juliet."

Kenta was giving terse commands to the MedSurg bot in the other compartment. Whatever was coming sounded like a big deal. Chris took Annika's hand in his, intent on finishing his story even if it meant rushing. "But what's cool is they were special probes. Once they got here, they landed on whatever they could find—asteroids, Romeo, everything. Then they mined rocks and metals to build more probes.

That was their main job. To build more of themselves."

THEY BUILT BABY ROBOTS?

"Yeah. And when there were enough of them, they scouted out the system together. Eventually they were smart enough to see that Juliet was habitable. So, they got together and beamed all that information back to Earth. That's why Captain Piper felt good that his mission would be successful. He already knew what was waiting here before he left."

Annika sat on the bed, captivated by Chris's narrative. He always knew he could tell a good yarn, and he gave her arm a squeeze to punctuate his success. But after a few moments her face fell, and she stared down at her tablet with sadness in her eyes. No, not sadness. Resignation?

She tapped the keys on the screen.

SOMETIMES I FEEL LIKE A BABY ROBOT.

He scowled. What the hell was that supposed to mean?

Before he had a chance to divine the intent behind an eight-year-old vocabulary, Chris found his train of thought interrupted as gruff words intruded from the med bay. Kenta was listening to the comm and telling Bell something about a combative patient, how one dose of sedatives wasn't enough. Both had dressed in surgical scrubs. He watched the two physicians flank the robot arm extending from the track in the ceiling.

Tension flowed from the other room, thicker than water rushing downstream.

His bed sheets rustled. He turned to find Annika sitting bolt upright. Her expression had shifted into a stark intensity, as if she had heard a distant sound but couldn't quite figure out what it was.

"Hey," he asked. "You okay?"

Annika ignored him. Instead, her gaze tracked along the bulkhead, staring at the wall as if she could see right through it. A moment later she was facing the entrance.

The hatch slid open and the med bay ingested half a dozen troopers.

One of them came in strapped to a stretcher, moaning and agitated. The rest wore CORE helmets. Chris noted that one of the stragglers held a Vector pointed at the general vicinity of the injured trooper.

This wasn't something a preteen girl needed to see, Chris decided. Time to test the MedSurg bot's multitasking abilities. "Epione, shut my door," he said.

The interior hatch slid in its track, leaving a glimpse of a dismayed Bell standing over the new patient before it clicked shut. Chris reached over and put his arm around Annika to reassure her. "I wonder what—"

He froze.

Annika's eyes had constricted to pinpoint-sized pupils as they burned a hole through the wall into the other room.

16

USIC *Vigorous*
Lagrange Point 4, Alpha Centauri A
01 April 2272

It was only a dream, Chris told himself. Another horrible dream.

He was questioning a lot of things on his mind lately. His recollection of the hangar. Their extraction from Juliet. Even the progress of his wounds healing. All of it might have been just a collection of phantoms, his brain slipping through a narcotic fog of painkillers—meds he had to manage on his own now that Kenta had kicked him out of the med bay.

Annika had stared at that trooper just like she had at Izzy.

No, she was just concerned. She blinked after the door closed.

But I saw her eyes.

It was the lighting. You looked again and they were fine. Her eyes were fine.

They why did they separate us?

Kenta told you why. They needed the room for survivors from *Alexander*.

How long ago was that?

Good question.

He looked at the calendar on his tablet and struggled through the haze of his memory. Two days? He had trouble counting lately, and the mental effort to do math made him anxious. Plus, Kenta had said something about rejuvenation drugs and the possibility of "undesirable growths" if his cortisol levels stayed too high. He wasn't sure what that meant. It didn't sound like something he cared to find out.

He could read, though. And escaping into a novel had proven so far to be a good thing, a small reprieve from the cast of weird actors that lived in his dreams and danced to the symphony of aches and pains. He couldn't remember the last time he'd read fiction. All the noises faded to the background as the written word scrolled across his neural stub.

All that tranquility went out the window when Laramie yanked open the door to his berth. "There you are."

"Um," he managed.

Her silhouette loomed imperiously through the hatch. "Do you know how long I've been looking for you?"

"Kenta said I could finish my recovery in my bunk. What's it matter?"

Laramie stepped inside. Chris could tell she was amped—even in the dim lighting of the berth, he could see her chest heaving as if she'd run up a flight of stairs. He watched her scan the other bunks until she found Staff Sergeant Lenox radiating an intermittent rumble through his slumber.

He nodded at Lenox. "He's a hard sleeper."

"Is he?" she said, apparently wondering if that qualified enough for privacy.

Chris bookmarked the passage on his tablet and blinked away the neural feed. Laramie was just standing there in the doorway, hesitating. Uncertain.

"You okay?" he asked.

"We found a survivor. Onboard *Alexander*."

"I know. I got a glimpse when he came in."

"He's like Annika."

Chris stiffened in his bunk. "What's that supposed to mean?"

"Jack Bell has them both in med bay. He says whenever they get close to each other, their eyes change. That they both have constriction—"

"Annika doesn't have constriction."

"—but that it's different somehow, not like what's driving the epidemic—"

"Did you hear me?" He heard his voice getting harder, as if a hidden operator were turning up the intensity dial. "Annika isn't infected."

"Chris, I *saw* him." Her voice wavered.

"Him who?"

"The *survivor*." Laramie closed the hatch, leaving them in the relative darkness of the berth. "I took his helmet off. He was right in front of me. His eyes—I had my pistol pointed right at them. He *has* it."

"If that were true, we wouldn't be talking right now."

Laramie sat abruptly on the floor, drawing up her arms as if shielding herself from some arctic blast.

"Did you see sparks?" Chris asked.

"Well ... no."

"Did you feel any euphoria?"

"No."

"Then it's something else. Constriction isn't some weird eye fungus, Laramie. It's a deterioration of the mind. Did you see this guy do anything showing he could still think?"

"He wrote his name on a tablet," she said. "We sedated him in the Javelin, but Kenta and Bell revived him. They asked him his name and that's when he wrote it down. Will Jameson. He's a RESIT Dagger sergeant."

"There you go. No constriction."

"Then how do you explain Izzy?"

Chris started to retort, but the words failed to materialize. The constricted possessed a short list of hobbies: clustering in those weird circles, and hunting for fresh prey. They didn't write their names on tablets, and they sure as hell didn't use laser cutters. Corpsman Watanabe had something else going on, case closed.

But the armory guard was kneeling head-first on the deck. Izzy was the only one around, and he had the eyes.

Annika had the eyes, too, and she continued to be highly functional.

She also saved your life with a stare.

No. It had to be something else.

Laramie was watching him from across the berth. Judging by her reaction, Chris realized he must have been wearing his emotions on his sleeve.

"I'm sorry," she said. "I know how close you are to Annika."

"And she's going to be fine," he finished.

"She's not, Chris."

"*Yes, she is.*"

The anger flared back up. He could feel the flush of heat in his face, the tirade of profanity ready to charge forth from his voice box.

A small voice in the back of his head told him to stop. Laramie wasn't trying to goad him. Her insistence wasn't meant to hurt. And he understood and valued tough love, even if in this case the assertion about Anni was completely, flat-out wrong.

Chris sighed. A friend right now probably wouldn't be a bad thing.

Was he willing to take a risk?

Words started slipping out before he had a chance to stop them. "Look, Laramie. I don't have any family. I'm an only child. My parents are gone. I don't have any kids—at least, none that I know of. I've been a lone wolf my whole life."

His pulse quickened, vaguely reminding him of Kenta's warning about *high cortisol* and *undesirable growths*. Jeez. Marines weren't supposed to have feelings. He wasn't good at this kind of talk. It was a far cry from his expertise in pushing people away and shooting bad guys in the head. Yet something deep inside of him wanted to peel off that armor and become a human being again. Even now he wasn't sure he could do it, excavating emotions buried long ago in an emotional basement.

He stole a glance at Laramie. She sat in silence, watching. Waiting.

Shit.

"I've known Anni since she was *three*," Chris said, rubbing his forehead. "I moved off-world for a fresh start, ended up on Juliet. Pulling security for the governorship was the best gig I ever landed. I worked with Dak Hewitt during his campaign, got to know him, got to know Larissa, got to know Brouard, their son. Great people. And Anni was the baby. We hit it off, me and the kids. Hewitt was always dealing with state stuff. And you've seen Larissa in the vids, she was always entertaining and working on her causes. Not exactly the mothering type.

"So, Anni and Brouard and I just sort of adopted each other. They called me 'Uncle Chris.' Since working security is around the clock, I was always around them. I'd play with them sometimes. Brouard had this toy castle set where I'd help him march little knight figures around and kill monsters. Then Anni would come in, and the next thing you knew the monsters were having a tea party." Chris realized he was smiling. "Five years of that, watching them grow up."

"Sounds like you were close," Laramie said.

"Yeah."

The smile started to slide off. "When things started going bad, though ... it was bad. You'd think something like constriction, that is an existential threat. You would hope something like that would pull people together. It didn't. It brought out the worst. Martial law. Neighbors reporting each other. Food shortages, every man out for themselves. The whole fabric of Juliet, a culture where everyone always helped each other, it just fell apart. General McManus and the governor had these terrible arguments, screaming at the top of their lungs about the body count going up. Security got more difficult. Then McManus staged his coup. The last thing Hewitt said to me was to do everything I could to keep those kids safe."

"He trusted you."

"He shouldn't have. I failed. Brouard got shot in the chest. He was ten."

Chris shook his head at the memory. Four goons in police body armor firing at them without so much as a warning. He could smell the ozone hanging in the hallway as he and Finn returned fire. He could hear Calista screaming her lungs empty in terror from behind a storage crate. He tried to blink it away.

"I can't let that happen to Annika. I won't."

Laramie cleared her throat. "I'm sorry."

"Yeah."

The silence returned. Chris blinked some more, his eyes wetter than he remembered. He drew an unsteady deep breath to flush it all away. It hadn't been his intention to go there.

A random slice of pain in his abdomen brought him back. He glanced at Laramie. It had only been a few minutes earlier that she had charged his berth with anxious energy. Chris found her presence reassuring.

"Bell could be wrong," she said. "He says all the time they still don't understand how constriction works."

He couldn't tell if she meant it. Maybe she was just being conciliatory.

"Let's hope," he said.

Her eyes crinkled at the corners with her smile. A second later her expression turned back to serious as a comm message came over her earpiece.

"I need to go," she said.

"Of course. Something going on?"

"Wyatt's passing down an order from Beck." She frowned. "I'm being called to the bridge."

"That's not a normal thing, is it?"

"Very much no." She stood up and rubbed her hands together, seemingly uncertain of how to exit their conversation. "I'm sorry."

"It's all right. I'm glad you came by."

For a split second, Laramie smiled again. Then she was through the hatch and gone.

A strange, guttural echo sounded nearby as Sergeant Lenox rumbled in the bunk.

Alone again, Chris flipped over his tablet and tapped a key. The neural stub came back to life and obscured his vision with a dark blur. A panel of words sprang into existence on top of it.

The Memoirs of George Sherston. The novel of a soldier who left home looking for adventure, only to find the horrors of Earth's World War One. Industrial slaughter between the trenches. The loss of countless friends. A complete failure of leadership and a government. All of them took their toll on a hungry, innocent kid who came back broken by death and furious at the world around him.

Chris could easily imagine such a story being equally about him.

17

In the academic sense, the captain's quarters were among the largest private berths aboard *Vigorous*. A private office and adjoining head increased the total volume fifty percent over the other officers' cabins. But the engineers who designed the troop carrier atoned for this sin by cramming as much furniture as possible into the floorplan, masking the action with clever names so their military contractor could charge higher rates. A folding desk and retractable chair became a "multi-use office and bunk." The stacked sink, toilet, and shower combined into a "personal hygiene compartment." The crown jewel came in the form of a large holo monitor mounted over the desk. It dominated the remaining airspace like a great gargoyle leering down from the corner of a cathedral.

Kate Kazimira, skipper of the *Vigorous* and career spacer, hated that monitor.

She wasn't a large woman. She didn't get feelings of claustrophobia. It was just that the hardware was unnecessary. She supposed it was a testament to the days before neural stubs. Two of the adhesive transmitters would create an instant virtual reality headset with the largest computer screen imaginable, beamed right into the wearer's optic nerves. That was what she was looking at right now. It allowed her a level of flexibility that couldn't be matched by the hardened 3D display across the cabin.

Unfortunately, even with the comfort and productivity of the neural stubs, the multiple passes Kate had made through the *Alexander's* bridge logs weren't providing a very happy experience.

A chime at the door caught her attention from the beyond.

"Yes?"

A muffled voice came through the hatch. "Beck."

"Come in." She blinked several times to clear the computer-generated image.

A metallic clank reverberated through her cabin as the latch mechanism released. The door swung open and the RESIT troop commander stepped across the threshold, carrying a plastic bag filled with ice in one hand and a metal flask in the other.

Kate's eyes flicked over to the flask as Beck closed the hatch. "I could use some of that."

"Scotch tonight. Out of vodka." The major put the flask down and produced two glasses from the locker under the holo monitor. He hesitated as he placed them on the desk. "You still want ice, I assume?"

"Yes, please."

Kate leaned back against the wall of her bunk and smoothed away a loose strand of brown hair. Beck poured the flask. This had been their ritual for years. A couple days a month, a chance for drinks and talk and mutual support. It wasn't a physical relationship. But on long deployments, she'd come to rely on Beck's companionship to keep her going almost as much as the thoughts of her husband and daughter back home.

Beck held out a glass. "Cheers."

"Cheers."

She took the glass and swirled the brown liquid around the ice chunks a few times before downing it in one gulp. The Scotch burned her throat. Her eyes squeezed shut for a moment before she could blink away the momentary tears. When she opened them again, Beck watched her from the desk with his own drink still in his hand.

"I didn't know we were doing shooters tonight," he said.

Kate held out her glass for a refill.

Beck hesitated for a moment before decanting another pour. Then he added to his own cup as if concerned he'd better get his share while he could. The whole time, his eyes never left hers.

A quick sip this time, Kate decided, and she swished the Scotch around her mouth. She felt herself relax a tiny bit.

"Have you looked through *Alexander's* bridge logs yet?" she asked.

"No, still working with Marley on what the hell happened in the hangar." Beck's glass still didn't move. "I figure the fleet stuff is more your house."

Kate nodded. That wasn't far from the truth. Beck commanded the troopers, so when it came to boardings or other direct action, he was the one with the real training and experience. Likewise, she'd spent her career in charge of spacecraft and getting them through the empty black. It was a division of responsibilities that worked well for RESIT. But sometimes Kate wished she had another fleet officer against whom she could bounce ideas.

She caught herself frowning. Beck had proven many times over to be a brilliant tactician. Her old prejudices were selling him short.

"I've been through the logs," she said.

Beck studied her for a few moments before he spoke. "You're bothered. Is that because of what you found, or what you didn't?"

"The first one."

"Do tell, then."

"Colonel Marwat had two hundred constricted aboard his command carrier at the time they were attacked."

The major put his glass down on the desk without taking a drink.

"Two hundred constricted," he repeated.

"That's right."

"Why?"

Kate shook her head. "You know Colonel Marwat's reputation. Guess."

"Humanitarian relief?"

"Yup." She swirled her glass and tried to drain the last traces of alcohol mixed with the ice melt. "RESIT patrols started finding infected crew. A routine inspection here and there, some personnel who look sick or borderline catatonic. Then more. And more."

"Two hundred," Beck muttered again.

"They were leaving the planet, Gustav. No containment."

He nodded slowly.

Kate blinked the neural stubs back on and scrolled back through the transcription to her earlier bookmarks. Bright yellow tabs called her eyes to the key passages. "Here, I'll give you the high points. The Julietan government sent a flash message about a potential infectious disease making it off planet back in July '71. Marwat increased the patrol frequency and doubled shifts at some of the system key checkpoints. They started finding crew with symptoms. They started finding too many with symptoms. Marwat made the call to pool them together in one place and get them treatment."

"I thought constricted couldn't be treated," Beck said.

"This part of the log is a year old. Did they know that back then?"

The major allowed a slight nod. "Maybe not."

Kate continued to scroll through the log file. "That's my guess. What he was probably thinking was how inefficient it would be to ferry clinical teams between many different vessels. A lot better if you set up a treatment ward. And our boarding teams saw that, right? Lots of civvies in *Alexander's* B-ring. One place with access to physicians, diagnostic equipment, medications, robotics. You batch them up, try to get them well."

"Until they don't." Beck's face remained dark.

"Until they don't. But even then, there would be a MedSurg bot to manage treatment."

"I suppose."

A silence fell over the cabin that Kate hardly noticed. She was searching for one particular bookmark from Marwat's log. When she found it, her stomach fluttered with a mix of excitement and dread at the opportunity to share the revelation.

"Gustav," she said. "I want you to listen to this part of the log. It's from two months ago."

"Okay."

"Epione, play my highlighted notation," she said, her voice louder.

"Yes, Captain," the ethereal voice replied. A momentary delay preceded another voice from the speaker in the ceiling. This one was male and held a slight Pakistani accent.

"*New development today. By and large, the refugees we've taken aboard have gone through the same pattern of deterioration, lethargy followed by an almost catatonic state. Doc Riggins has his medical team inserting IVs to maintain hydration.*

But in every case so far it really hasn't mattered. Once one of his patients goes into the slump, it's just a matter of time before we're sending a drone in to bag up the body.

"*And then, today, we get a complete surprise. A crewman named Mills, who had been given a cot in the enlisted mess after being unresponsive for nearly ninety hours, wakes up, shambles over to cold storage, and makes a sandwich.*"

Kate blinked to restore her vision. She wanted to see Beck's reaction. The major was staring at the deck, stony-faced.

Marwat, on the other hand, sounded hopeful. "*A sandwich. Can you believe that? We have refugees expiring left and right because they won't eat, won't drink, and this son of a bitch gets up and raids the pantry. It wasn't pretty, mind—just a tortilla and a smear of protein. But he put the thing together and gummed it down before he went back to his corner.*

"*Riggins has told me to not get my hopes up. That one random event doesn't mean anything. But I can't help but get a little excited at the thought that some of the treatment might be working. We're finding too many of these infected spacers, and reports from Juliet aren't very encouraging. If we're able to contribute something toward finding a cure, or at least some kind of care plan, we might help find a way out of this thing.*"

"Epione, pause," Kate said.

Beck was still frowning, unfazed. "So, one of them got hungry," he said.

She held up her hand to silence him. "Epione, play the next bookmark."

"... *together. We watched the security footage as four patients got up from one of those little circles they kneel into and entered the mess together. They all ate the same thing—a couple tortillas, nothing fancy, almost as if they were just looking for any calories they could get their hands on. Then they went back to their respective cots. It was fascinating to watch. They didn't seem to communicate with each other in any explicit way, yet were able to cue off of Mills as he led the way back.*

"The medical drone did its rounds about an hour later and took vitals on the four. All showed continued decreases in body mass, but if they go back for another meal like Mills has been, we're expecting those losses to flatten out. And that will give us more time to provide treatment. We've been at this for months, trying this drug and that, experimenting with different therapies. And now, finally, instead of watching these poor souls starve and waste away, there's a sliver of hope that we'll be able to help. I just wonder if it will be enough to get them on the road to recovery."

"Epione, pause." She looked at Beck.

"They're learning from each other?" he asked.

"It appears that way."

Beck's eyes wandered around the cabin as he thought for a few moments. When they settled back on Kate, she could see the skepticism in them.

"Not dying of hunger anymore. I want to say that's a good thing," he said. "But I can tell that's not where you're going with this."

"No."

"What is it, then? They don't starve, they don't die? The threat of disease lasts longer?"

Kate felt the grim smile slide across her face. Beck had a strong intuition, but he hadn't grasped the punchline. "Epione, play the last bookmark in this section."

Colonel Marwat's voice resumed on the speaker, noticeably ragged.

"It's oh three hundred hours and we're still at general quarters. We've had a situation with the constricted. There's a group of about twenty that has been feeding themselves for several days now. We thought that might be a sign of progress, that treatment was finally killing off the infection, letting these people start the road to recovery. Instead ... well, I'm not quite sure what to make of it.

"Yesterday morning they got up out of their little circles, walked in complete silence over to the pressure bulkhead, and unlocked the hatch. I don't know who had a passcode. I didn't think in their condition they'd know what a passcode was. But sure enough, the next thing we knew was they were

making a push on the lift access deck. A security team intercepted them and one trooper managed to signal an alert. That's it. That's all they managed. The next thing we knew, the whole team had crumpled on the deck like rag dolls. No physical confrontation, no shots fired. Just ... down. And the constricted were loading up on both lifts to come down to the main hull."

As Kate watched, Beck's face grew even darker. His eyes burned a hole through a point somewhere on the far wall.

"Master at Arms Miller set up a blocking position at each lift deck and manned them with full squads. I've got to give him credit for the speed of his response. But what really made the difference was dumb luck. When the constricted split up— which they did without speaking or using communication of any kind—one group went down the first lift right away. The second had to shamble over to the other spoke. That delay is probably what saved us.

"Our troopers engaged with the first group as soon as they appeared. They took down multiple constricted, but three or four of them managed to avoid being hit. Then they ... I don't know how to describe it. Stared at my men. Glared at them. Miller and the others dropped to the deck in an instant, screaming. I watched the security footage, couldn't take my eyes away as my troopers flopped around in agony. I saw their arms clamped around their heads, trying to make it stop. And the

constricted refugees just walked out of the lift, like some kind of monster out of a horror vid.

"That's when the second platoon showed up to reinforce Miller. I don't know if the constricted didn't see them, or if they were just preoccupied with torturing the first platoon. But Sergeant Wozniak took them all out with Vector fire. Then they ran back to the second lift just in time to hold the position. Luckily, the constricted groups weren't split evenly, and this one only had six. Woz took them all out before they got attacked the way Miller did."

The recording played dead air. Beck cleared his throat as if to speak. But Kate held up a hand, wanting to make sure he heard the last part of this section. The most important part.

Marwat spoke slowly as he organized his thoughts with care.

"We've been picking up constricted spacers for months. Most of them starve to death. We've been running tests, treating them, observing them, trying to help them. We've been approaching them as refugees in need of care. But what we saw today? They're not getting well, but they're certainly ... changing. Adapting. A bunch of weak, malnourished spacers in a near-vegetative state relearned how to eat, then open a passcode-protected hatch and use a lift.

"We're due for another vid call with Juliet Emergency Management. I'm going to brief them on the events today. I know the director is nervous

about our humanitarian efforts and the risk of
exposure. This is not going to help his unease, but
it's going to take all of our brainpower to figure this
out. Marwat out."

Kate blinked the neural stub transcription away
and turned her attention to Beck. "That was his
last personal log entry. Any thoughts on that,
Major?"

"Troubling trend," he said simply.

"They're learning how to use tools, Gustav."

"Like Corpsman Watanabe and the laser
cutter."

"Exactly. We had one aboard *Vigorous*."

The major rubbed his fingers together, thinking
long and hard about what he had heard. "So what
do you think happened to *Alexander* after that vid
call?" he asked.

"I think Juliet told him to kill all the refugees."

"And how would Marwat respond?"

Kate sniffed. "He'd tell them to go to hell.
Constriction or not, they were people needing
help."

Beck nodded. "And then they showed up to
blast him to hell, giving us nothing but a dead
end."

"No. Not exactly."

"Oh?"

"Gustav, where would you put a bunch of
vessels with no crew?"

"Park them in orbit somewhere," he said, shrugging. "Put a destroyer on station to keep them secure."

"That's right. But say you didn't know how long it was going to be for. Orbits decay. Gravity is always pulling. Where would you put them?"

"A Lagrange point."

Kate nodded. "And where is *Alexander* right now?"

"Bering ... *gate*," he said, drawing a breath as soon as he said it. "Which is at a Lagrange point, just like the gate at the other end. I'll be damned. RESIT moved all the impounds to Alpha B."

"I'm sure of it." Kate splayed her fingers and ticked off the logic point by point. "You keep them away from refugees to enforce containment. It's far, twenty-three AU, but RESIT Dagger could still get there without a quantum gate if they had to. And there are resources there."

"The old Liu shipyard. Back from when we thought we might colonize Alpha B."

"It's decommissioned, but it's still an asteroid with fuel and facilities."

Beck was nodding vigorously now. "All right. We head there, grab these guys and beat some sense into them. I'm in. Are we going the long way or the short way?"

"They'll see us coming for weeks if we go the long way."

"Then we go through the gate."

"We go through the gate," she agreed.

Beck held up his Scotch in salute before downing it in one gulp.

Two sharp tones pinged in Kate's ear over the command channel on the comm. One chirp meant it was for her. This one was the major's.

Beck pressed the bone-induction mic behind his earlobe. "Beck here."

His eyes slid over to Kate with one of his famously hard stares.

"Marley's found something. Care to join me?"

18

Ready Room B was becoming a regular destination for Wyatt. He entered the berth to find Major Beck already seated at the table. His adjutant sat to his right, his eyes glassy as he read something from a neural stub, followed by a female bridge officer. On his other side, Laramie was squeezed next to Elton Forrestal, the former deputy chief of staff for Governor Hewitt. Elton sat with his arms folded and looked as unfriendly as he had been when Wyatt met him in the safehouse.

The biggest surprise was the presence of Captain Kazimira. The skipper of the *Vigorous* sat in the first row and watched Wyatt as he entered. Her expression remained neutral, but Wyatt couldn't help but feel judged as her eyes followed him.

"Reporting as ordered, sir," Wyatt said.

Beck gave him a nod. "Thank you, Lieutenant. We're just waiting on—Dr. Bell, come in."

Wyatt moved aside as Jack Bell stepped through the hatch. The health director looked even more bewildered than Wyatt felt. No, not bewildered. Exhausted. Wyatt could see it in his eyes, his posture, his disheveled appearance. Eyes brimming with fatigue slid over to the major, waiting to be directed.

"Doctor, have a seat," Beck said. "Lieutenant Wills, would you close the hatch?"

"Yes, sir." Wyatt secured the door behind him. He barely had a chance to turn around before Beck motioned to his adjutant.

The holo monitor came to life at one end of the room. Beck didn't waste any time. "Do you know what that is, Doctor?" He pointed a rigid finger at the image, but his eyes never left Bell.

Wyatt certainly didn't know the answer. The three-dimensional display showed some kind of multicolored chart, with telemetry and red-yellow-green indicators peppering the margins.

Jack Bell shook his head. He looked like he might fall asleep. "No."

"That is the application panel for quantum gate control. The helmsman uses it to ensure *Vigorous* goes through the gate at the right time, with the correct alignment. Wouldn't want to crash into anything."

"Okay."

"Now, you see that line graph in the upper right?"

Wyatt followed Beck's finger as it slid upward. On the holo monitor, a flat line chart transformed into a hemorrhage of peaks and valleys.

"I see it," Bell said.

"That tells us the entanglement tunnel is open. We don't even approach a gate unless our sensors confirm it's active. Are you with me so far?"

"Yes."

"Here's the rub. Thermopylae wasn't active when we measured this."

The doctor stared blankly at the holo monitor. "I change my answer. I'm not following."

"The gate wasn't open. The sensor readings should have been flat."

Jack Bell squinted at the graph, apparently trying to catch up to the implication Beck left hanging. "What is it measuring, then?"

The major glanced at the bridge officer. "Marley, bring up the clip."

With a few flicks of her finger, the woman next to him slid a pair of new images onto the holo monitor. One was another line graph, its data completely flat. The second was a video still from a security camera.

Wyatt felt his heart skip a beat. He recognized the woman now. They were looking at the footage from the hangar, when Chris had come across Izzy cutting through the deck.

"Are they synched?" Beck asked.

"Yes, sir."

"Play them."

The security feed stuttered forward. Corpsman Second Class Isi Watanabe lurched across the hangar deck with laser cutter in hand, inexorably closing on Chris. Wyatt could see the bloody gash in Chris's abdomen as he struggled to crawl away. In the panel next to the video, the line graph remained flat and uninteresting.

Chris slumped against a locker. Izzy closed in and raised the cutting torch.

Out of nowhere, Annika dashed from the shadows. She threw herself between the two men and covered Chris's body with splayed arms, protecting him the way a lioness might defend its cub from a rival.

Annika's face grew fierce. Izzy staggered.

The line graph went haywire.

Multiple eyes watched the video feed without interruption. Beck let it continue to the point where Izzy turned around and went back to his sabotage. The line graph died back down to its baseline, and he motioned for Marley to stop the playback. The holo monitor ended with an unobstructed view of Chris, his face a mix of bewilderment and horror as he stared at the little girl leaning against him.

Jack Bell leaned back in his chair. The fatigue had vanished. His eyes held a sharp focus and didn't leave the monitor.

"Fascinating."

"I was hoping for a little more than that," Beck said.

The doctor spoke softly, his voice far away. "This is ... we've been trying to isolate the transmission vectors for constriction since the beginning. Airborne, direct contact, ingestion— nothing. No bacteria, no viruses. No toxins. We've had the entire health apparatus of Juliet and have come up empty every single time." He struggled with deep thoughts as he stared at the monitor. "Then, this. Just fascinating."

Bell blinked and looked around the room as if suddenly surprised he wasn't alone. His eyes ended up on Wyatt.

"This is hard, you understand," Bell said. "It's hard to take complex subjects and articulate them for a lay audience."

"Try," the major said.

"Okay." Bell drew a deep breath. "The human brain, it's complex. Not just biologically but cognitively. Our *thinking* takes place at a quantum level. Science didn't understand this for a long time. It wasn't until about fifty years ago, Dr. Richard Hermann of the Bern Institute wrote his dissertation—"

Beck held up his hand. "I don't need a history lesson, Doctor."

"Right," Bell said. His expression turned thoughtful as he searched for the right analogy. Then his face suddenly lit up. "Thompson. I actually had a discussion with him the other day that can act as a framework.

"Think of your brain as hardware and software. The gray matter in your skull? That's hardware. It's important, don't get me wrong. You can damage a drone and it won't work properly; likewise, if you damage your head, you can see any manner of cognitive or behavioral disorders.

"But for hundreds of years, we still had a missing link between physics and neuroscience. The breakthrough from Dr. Hermann was about the software. He proved, experimentally, that while thinking gets processed *through* the hardware of your gray matter, your software— your consciousness, your self-awareness, your *you*— doesn't *originate* there. It occurs at a quantum level. We still only understand a fraction of it, but it's there, and it's distinct. Dr. Hermann determined how to measure it. And he showed that your brain is just a processing unit, that the software code, if you will, exists at a whole different level."

Bell fell silent, scrunching up his eyes in thought.

"Doctor?" Major Beck prompted.

Bell shook his head, muttering to himself in some kind of internal debate. "No, no. That wouldn't ... but of course, this changes everything, and maybe we could ..."

"*Doctor?*"

Jack Bell's eyes flicked open with a renewed intensity. "Major. I've studied this. I've used Dr. Hermann's measuring techniques myself. Until now, every measurement we've ever done around quantum thought has been confined to a particular individual. Which makes sense, right? They're *your* thoughts. They stay in your head. We've never duplicated ESP. The mind reader at the carnival is still a hack."

Jack Bell turned to the holo monitor. "But this? This might be the first recorded instance where that isn't the case. Imagine that. Thoughts, instructions that take place at a quantum level, no longer confined to one individual's gray matter. I don't know how else to explain this."

The health director stood up and started pacing in front of the holo monitor. The rest of them watched in silence. Wyatt found himself thinking back to the spaceport, fleeing through the concourse as dozens of faces peered at him with pinpoint eyes. He had almost stopped running. An irresistible urge had come over him, one he could have sworn had been his own, to cease his pointless escape and stay behind. To stay with the constricted masses who stared at him from all around.

He had heard the voices calling to him. *Voices.* Is that what it felt like to have your thoughts interjected with someone else's?

Someone else.

Who?

Major Beck decided the room had had enough time to ponder the imponderable. He spoke with the authoritative tone of command. "Doctor Bell, I'm interested in two things only." He pointed at the monitor. "Is there something about that little girl that can stop the transmission of this disease? And if so, does the data we collected help you duplicate it?"

Bell turned toward the bridge officer. "Miss? Would you play the clip again for me?"

Over the next several minutes, everyone watched multiple times as Annika threw herself between Chris and Izzy in the security footage.

Jack Bell remained silent except for requests to zoom in or rewind. Otherwise he paced across the deck, deep in thought, his fingers steepled under his chin.

After the fifth repetition, the doctor seemed to break from his meditation. He turned toward the room. "Major, I think the answer to your first question is yes. Corpsman Watanabe was infected—I don't have an explanation for all the variances, but in my assessment he clearly has constriction. We can see here he's advancing on Master Sergeant Thompson. But Annika Hewitt also clearly displays the classic constricted pupils while she does something that turns him away."

"Turns him away," Beck repeated. "What do we need to do to bottle that up?"

"Very simple." Jack Bell stopped pacing and crossed his arms. "I need to take her back to Juliet."

19

The major arched an eyebrow. "Come again?"

"Are you familiar with Los Cuernos?" Bell asked.

"No."

"The university there is the top research center for neuropsychology. One of my colleagues is their professor emeritus and developed models related to the dynamics I just described—quantum mechanics and its role in thought. We need a facility like that, their labs, and the expertise of him and his research team. That's the only way we can analyze this. It's the only way to formulate a response."

Captain Kazimira cleared her throat. "We're not going back to Juliet, Doctor."

"We must. There's no other way to explore this."

"If we took a risk and broke our comms blackout, maybe we could allow you to send a transmission to your colleagues," Beck said. He traded glances with the skipper. "Send them this data, see what they make of it."

The doctor laughed. "I don't even know if my colleagues are still alive. And even then, there's a lot more testing and analysis we would need to do if we're going to make anything useful out of this. Your navigational sensor data was an accident. They have neither the detail nor the data models to do anything. No, no. I need to take Annika Hewitt to a real research center."

Kazimira leaned forward and fixed her gaze on Bell. "I said that's a no-go, Doctor. You'll need to come up with alternatives."

Bell folded his arms with the same flair of defiance Wyatt remembered when they abducted him from his office. "You pull me away from my patient—the most important patient you will ever have, by the way, that little girl in your med bay. You show me this supposed phenomenon on your monitor. Then I suggest to you the importance of what it might represent, but you refuse to take the most basic steps to potentially stop the death of millions?" His words took on a sarcastic tone. "Explain that to me, *Captain*."

Kazimira abruptly stood up.

Wyatt stiffened. The skipper maintained her professional demeanor, but the look in her eyes made Wyatt wonder if Bell was destined for the brig.

"Marley, bring up the exterior camera," Kazimira said. "Show us Bering Gate."

A moment later, the holo monitor switched to the blackness of space. A tiny metal ring in the distance reflected the light of Alpha A. The captain pointed a finger at the image.

"I have a command carrier that was destroyed by its own RESIT Team, Doctor." The skipper's words were calm but carried a quiet intensity. "That gate is where they went afterward. In six days, it's going to open again and offer us our chance to hunt them down. We're not leaving."

Bell wouldn't back down. "I know the body count taking place on Juliet right now. What's more important, saving millions of lives, or erasing a few hundred?"

"We're not leaving the gate, Doctor."

"Captain. Please."

A man's voice cut through the momentary silence. "Captain, a moment?"

Arguing ceased. Multiple sets of eyes swiveled to Major Beck. His normal expression of a man about to kick all their asses had faded to something more thoughtful. He stood from the table and motioned for a sidebar with Kazimira.

Wyatt strained to hear their conversation. When he couldn't pick up anything, he looked around at the others. Everyone was watching the two most senior commanders in the room.

The skipper's eyes had shifted. With a start, Wyatt realized they were resting on him.

"Marley, have the bridge hail *Sawtooth* and patch them through," she said.

"Aye, sir."

The hair on his neck stood on end again. That was the Fast Attack assigned to *Vigorous*. Why was Kazimira wanting to talk to them?

The comm crackled with an accented voice. "Sawtooth *Actual*."

"Otto? Kate."

"*Yes, Captain.*"

"How many grav couches can you fit on your ship?"

"*Grav couches—say again, ma'am?   I didn't copy.*"

She repeated the question. Wyatt started to feel uneasy. The two gees that *Vigorous* could push were plenty hard on healthy physiology. For injured troopers, the med bay used portable grav couches, gel-filled cocoons with peristaltic massage mechanisms to assist with breathing and circulation. They were sometimes used for high-acceleration transits. They were always beyond uncomfortable. In the acronym-fueled lexicon of RESIT, troopers called them IVRs—short for industrial vomit recirculators.

The comm snapped back to life. "*Captain, this is* Sawtooth. *We think six. We'll have to unload provisions from the hold to even make that work. Do you mind if I ask why?*"

"Wait one," Kazimira said.

The skipper sat back with Major Beck and Marley, the bridge officer. They were working out something on Marley's tablet as they conversed back and forth in low voices. Wyatt saw Kazimira arch her eyebrow. Beck just nodded at her.

Kazimira turned toward Jack Bell.

"Doctor, it's your lucky day. I'm going to put you on a Fast Attack. Commander Otto will get you to Juliet."

"That's excellent," Bell said. "Thank you."

"Don't thank me too much. To make this work, you're going to be under four gees inbound and four gees back. That will give you forty-eight hours on the surface if you're lucky."

The doctor's eyes widened in disbelief. "Forty-eight hours? I need weeks!"

"That's the offer, Doctor Bell."

"Just leave me planetside with my patient. We can figure out how I get back at some later point."

"I don't think so. You and Miss Hewitt are too valuable." She glanced at Beck. "That's why Lieutenant Wills will be bringing a ground team to accompany you. When it's time to leave orbit, you *will* be onboard *Sawtooth*. Understood?"

Bell snorted with indignation, but even he could read Captain Kazimira's demeanor. Her decision stood resolute like a stone statue. After a few moments, he bowed his head. "Understood."

"Then get moving."

Wyatt felt the blood drain from his face. Four gees. For two days. *My God.* Jack Bell had no idea what he had just gotten into.

The doctor did seem to understand the time pressure, though. He gave Major Beck and Captain Kazimira a quick nod, grabbed Elton by the arm, and hustled toward the hatch. Wyatt turned to follow. But as he went to exit, he saw Beck's eyes tracking him and had no doubt as to the message behind them.

Don't screw this up.

20

Six couches.

Wyatt, Jack Bell, and Annika filled out half the roster. Teo would pilot their Javelin, so he would need a couch while they towed it during transit. Laramie and Kenny would act as their security detail in case they ran into trouble.

But the compressed timeline caused problems. Two days allotted to the surface meant no time for Bell's carefully controlled experiments.

After a lot of arguing, Bell proposed an alternative as the only way to make the mission work. He wouldn't test Annika just by herself. He would need a second constricted person. Then and only then, by allowing the university's superior equipment to pick apart the quantum interactions, would they have the data at a granular enough level to eventually explain how constriction's transmission worked.

Wyatt wouldn't approve the idea of hunting down and capturing an infected citizen. Too dangerous and too many unknowns in such a short period of time. That meant they needed to bring someone who had constriction with them.

So, it turned out they needed to include a seventh person.

Corporal Dean.

Wyatt didn't want to do it. No one had any doubt that the armory guard was compromised. It just seemed incredibly unsafe despite Dean remaining in a medication-induced coma since the altercation with Izzy. Only after Kenta vouched for the efficacy of the sedatives did Wyatt begrudgingly agree to go along with it. The idea still gave him the chills, but he was a RESIT trooper and he would do what he needed to do as part of the mission.

That left one last conversation to have before they disembarked. It didn't go well.

"What in the *hell* do you mean I'm not part of the mission?" Chris raged. The Marine glared at him in the med bay, half-undressed as Kenta readied him for another round of injections.

"Four gees are no joke, Chris. There's no way you could take it with your injuries."

"Oh, and Annika's allowed?"

"She doesn't have a hole in her side."

"She's a child."

"She's healthy."

A stream of profanities including words Wyatt didn't even recognize flew through the air. "If Annika's on the team, I'm going," Chris said. "Plain and simple."

Wyatt jabbed the Marine's abdomen with his fingers. Chris doubled over, giving Wyatt just enough time to step back before his target tried to break his hand.

"Now, think of feeling that for five hours at a stretch," Wyatt said. "This is going to be a tough ride. We're going to be squashed flat, unable to move. And the whole time, that's what your wound is going to feel like from the weight of your own body."

"I can take the pain."

"It won't do anyone any good if your ribs heal back permanently deformed. Anyway, Major Beck wouldn't allow it. You're still not cleared for duty."

Chris scanned the med bay in search of support. Doctor Kenta just shook her head.

For a moment, it looked like the Marine might slip into another epic tirade. Wyatt had known him long enough to be wary of the temper. But to his surprise, the fury on Chris's face melted away the moment his eyes fell on Annika.

He walked over to the eight-year-old girl standing next to an open storage locker. Laramie was kneeling next to her, finishing the fitting of a youth survival suit.

"Anni," he said. He took a knee and drew his face close to hers. "Anni."

Annika Hewitt didn't speak. She'd never spoken ever since Wyatt met her. But this time she didn't need to. Tears were already streaming down her cheeks as Chris struggled to keep his composure.

"Listen to me. You know where you're going. It's dangerous. Don't do anything stupid." He jerked his thumb over his shoulder. "Lieutenant Wyatt? You do what he says. You let Doctor Bell run his tests. You get in and out. That's it. Okay?"

She nodded. Then she threw her arms around his neck.

"I know, sweetie. I wish I could go with you. I'm sorry." Chris's voice buckled on the last words.

Kenny stepped through the med bay hatch. "Lieutenant. Teo's calling, says everything's ready for the transfer to *Sawtooth*."

"Time to go," Wyatt said.

Chris let Annika go so that Laramie could pull the last zipper tight on her survival suit. As Laramie stood up, Chris grabbed her by the elbow.

"Take care of her," he said.

"I will."

"Laramie. Please."

Her brow furrowed. "I promise."

Wyatt waited by the hatch, watching their eyes exchange some private conversation to which he was not privy.

***

Inside the Javelin, Wyatt watched on the holo monitor as they maneuvered past *Vigorous*'s drive rings. He could see the docking boom connecting the troop carrier with *Needle*, the slim hull of the Fast Scout seemingly mismatched with the four reactionless drive nacelles at its aft end. Then they turned toward the inky depths of space. As the minutes crawled by, Wyatt gradually became aware of a dim break in the void. The silhouette of another vessel appeared and gradually resolved itself into the sleek profile of a purebred hunter.

Reducing the magnification factor on the monitor only served to strengthen the lethal nature of *Sawtooth*'s trade. A laser turret sat mounted prominently on the top of the spacecraft, while multiple drone ports lined the edges of its belly. At the aft end, an overly large power plant promised enough energy to run down any vessel targeted for interdiction. The slender docking boom seemed like a disingenuous invitation to come aboard.

A series of stomach-winding turns maneuvered the Javelin into position. Once the clank of metal on metal stopped reverberating through the cabin, the dorsal airlock light turned green, and Wyatt unbuckled his harness. A turn in his chair caused him to immediately jerk back. Just a meter behind his station sat one of the headlights of their Jackal, the large enclosed rover RESIT sometimes used for surface operations. The vehicle took up most of the room in the cargo bay. Since Wyatt didn't know exactly what they'd be facing at Los Cuernos, he decided they might need a more discreet entry vehicle than a Javelin thundering in from above. Loading it had cost them half a dozen hours. He tapped the headlight with his hand and hoped he hadn't made a bad call.

While Teo engaged in procedural dialogue with *Sawtooth*'s bridge about tow lines and attachment points, Wyatt led the rest of their team through the docking boom. The other end was blocked by a wiry man with blue eyes and receding blond hair. He wore a lieutenant commander's pips on his shoulder.

"You're Wills?" he asked.

"Yes, sir." Wyatt delivered a salute. "Permission to come aboard?"

A bemused look creased the man's eyes. "Save the formalities for the big ships, Lieutenant. We keep it nice and simple. Otto Edelmann, commanding the *Sawtooth*." He extended his hand instead of saluting back.

Wyatt shook his hand and maneuvered through the hatch. He instantly understood Otto's perspective. The airlock was only marginally larger than the narrow docking boom. Floating into the main corridor beyond, Wyatt saw a maze of exposed pipes and junction boxes instead of the smooth interior familiar from most ships. There didn't even seem to be enough room for two people to float past each other.

Otto watched him with a cocked eyebrow. "Never been on a Fast Attack before?"

"No, sir."

"Well, don't worry. Pretty sure you won't get lost."

Wyatt followed their new guide into a larger berth that he realized should have been the cargo hold. Six portable grav couches sat latched to the deck and walls, each with a bundle of cables running to an open power panel among the labyrinth of pipes on the ceiling. A crewman with the word ENGINEERING on his pressure sleeve floated from couch to couch as he ran test routines on his portable table.

Otto waved his hand across the room. "There's a tiny bit of cargo netting over there for everyone's belongings. Make sure no one's wearing anything sharp before they climb inside their couch. Is ten minutes enough time to get sorted?"

"Ten—that's it?" Wyatt said. "Get in and go?"

"Yeah, that's about the size of it. You want a safety briefing or something?" The *Sawtooth* captain arched his eyebrow again.

Wyatt blinked, unsure of how to respond. It wasn't that he didn't know the operation of a grav couch. He'd just expected something with a bit more protocol.

He glanced over his shoulder at the others coming in behind him. Annika's eyes were as wide as dinner plates at the wonders of this new and exciting spacecraft. Bell and Kenny were struggling to get the unconscious Corporal Dean through the hatch without banging the IV pump against the wall. Laramie eyed the couches like an animal wary of predators. Wyatt couldn't help but feel they were climbing into a hot rod of old, all engine and fuel and testosterone. Even the air tasted like machine oil.

Otto cleared his throat. "Wills?"

"Sir?"

"Otto," he corrected. "Not sir. Look, I realize you're probably a little apprehensive about all this?"

"Yes, a bit," Wyatt admitted.

"Relax. My crew does this for a living." He pointed to the couches. "Everything's powered up and synched with the flight computer. We'll have the medical readouts on the bridge and can cut the drives if there are any problems. All your team needs to do is just lie there."

"That's it?"

"That's it. I mean, it won't be a picnic, but we won't be at this long enough to worry about cardiac stress from four gees."

Wyatt scanned the compartment again. He realized with a start that there weren't enough. "I only count six?"

"Yeh, that part about squeezing in an extra? Turns out we were wrong. But no worries. You'll be up on the bridge with me. I sent my first officer aboard *Vigorous* for some medical treatment. Long overdue."

"Oh," Wyatt said. "What was wrong?"

A gleam entered Otto's eye. "Cardiac stress from four gees," he said, and left.

21

USIC *Sawtooth*
Alpha Centauri A
04 April 2272

The confined bridge of *Sawtooth* allowed no room for imagination. The oval layout held four acceleration couches arranged in a two-by-two configuration, with holo monitors and control systems mounted to the walls so thickly that it made it difficult for Wyatt to even reach his seat. Once he reached the first officer's station, he wriggled into the gel-filled pads and cringed from the clammy, smothering embrace offered by the peristaltic stroke mechanism sliding around his limbs. In his mind, Wyatt knew that the stiff metal fingers would supplement his circulatory system while under sustained high acceleration. In his soul, the entire experience screamed suffocation and entrapment.

Otto seemed amused at his discomfort. He pointed to a contoured storage box on the right of Wyatt's couch. "Your CORE helmet goes right in there. Obviously, you won't need that unless something bad happens."

Wyatt managed a minimalistic nod with his chin. Otto patted him on the chest and returned to finish preparations with the rest of his crew.

Momentarily alone, Wyatt was left to wonder what the hell he had gotten himself into. Human physiology had evolved over tens of thousands of years to produce a mechanism optimized for upright, bipedal locomotion. To flip a body horizontal and subject it to four times its apparent weight wasn't comfortable, but people managed. Fighter pilots. Race car drivers. But none of them had to sustain that load for days, or weeks, or careers. Weren't drones adequate for chasing rogue spacecraft or performing covert missions? To subject human beings to this ungodly situation surely violated their manufacturer's warranty.

A set of peristaltic rods rolled over his thighs, violating his person with a mechanical squeeze.

The video feed on the holo monitor above his station cycled to the camera locked on their Javelin. "Load confirmed secure," a voice announced.

"Understood," Otto said, out of view on Wyatt's left. "Getty, is our course locked in?"

"Aye, sir," a man replied near his feet.

Wyatt rubbed his fingers together, just about the only thing he could find to fidget with. He suddenly felt giddy.

"Take us out," Otto said.

Wyatt's torso settled into the acceleration couch. At first the sensation was pleasant, a return to the natural weight that God designed the human form to endure. But their power plant didn't like restraint. It pumped more radiation to the reactionless drive system, and Wyatt found himself in a sudden and unforgiving crush. It was as if the hand of some invisible giant had grabbed hold of his body and intended to pop him like some piece of mashed fruit. Ironically, only Wyatt's cybernetic leg spared him any pain, calloused as it was against the joy of feeling.

Much of the ride proved boring. They did take breaks. Protocol afforded them one hour of free movement every four hours of confinement. The challenge was that there just wasn't any room aboard the spacecraft. The design of the Fast Attack clearly centered around strapping in for multiple gees or floating about in none. There were no decks, no semblance of up or down like on a troop carrier, leaving Wyatt and his team to grapple with disorientation and vertigo. Jack Bell had a particularly hard time. His stomach reveled in its newfound freedom by purging into a sick bag.

Mealtimes weren't much better. For their first dinner, Wyatt floated inside the tiny galley and nursed his new migraine. He barely noticed Laramie floating up next to him.

"This sucks," she said.

"I know."

"You should have taken Carlos instead of me."

"Then it's a good thing you're here so I don't have to listen to any whining." He glanced at her to see if she got the hint.

Laramie ignored him, instead frowning at the small food warmer in the bulkhead on the other side of the galley. The helmsman from the bridge was loading another zero-gee ration pouch into it. A name tape on his chest said *Getty*.

"You can eat first if you want," Wyatt said. His forehead pounded away inside his skull.

"No."

"Seriously, it's okay."

"No."

For a moment, he wondered if he'd misheard. "You not eating is like Carlos not complaining."

"I don't think I'd keep it down." Her voice sounded funny.

The helmsman near the food warmer let out a chuckle. Dark eyes twinkled under heavy eyebrows. "You guys worry too much. You can't get sick at four gees."

"You can't?"

"No. The acceleration holds it in."

Laramie turned a dull shade of green before leaving through the hatch.

The journey did not get easier. Wyatt found sleep elusive. When he did manage to doze, he would dream of monsters scratching at him with scaly, clawed fingers. His mind drifted to deep-sea crews battling psychosis from the pressurized environments that altered emotions and logic alike.

After the next interval, Otto took pity on him and offered him some pills. Wyatt didn't remember much after that.

He did, however, take note as they closed on Juliet orbit a day and a half later. Otto had reoriented *Sawtooth* for deceleration, but instead of an orbital insertion, the captain only bled enough speed to put them into a hyperbolic trajectory across the planet's path.

"Why aren't you taking us into orbit?" Wyatt asked.

Otto cocked his eyebrow again in an expression becoming very familiar to Wyatt.

"That's not what we do," he said.

"What do you mean?"

"This is a Fast Attack, Lieutenant. We intercept and disable. A lot easier to do when no one knows where you are."

"Like in orbit," Wyatt finished.

"Like in orbit." He cracked a grin. "We didn't come here to get jacked."

Wyatt nodded. The last time he had been in a Javelin above Juliet, a different Fast Attack had nearly burned them out of the sky. "Well, as long as you're back by the time we need to rendezvous, we'll be fine."

"We'll be here. Grav couches and all."

A grimace crawled over Wyatt's face. "Yeah."

"You get used to it after a while," Otto said.

"Really?"

"No." The grin came back.

Wyatt tried to compartmentalize his discomfort so that he could better focus on the now.

As they approached Juliet's atmosphere, the tone aboard *Sawtooth* turned markedly serious.

Otto's banter slipped into a businesslike cadence that set a professional tone for his crew. The helmsman, Getty, ran his fingers up and down a pair of control yokes that seemed decidedly antique inside a spacecraft capable of interstellar trajectories. The weapons officer next to him watched for any other vessels on the threat monitor. Together, the three bridge officers acted as if they were a single organism, finishing each other's thoughts and actions with the coordination of a juggler's hands. Meanwhile, Juliet's atmosphere resolved itself into a thin blue film on the holo monitors.

"We're in the pipe," the helmsman said.

"Cut engines," Otto replied.

"Aye."

Otto popped himself out of his command couch. "The train's arrived at the station, Wills. Time to get aboard your dirt bumper."

Wyatt didn't need to be told twice. He quickly marshalled the others and ordered them to the Javelin. Jack Bell and Laramie looked remarkably gaunter than he remembered. Teo and Kenny seemed unfazed by the journey. Annika was clearly relieved, though Wyatt suspected that would quickly change during the battering of reentry. And Corporal Dean seemed to be holding steady on his IV laced with sedatives. Within thirty minutes they had all strapped into their seats for the trip groundside.

"*Sawtooth,* this is Savage Echo, tow hooks are released," Teo announced from the flight deck of the Javelin. "We are clearing docking boom in three ... two ... one ... clear."

"*Copy that, Savage Echo. We read you clear as well. You are free to maneuver.*"

"Roger that."

"*Oh, and Lieutenant Wills?*" Otto added.

"Yes, sir?"

"*Good hunting. I hope you find what you're looking for.*"

"Thank you, Captain."

Wyatt closed the channel as the Javelin began its own deceleration burn. He looked down the cargo bay until his eyes rested on an eight-year-old girl sitting across from an unconscious RESIT trooper, wondering if they would indeed find what they were looking for.

22

While the Javelin plunged through ever-thickening atmosphere, Laramie had to clench her teeth to keep them from rattling. Incandescent plasma blazed through the flight deck canopy and bathed the interior with a bright orange light. When they slowed past the sound barrier, Teo ignited the engines to add to the cacophony of rushing wind. The jolt slammed Laramie into her seat. Immobilized by the weight of reentry, she watched as the nose camera fed her images of moonlight shimmering across a broad forest of bamboo-like grass.

Not that long ago, this same journey from orbit had been in a damaged vehicle that threatened to break apart during reentry. This time, cruising along in level flight, the Javelin felt smoother than walking on solid ground. She leaned across the aisle and shouted at Wyatt. "A little different than our last visit, huh, LT?"

"I was thinking the same thing." He turned toward the flight deck. "Where are we at, Teo?"

"About a hundred klicks north of Los Cuernos."

"What's our ETA?"

"About twenty minutes," the pilot replied. "The bad news is I'm not seeing a lot of choices for an LZ. This bamboo is everywhere."

Laramie peeked through the hatch. Teo was sliding his fingers across the holo monitor, searching a topographic map with the help of the Javelin flight computer. The little cactus he took everywhere sat proudly in its zero-gee bulb on top of the monitor. Supervising.

"Put us down where you can," Wyatt said. His tone sounded like he had expected that answer. "That's why we brought the Jackal."

Teo ended up circling the town in a wide arc, eventually finding a small break in the contiguous copses of bamboo shoots. He set them on the ground and powered down the engines. Laramie unstrapped from her chair and marveled at how their time on *Sawtooth* made the gravity of Juliet seem downright weak. She felt positive she could jump ten meters in the air.

No, it wasn't the gravity that made her feel like this. It was the chance she had to find out what the hell was up with her family. A quick trip over to the post exchange would give her all she needed to place a simple video call to her parents. What would she say? *Do you know about constriction? Drag Jessamy and her boys off the range. Warn Mat and the other brothers. Load up on supplies, keep other people away, and don't trust the government.*

Stay hidden and stay safe.

The plan was a simple one. They would leave the Javelin behind and rumble to the university in what they'd claim to be yet another military surplus vehicle repurposed for ranch work. She and Kenny moved outside to form the barest of perimeters while Wyatt untethered the Jackal. Laramie positioned herself underneath the ascent booster extending off the back of the Javelin like the thorax of some massive insect. The pale glow of Romeo bathed the skin of her bare arms.

My home.

The whine of a turbine engine dispelled her reprieve. Behind her, the four massive wheels of their reconnaissance vehicle crunched down the ramp. A butterfly door popped open to reveal Wyatt waving at her from the driver's seat.

"You should let me drive, LT," Laramie called out.

"Why?"

"Lieutenants often get lost, never to be seen again."

"Right. I'll take my chances this time, thank you."

Bell and the others were already aboard the Jackal. Teo would be staying behind, so Wyatt spent the last few minutes briefing him on which comm channels to use and how often to check in. Then the engine rumbled to life and they headed toward Los Cuernos. Through the windshield, Laramie caught a glimpse of the town near the distant mist of the river. Then the vehicle plunged into the darkness of the bamboo forest.

Kenny alternated his attention between the windshield and the tiny porthole near his seat. "What does Los Cuernos mean?" he asked.

"It's Spanish for *the horns*," Laramie said. She turned around and pointed through the tiny window in front of her. "Did you see that river a moment ago?"

"Yes, ma'am."

"It's man-made. There's a dam leading to a large gorge right past it. If you went to the bottom of the gorge and looked back up, you'd see two outcroppings that stick out on either side of the dam." She held up her hands on either side of her head. "Horns."

Bell gave her an odd look as he eavesdropped. "How do you know where it got its name?"

"My folks live around these parts," she said, barely able to hear herself over the interior noise. "A couple hundred klicks away. But this is the main supply depot for the western ranching counties. I actually dated a guy who went to university here."

"Did you ever think about attending?" Bell asked. "Instead of joining RESIT?"

"I'm a country girl, Doctor. I work for a living."

Condensation obscured parts of the windshield as the Jackal followed dirt trails through the bamboo. The holo monitor on the dashboard showed a tactical map that had them closing in on the town. Laramie rubbed her hands together in anticipation. She just needed thirty minutes to drop into the post exchange. Maybe even fifteen. Then Wyatt could help Bell do his little experiment, and Laramie would rest easily with the knowledge that the McCoy clan would weather this storm just like they did hopper swarms and bad weather.

A sudden burst of light flooded the cab. Outside the armored windshield, Laramie saw the forest fall away as Alpha Centauri A peeked above the horizon in a good morning sunrise. Straight ahead, a clearing appeared with multiple outbuildings and connected fences. To their left, a paved road emerged from the dirt and extended past more structures until it reached the waterfront, where a retaining wall lined the edge of the river a meter or two below.

"Slow down," Bell advised. "We don't need the police stopping us because we come blazing in with some sort of tank."

"Police?" Wyatt said. The concern came through his voice clear as day.

"No. This isn't Venice, Lieutenant. We just have to act normal, low-key."

Wyatt pulled the Jackal behind a large shed made of dark carbon-fiber panels. Once he cut the engine, everyone unstrapped and grouped together for a final huddle. Wyatt glanced down the cab at the unconscious form of Corporal Dean in the back.

"How are we going to be low-key in getting *him* to the lab?"

"The university's got three-wheeler runabouts." Bell pulled out a pair of identification cards from a pocket in the chest of his utilities. "My credentials will let us borrow one."

"How many passengers can you take?"

Bell gave him a look. "Well, at least a driver and a body."

Laramie saw Wyatt's eyes harden. He didn't look convinced. But after a long stare down with Bell, he just shook his head and looked at his watch.

They climbed out of the Jackal. Laramie could smell the scent of wildflowers mixed with mildew from a nearby maintenance shed. Her eyes followed the power cables from the shed's roof until it split into smaller lines connecting to buildings lining the river. These smaller boathouses each straddled a wide carbon-fiber dock with some sort of watercraft tied up at the end. A few of the boats appeared to be racers, low and sleek and expensive.

"Will you look at those," Kenny said. He marched quickly toward one of the nearby boats.

Laramie startled when she heard Bell's voice right next to her ear. "College of Marine Science," he said.

"What?"

"It's one of the newer schools. Not nearly as established as the College of Medicine."

"Marine Science," Laramie repeated. She pointed at one of the wedge-shaped hydrofoils. "What do they teach? How to race all day?"

"No—the university sublets the dock space. You know, to give the rich patrons a reason to come by and donate."

"Huh."

Kenny was circling the boat immediately in front of them and marveling at the massive engine cowling. He seemed like he was in heaven, his hands tracing the lines of the aerodynamic hull.

Bell took a couple steps toward him. "What do you think?"

"I used to race these," Kenny said.

"No kidding?"

"Yeah. I was never good enough to make it past regionals, though."

"On Juliet?"

"No. Earth."

"Well, I imagine regionals on Earth is pretty damn good," Bell said.

"Not bad, I guess." He glanced around. "Wish I could chat with the owners."

"Don't see anyone. Must be a workday."

This time it was Laramie's turn to eavesdrop. She had no idea about this little tidbit of Kenny's background. "You raced hydrofoils, Ken?"

"Yeah."

"Your folks have a lot of money or something?"

"Yeah."

She blinked, dumbfounded.

"Why did you stop?"

He shrugged. "Because I decided to join RESIT."

Laramie was struggling to contemplate such a life choice when Wyatt called for them to rally near the Jackal.

"Let's go over the plan one last time," he said. "Kenny, you stay here with the Jackal. If we have problems and need to abort, you're our quick reaction force—come in, pick up, extract. Got it?"

"Yes, sir."

"Good. Assuming no issues, Laramie, Bell, Annika, and I will hike into town. We're going to head straight to the university campus. Bell, you're going to have to talk us past whoever needs to give us access to the lab and get us inside. You know what you're going to say?"

"Just leave it to me, Lieutenant. All I need to do is get a hold of my former colleagues. They'll take care of us."

"Good. Just limit the visiting if you can. We need to set up this experiment and get it done. We're on a clock."

"Understood."

"Okay." Wyatt looked at Laramie. "Once we're in and everything's legit, you and Annika are going to stay with Bell while I come back and get Corporal Dean. I'll bring him to the lab, we revive him, Bell does whatever he needs to do, then we haul ass back to the Jackal. Got it?"

"Got it," she said.

"Good." He surveyed the cabin until his eyes fell on Annika. "Any questions?"

The little girl shook her head.

Wyatt showed her a tiny smile. He glanced at the chronometer on his wrist. "All right. We've only got thirty-one hours. Let's move."

Laramie took point. As they moved toward the town proper, the loose, corrugated panels of the outbuildings gave way to more substantial structures built from stacked cargo pods. Up ahead, Laramie saw the paved road veer away from the water as it wound its way toward downtown, splitting an ever-growing cluster of buildings that grew taller and more modern the further in they went. Memories flooded her brain of the trips with her father to buy new tools or get some jewelry for her mom's birthday. She remembered coming here for a harvest festival as a little girl, her first trip to what she thought was the biggest city anywhere. How simple life had been back then. How thrilling. How safe.

How come they hadn't seen any people?

Her attention shifted to a sharp, oily odor carried by the breeze. Laramie stopped, her boots scraping the tiny pebbles on the pavement.

"What is it?" Bell said.

Laramie closed her eyes and inhaled. The scent lessened but was definitely there. Something was on fire.

"I smell it," Wyatt said.

She turned back to the road and scanned the rooftops, shielding her eyes from the morning sun hanging low in the sky. A moment later she spotted a plume of thin, black smoke rising from a cluster of residential buildings. "Over there," she said, pointing.

Wyatt raised his arm in the other direction. "And there."

Laramie saw it, too: more clouds billowing up from the ground, dissipating in the wind above the rooftops. She now noticed several plumes originating just up ahead, out of sight.

"I assume there's a fire department here?" Wyatt asked.

Bell snorted. "Of course there is. This is a city, not some backwater pit—"

The doctor went abruptly silent.

"Doctor?" Wyatt said.

No reply. Laramie turned and looked over her shoulder. Bell's eyes had grown wide, his feet planted firmly in the dirt.

"Jack?" Wyatt said.

The doctor blinked. His eyes darted across the landscape, then settled directly on Laramie. She couldn't put her finger on the emotion they held. Fear?

"I'm sorry," he said.

Something in her stomach twisted into a knot.

Wyatt was speaking. Laramie didn't hear him. She had already turned to run toward the flames.

23

Death lay everywhere.

Bodies covered the street. Men, women, boys, girls, all lying on the ground, rudely and simultaneously interrupted from whatever they had been doing when the moment struck. Thousands of eyes staring without a trace of the spark that once lived in them. The overpowering stench of rotten flesh mixed with smoke and ash and smoldering piles of rubble.

Everywhere, as far as the eye could see, the residents of Los Cuernos blanketed the ground like a mass of insects that had been suddenly and ruthlessly exterminated.

Remnants of the event poked through the carnage. Pockmarks bruised the ground every fifty meters or so, eerily similar to the marks made by cluster bombs Laramie had seen used against Oscars on Tiamat. Long scorch marks were all that remained of a farmers' market. Another crater indicated the position of what once had been an ambulance, with only a twisted vehicle chassis left to wrap around the sirens.

Laramie tried to process what she saw. Somewhere deep in her brain she recognized a mass-casualty event. Without thinking, her RESIT training made her scan the scene in front of her, her eyes searching the horror for anyone moving, anyone who might have survived. A swath of light blue caught her vision. She stepped toward a little grassy patch next to a children's playground. There, half underneath a merry-go-round, she saw the body of a little boy contorted into an impossible pose. His limbs twisted in a way that made the terror on his face even more horrible.

Everyone was dead.

Everyone.

The world swam. Legs buckled. Laramie found herself sitting on the dirt, unable to see, incapable of breathing any air. These people. *Her* people. Families just like hers, children just like her sister's, cut down where they stood. She could tell from the layout of the carnage that nobody here had been constricted. Nobody had been kneeling in a ring, forehead to the ground. These were just regular folks doing their lives, eating lunch, playing, talking. Living.

Had any of her own family been visiting? Her dad probably rode the maglev in once every other week. Her brain rattled through the faces of her mother and father. Jessamy. Her brothers Rik, Mak, the twins. Nieces and nephews. Her grandma. They all called Juliet home.

How could this happen?

Vaguely, Laramie caught the wisp of a conversation behind her. Something about nerve gas yield and dispersal patterns, bomblet payloads and Ibex drones. She swiveled on her rear until she could see the source of the voices. Bell and Wyatt stood next to each other just a few meters away. The LT held a gloved hand over his nose, horror in his eyes. Doctor Bell just stared at the carnage with the detached expression of an academic grading an assignment.

Monster.

Her body moved without her. The buildings blurred, the sky twisted. The unmistakable sound of a Ka-Bar being drawn from its sheath. Someone yelling, not her. Bell's face, wide-eyed, getting closer and closer ...

A sharp pain in her forearm accompanied another blur that abruptly stopped her forward motion. Something was grabbing her wrist and blocking her. Part of Laramie's brain, the rational part that recognized her lieutenant struggling to twist her knife away, pled for restraint. This wasn't what she should be doing. But the well of agony was too deep, the overflow unstoppable.

Bell was just behind the LT. So close. She could almost reach him.

Wyatt was yelling at her. "Staff Sergeant! Stop!"

"*Why?*" she shrieked.

Laramie's voice sounded otherworldly even to her own ears, spoken by a stranger she had never met. She pressed forward, her forearm against Wyatt's, the Ka-Bar flashing over his shoulder as she desperately fought to get it under Bell's chin. She screamed again, spittle flying from her lips. "*Why?*"

Something twisted her arm. She tried to move her knife, but the next thing she knew, she wasn't holding it anymore. Someone was saying her name. Someone was holding her back. No, holding her up. She tried to blink away the tears but more came in their wake, until finally the grief carried her away to someplace dark and lonely.

Laramie was sitting on the ground again. Wyatt's arms wrapped around her, holding her down. Consoling her.

"Why?" she said again, but this time her voice was tiny and weak.

"I'm—" Bell said. The doctor looked at the ground. "This is what Firebreak is."

Swirling deep in her memory, the word stirred like a dragon slowly coming awake. *Firebreak.* Preemptive murder. Culling specific population centers based on constriction's transmission vectors. When briefing Major Beck, Bell had likened it to denying fuel to a wildfire blazing out of control. She'd assumed he meant surgical strikes. Not cities full of innocents. Not tens of thousands.

Eventually, with her throat raw and her eyes empty, she pulled herself from Wyatt's shoulder. The lieutenant helped her to her feet with an unsteady wobble. She noticed he didn't let go of her arms.

"Laramie," he said, softer this time.

The brown soil stared back at her from her feet. She felt drained. Numb.

Wyatt moved his face directly in front of hers. "Hey, listen to me, Laramie. I need you with me.

We have a mission to do. It's the only way to stop this. The *only* way. Do you hear me?"

Her nose was running rampant down her face.

"Laramie? Snap out of it. I'm sorry, but we have got to get this done."

Of course they did. She snuffled a few times and nodded, pulling back and wiping her cheeks with a gloved hand. Pull it together. Be the professional. Stop this from happening at other places.

A tiny voice screamed in fury from inside. *What about your family? Where were you for them?*

"We good?" Wyatt said.

She met his eyes. They stared back with intense urgency.

She managed a small nod.

"Then let's get this damn thing over with," he said.

***

They formed up into a skirmish line, RESIT troopers on the edges, Bell and Annika in the middle. Bell led them to a main road where time seemed like it had stopped. Vehicles sat motionless in the traffic lanes after colliding with each other as drivers suddenly expired. Bodies littered the sidewalks in clumps, their faces snapshots of agony.

Laramie glared at the health director as they marched. The doctor wouldn't make eye contact.

"The drones that came here," she said. "Did you say they used a nerve agent?"

"Yes," Bell said, his voice detached and small.

"What about people hiding indoors? There might be survivors."

"The payloads were designed for urban areas. Maximum penetration and lethality." Bell shook his head as if coming to grips himself with the brutality of his containment plan. "But that doesn't matter. Ground-based drones would have come after, like the one on the freighter."

A glimpse at a small grocery store confirmed Bell's assertion. The glass storefront lay shattered over the sidewalk, and she could see the scorch marks from laser fire on the structural columns. She spat in the dirt. They should go look anyway. Rescuing lives remained a key tenet for RESIT, whether in space or on land.

But Wyatt's words reminded her of their timeline. They needed to complete their mission and get Bell his data. It would be the only way to stop McManus from murdering more citizens in whatever this mad strategy entailed.

She scowled at Jack Bell again. One of the key architects of Firebreak, a protocol for unholy and industrialized murder, was walking next to her because he claimed he had found a way to shut off what he had built.

We've made a deal with the devil's henchman. What does that make us?

Laramie could see the main college now, a cluster of gleaming carbon-fiber buildings that were only two or three stories tall but with massive footprints that stretched wide across the campus. One building dead ahead was surrounded by a wide, green lawn, with a large telecommunications array on the roof that scraped at the clouds. Two smaller buildings flanked the road up ahead like some sort of medieval gatehouse. A collection of flagpoles and pennants graced both of them.

"Where's the lab?" Wyatt said.

Bell pointed toward the building with the roof array. "That's the College of Medicine. The Department of Neurosciences takes up sublevels one and two, underground." He glanced around at the corpses littering the lawn in front of the doors. "I think you can radio your man to bring up the truck. There's not really any point in keeping a low profile."

Laramie felt her lip turn into a snarl. No wonder Chris felt the way he did about this man. How could this bastard be so cold?

If Wyatt had any similar feelings, he kept them buried. He switched on the comm. "Battle Two, Battle One, do you copy?"

"Two, I copy."

"Bring the Jackal up, Kenny. This place is a graveyard. There's no reason to keep you out of sight."

A moment of hesitation on the comm. "Aye, sir."

Ten minutes later, the four-wheeled ground vehicle rumbled toward them under the whine of a gas turbine engine. Laramie released the butterfly door and manhandled Corporal Dean through the narrow opening. But when she started to throw him over her shoulders, Wyatt held up his hand to stop.

"What?" Laramie said.

"I'll take him."

Part of her thought she should protest. Carrying a body wasn't a job for an officer. But she didn't resist as Wyatt pulled Dean into a fireman's carry.

His eyes didn't leave hers. "Come on. The sooner we start, the sooner we can get the hell out of here."

24

On the flight deck of his Javelin, Chief Warrant Officer Teo Parata gazed out the armored windscreen at a swarm of insects dancing against the blue sky. A gentle breeze rippled through the green-gray grass in a way that made the fields seem alive. He had excellent visibility; the edge of the bamboo forest lay a hundred meters away, and there was no way anyone or anything might try to approach without being spotted. Then again, lots of hostile organisms lived on Juliet. Being alone was dangerous.

Well, he wasn't totally alone. A tiny mammillaria cactus protruded from the opening or a zero-gee water bulb suctioned to the control panel. Some pilots taped up pics of their girlfriends for good luck, but that never seemed to work for him. Instead, he kept a thorny Earth plant named Bruce.

Prickly and hard to eradicate. Just like him.

An orange threat light illuminated just below the water bulb.

Teo refocused his attention on the control panel. "Tac, what's the alarm?"

"Unidentified contacts approaching in sector six-six," a synthesized female voice replied. "Four signatures. Range, thirty kilometers, bearing one-eight-five at twenty kilometers per hour negative closure."

Teo frowned. The blips were about a thousand meters above the surface and drifting northwest of Los Cuernos. The first time they appeared and disappeared so quickly that Teo didn't think much of it. Now they were back, and he didn't need the analysis of the Javelin's passive surveillance array to recognize an aerial search pattern.

"Tac, mark the four bogeys in sector six-six as unknowns and track ongoing."

It took only a moment for the Javelin's computer to comply. The warm, female voice did little to comfort him. "Bogeys are marked Utah One through Utah Four."

"Can you profile them?"

"Negative, our optical array is unable to profile at this distance."

Teo watched the blips travel in a slow arc across the holo monitor. He mentally measured the distance from the corner of the monitor to his current position, then added the distance from the Javelin to the town. If this was indeed some kind of reconnaissance, the bogeys would be on him within the next two hours.

Then again, maybe they were something else. Teo had seen his share of weird on this planet, including a pack of furry Muppets that had tried to eat his crew chief the last time he'd been here. For all he knew, these bogeys might be some kind of fanged bird with a corkscrew tail and unicorn horn.

The blips went off the screen again.

Maybe it was nothing. Teo would just keep an eye out and hope that there wouldn't be a need to break his orders for radio silence.

***

Clusters of bodies lined the glass-walled entry of the university lab. Wyatt saw teenage boys slumped against tables, young women clutching tablets to their chests. Now they lay in contorted poses, limbs jutting abstractly into the air from rigor mortis.

Students. Children, really. Innocent save for the fact that a computer algorithm had decided they needed to die. Wyatt's stomach churned in revulsion, though he wasn't sure whether it was from the stench or the display of horrific mass murder.

"This way," Bell said. He covered his face with a rag to block the smell.

They wound their way through several corridors until they reached an area filled with glass-paneled offices. The words DEPARTMENT OF NEUROSCIENCE announced their new location, below which Wyatt saw *Quantum Mechanics Studies* stenciled at eye level. They entered a reception area with low, plush couches positioned around a small coffee table cluttered by magazines. An official-looking counter cordoned off the administrative section, behind which a young woman lay sprawled out on the floor. Wyatt noticed one of her shoes was missing.

Bell waved them to a door in the back. "The lab is back here. Staff Sergeant, you'll need to burn the lock."

Wyatt could almost feel the heat from Laramie's glare. "How can you just ignore all these people, Bell? Look at them."

"If a strike was ordered on this town, it was because they were about to be infected. The data models don't lie."

"They're dead because of you."

"Hey! This is my home too," Bell snapped. A glimpse of pain flashed in his eyes. "We are fighting for survival, Laramie. This disease is *wiping us out*. There is no other way."

"Enough," Wyatt barked. The weight of Corporal Dean across his shoulders seemed to be growing by the minute in the heavy gravity. "Laramie, burn the lock."

She shot Wyatt a look as she walked to the door. When a blob of metal finally slipped from the handle, she stepped back and scowled at Bell.

"Your legacy awaits," she announced.

The doctor's face darkened. "Don't."

"Door," Wyatt said.

They pressed forward. Glass gave way to opaque panels that held message boards and their proclamations from university administration. Bell took them down several sets of stairs and past supply rooms and offices. It didn't take long before they entered another section of the building marked with a sign that said ENTANGLEMENT LAB.

Laramie had to burn through yet another set of door locks at the end of a sterile-looking hallway. Bell pushed open the double doors to reveal a cavernous room with a low ceiling held up with stout support beams. Metal rails hung from the beams and supported arrays of lights and cylindrical shapes over their heads.

Annika immediately scurried over to a hulking metal cabinet next to long tanks of pressurized gas. Curious fingers started to fiddle with bright orange dials.

"Don't touch that one, please," Bell advised.

Annika withdrew her hands in disappointment.

Doctor Jack Bell, physician and former Chief Analyst at the Julietan Department of Health, pressed deeper into the massive lab. He inspected arrays of equipment and testing booths, workstations and holo displays, scanning with deliberate intent for some goal known only to himself. His eyes finally locked on a long, rectangular trench embedded in the floor on the far side of the room. A heavy metal canopy that reminded Wyatt of ancient twentieth-century military pillboxes squatted over the dugout, with narrow slits that lined the sides like viewports on a tank. Above it, a large array of cylinders and pipes hung from the rails on the ceiling.

"There," Bell said.

Wyatt shrugged Corporal Dean's body off his shoulders and let him fall to the floor. His thighs groaned in relief.

Laramie paced around one end of the booth and peered into the interior. "What's this thing all about?"

"It's a particle detector." Bell tugged at a section on the wall and it swung open like a door. "I suppose you could think of it as the lab version of your spaceship's nav system. Only this one is designed to measure brain activity at a quantum level."

"And you're sure this will get us what we need?" Wyatt asked.

"Hardly. If my colleagues were alive, and we had three months to design the experiments, maybe I would give you a different answer." Bell sighed. "But this will have to do."

For the next hour, Jack Bell powered up equipment and prepared the testing area. Consoles lit up and holo monitors came to life as he flitted between various workstations around the room. Then he sat down at a workstation near the detector and withdrew into his own thoughts, furiously typing on the keyboard. Laramie contented herself by mowing through a field ration. Wyatt was left to keep an eye on Annika before her exploration got her lost.

At 1420 hours, Bell stood from his workstation. He surveyed the others as if he had come down from a mountaintop with a set of stone tablets.

When his eyes fell on Corporal Dean, he started marching toward the motionless body.

"Please help me bring the trooper into the detection chamber," he said.

Wyatt forced himself to his feet despite the protest of both his natural and artificial legs. Even after days at high acceleration aboard *Sawtooth*, the heavy gravity of Juliet seemed punishing. It was as if the planet itself was objecting to the nature of their mission.

The two men dragged the unconscious trooper through a heavy hatch in the canopy of the particle detector. A short ramp descended below floor level. At the bottom, the rectangular interior of the test rig stretched ten meters along the long edge. A one-meter monopod extended from the floor at one end, with a single patient bed connected to a ball joint that allowed rotation around multiple axes. A belt and several limb restraints poked through the padded surface.

Bell glanced around the detection chamber. "Put Dean over there, near the middle of the chamber."

"Aren't we putting him on the bed?" Wyatt asked.

"No. In the middle."

They dragged the corporal further into the testing rig and set him down on the ground. Wyatt bent over to check the IV pump. It would need another cartridge of sedatives before much longer. He looked up to tell Bell, but the doctor had already exited the chamber.

Wyatt hurried up the ramp. He found Bell standing over Annika, his hand extended. "Miss Hewitt. We're ready for you."

Annika looked up from her school tablet. She didn't move.

"You're not testing one at a time?" Laramie asked.

"Of course not. We put the girl and the constricted trooper into the detector. We revive the trooper. Then we record the quantum interference when he moves to infect her."

"Revive—" The staff sergeant's eyes widened. "What the *hell*?"

Bell looked incredulous. "What did you think we were here to do? Sit around and eat ice cream? The whole point of this was to put her together with the corporal and measure the quantum interactions."

"You never said you were going to test Dean at the same time, and you never said he was going to be awake."

"I assumed you had a grasp of the obvious."

Wyatt turned his attention to Annika. So far, he had been utterly impressed by how well the young girl had contained her anxiety throughout the mission—on the Fast Attack, during reentry, even walking past dead bodies in the streets. It only took a glance to see that the veneer was starting to crack.

Laramie stepped dangerously close to Bell. Even without her Ka-Bar, her demeanor exuded lethality. "I saw the restraints on that bed in there," she growled. "You think you're going to strap her in like some animal waiting for slaughter?"

"Those restraints are necessary ... they keep the subject positioned in front of the detection equipment so they can record—"

"Bullshit!"

"Is it?" Bell slapped his hands against his sides in frustration. "We have an out-of-control pandemic, and our last line of defense involves killing thousands of people every day. You think figuring out how to stop all this is a waste of time?"

A metallic clatter echoed nearby. Wyatt turned to see Annika's tablet on the floor near her feet. She took another step backward.

Wyatt didn't like the idea of this experiment either. He couldn't help but feel Bell had hoodwinked Major Beck and Captain Kazimira by glossing over his intentions. But he also knew Bell was right. They had to learn more about constriction and how to stop it, and Annika was the key.

She had survived a close encounter once before. That was the bet. That was the mission.

He bent down on one knee. "Annika," he said. "Anni."

The little girl's eyes narrowed. Wyatt realized that only Chris called her that nickname.

"Do you remember when you were in the hangar bay up in space?" he continued. "When the other trooper, Izzy, was about to attack Chris?"

She frowned at him. After a moment, she nodded.

"You were fine after that, right?"

Her head swiveled back and forth. Not fine.

"But you stopped Izzy. And Chris survived. And you're okay, right here with us. Right?"

Hesitation.

Wyatt plowed on. "That's all this is. Doctor Bell just wants you to do whatever you did in the hangar with Chris. Just let it happen again. We'll have these sensors nearby so that he can record it with these special instruments. Then we might be able to copy it and use your trick to protect other people."

Annika watched Wyatt with a deep intensity, her eyes flicking back and forth between his own. Distrust oozed from every pore.

Wyatt realized belatedly that the lab had fallen silent. He reached out his hand. Annika leaned away from it like it was a deadly animal.

What should he do?

What would Chris do?

The weight on Wyatt's shoulders suddenly felt far greater than that of Juliet's heavy gravity.

"Hey," he said, trying to reset the conversation. "Do you remember when we were on the big freighter after leaving Juliet?"

Annika nodded.

"There was a robot that came aboard to try and stop us. Do you remember that? You watched that on the cameras?"

Another nod.

"I was really scared. All of us. Laramie. Even Chris."

Protest washed over Annika's face. Chris wasn't scared. Chris wasn't scared of anything.

Wyatt pressed forward, anticipating that that would be her reaction. "Yes, he was, Anni. It was really dangerous. But you know what? He saved us. He jumped on the robot with a breaching charge and blew it up. Even though he was scared too, he knew he had to do something about it. He didn't let the fear stop him."

She shook her head.

"That's what being brave is all about, Anni. Brave is being scared, but not letting it stop you when you know something has to be done."

Wyatt stopped there. He watched the emotions play out, her lip tremble, the tears welling up in her eyes. When she gasped for air, he thought she might be readying to turn and run.

Then, bravely, she reached for his hand.

25

Wyatt stood up and turned to Jack Bell. "If any of this starts going south, Doctor, I'm ending it. Let's go."

Laramie came over and extended her hand to the little girl. Annika took it in hers and the three of them walked slowly toward the detector ramp. Bell followed. When they reached the patient bed, the doctor adjusted the straps around her waist and shoulders to secure her against the padding. Annika kept her eyes closed, as if not being able to see would wrap her in a protective cloak of invisibility.

The next few minutes proved even more stressful. Wyatt checked the medication unit strapped to Corporal Dean's arm and found the bio-signs increasing. A brief panic set in that Dean might wake up before they were ready, that the experiment might devolve into a firefight before they even had a chance to start. He called up to Bell with a warning.

The doctor called out loudly from behind his workstation. "It's okay, Lieutenant. Switch the whole thing off and exit the detector." A second later he added, "Make sure the door is secure on the way out."

Wyatt tapped the tablet screen on the medication unit and shut off the IV. Then he turned to make a quick exit. He stopped just long enough to rest a hand on Annika's shoulder.

"It will be okay," he said.

She looked back at him, trembling.

God, I hope this isn't a mistake.

He exited the booth and pushed the door shut. As he reached the top of the ramp, he saw Laramie looking miserable over by one of the observation panels.

"Staff Sergeant," he said.

She lifted her eyes.

Wyatt repositioned his Vector in front of his chest. Then he pantomimed a punch through the air at the detection chamber. Get ready for action.

Laramie followed suit and shouldered her own weapon. Now both of them were covering the trench. If anything went wrong, if things got out of control, a couple laser shots would put Dean down in an instant. Wyatt just hoped that it would be before any lasting damage was done.

Bell's voice carried across the lab with a tinge of excitement. "It's happening!"

Through the thick glass of the observation window, Wyatt saw that Dean's eyes had flicked open. Two pinprick pupils were pointed off into space, staring at something a thousand klicks away. Then, to Wyatt's horror, the corporal swiveled his head and locked onto the girl in the booth with him.

Dean seemed oblivious to Wyatt and Laramie watching from three meters above the trench. He tried to stand but was having difficulty in the heavy gravity. Wyatt watched as Dean got on all fours and walked his body upright against the wall. Then he began a slow amble toward the girl strapped into the bed.

Annika was trying to get free. Eyes wide, mouth hung open, silent screams of panic as she writhed against the restraints. Wyatt felt his own stomach turn inside out. Was he really letting this happen? His conscience screamed at him to intervene. He had always thought of himself as a protector, a shepherd. It was why he joined RESIT. Now he was exposing an innocent life to existential danger.

What would Father Bradley say if he were watching? What would God say as He gazed down from heaven?

Is He watching? Or has He forsaken us again?

The whispers of prayer came unbidden to his lips. *The Lord is my shepherd, I shall not want...*

"I have a good reading," Bell said, his voice dull and matter-of-fact. "It's working."

He maketh me lie down in green pastures. He leadeth me beside still waters.

Corporal Dean shuffled toward the patient bed. His balance was off, and he moved with awkward, slow steps, yet his attention never wavered. The pinprick eyes remained locked on Annika with the gaze of a predator.

A distant click echoed from Wyatt's left. The sound of a safety being switched off. Laramie was leaning into her Vector, pointing it at Dean.

"Hold your fire, Laramie."

He restoreth my soul; he leadeth me in the paths of righteousness for his name's sake...

The constricted trooper kept moving.

What is Annika experiencing right now? he wondered. The lure of the siren call, to give in to constriction as the voices spoke of rapture? Or the sting of gold specks as her mind burned to a crisp?

Yea, though I walk through the valley of shadow of death, I shall fear no evil; for thou art with me...

Dean was only a few meters away now. Annika's face was locked in a mask of abject terror.

"LT!" Laramie warned.

"Wait."

"Look at her! We have to—"

"Hold your fire, that's an order," he said.

Annika's whole body trembled as Dean moved closer. The corporal was almost upon her. For a moment, Wyatt was afraid Laramie might just shoot him without orders.

And then it happened.

Annika's body stiffened as if being electrocuted. Even from the observation port, Wyatt could see her eyes shrink down to pinpricks. Her face contorted into a mask of fury, her lips pulled back into a snarl.

Dean reacted as if someone had punched him in the chest. He jerked to a halt. His expressionless face wilted with something that almost resembled surprise.

"Yes!" Bell yelled from behind the holo monitor.

The trooper stumbled back another step and closed his eyes.

Wyatt watched, transfixed. "My God."

Corporal Dean fell in a clumsy flop. A moment later, his body lay on the detector chamber floor in an ignominious heap, with limbs sprawled in all directions.

Annika was practically vibrating against the bed restraints. She kept her eyes locked on the constricted trooper a few seconds longer. Then, as quickly as it had started, all the visceral energy that had suddenly pulsed through her body seemed to vanish. She slumped downward, a marionette with its strings abruptly cut.

"Get her out!" Wyatt yelled.

Laramie didn't hesitate. While he covered Dean with his Vector, his staff sergeant rushed down the ramp and ripped open the containment door. Seconds later she had the bed restrains off and Annika's limp body slung over her shoulder. As soon as Laramie was outside of the detector, Wyatt slammed the door shut.

He turned to see Laramie on her knees at the top of the ramp, cradling Annika in her arms. To his surprise, the girl was awake again, blinking with normal eyes.

"It's okay," Laramie was saying, her voice unsteady and full of emotion. "You're okay."

Wyatt hurried over to the doctor. Jack Bell was busy scrolling his fingers across a touchscreen, reviewing his data.

"Did you get what you need?" he asked.

Bell seemed oblivious to the question. "Fascinating. Just ... fascinating."

"Doctor."

"Huh? Oh. Well, there was a massive recording event, I can tell you that. There's no doubt that there's some sort of quantum interaction taking place. No doubt at all."

"Is it what you need?"

"That will be up to the AI modeler." Bell's voice was distracted as he fiddled with the control screen. "You can only record what you observe, and observation itself causes decoherence—"

"Speak plain, Jack."

Bell turned and took a deep, annoyed breath. "Observation interferes with the core dynamic. If you put a thermometer into steaming water, that very act changes the temperature you're trying to measure. It's no longer a closed system. I need the AI modeler to undo that interference mathematically. Until then, I can't tell you yet if we have enough. Understand?"

Wyatt still wasn't sure if this new vocabulary could be considered English. "How long does that take?"

"Weeks. Maybe months."

"*Months?*" Wyatt felt his exasperation level rising. "Doctor, we have *hours* before we head back to the Javelin. We need to confirm your little experiment got all the data you need, because we are not coming back."

"Well, if you'll stop distracting me, I can continue down that path." Bell's words drifted off as he tapped the touchpad like a classically trained pianist.

For the next hour, Wyatt paced around the lab while they waited. Laramie moved Annika from the floor to a nearby office chair and was doing her best to tend to her. She seemed deeply disoriented. Wyatt noticed her head would droop every few minutes or so, like she couldn't stay awake. Laramie even tried to get her to eat something to build her energy back up, but the girl snubbed the ration pouch as if the food inside had gone sour.

Meanwhile, Corporal Dean remained motionless inside the quantum detector. Wyatt could see the body jumbled on the deck and pondered how different the outcome was than what he had seen with Izzy. On *Vigorous*, Annika had merely turned her attacker away. Here, it appeared to have gone much further than that. Wyatt wasn't even sure if Dean was still alive. He couldn't bring himself to go inside and check.

Late in the afternoon, Bell finally wrapped up his efforts at his workstation. The doctor stood from his chair and stretched with his arms wide, then started to walk toward Wyatt.

"I've done what I can do from here, Lieutenant," he said. "I put all the data into one of the department's AI cores. We just need to take it with us."

"Where is that?"

"In the server room, on the first floor."

"All right." Wyatt surveyed the lab a final time. "You sure we're done here? Once we leave, there's no coming back."

"I know."

"How do you want to prep Corporal Dean for transport?"

"We don't. He has constriction."

"You don't think your little experiment might be able to help cure him?"

Bell threw him an incredulous look. "There's no recovery from that, no matter what we learn from today."

Wyatt didn't like the idea of leaving anyone behind, but he could feel the truth in Bell's words. They had lost Dean the day Izzy stared him down in the hangar. "Okay. Let's go."

Bell marched toward the stairs. Wyatt followed close behind, while Laramie carried Annika clinging to her chest. As they climbed back up to ground level, Wyatt couldn't help but feel a sense of relief. It didn't matter if Bell could decipher the mechanics of how constriction spread. What they had witnessed in the detection chamber—the corruption of one's mind, thoughts, one's conscious self—felt like an unholy thing. And if not for the grace of God, Wyatt could have inadvertently been party to the death of an innocent little girl.

As they reached the top landing, Kenny's voice crackled weakly through the comm. "*—attle One, come in! Lieutenant?*"

"This is One. What is it, Kenny?"

"*Been trying to reach you, sir. Multiple aerial bogeys coming in hot.*" A momentary pause. "*They're getting close, I can hear the engines—*"

Wyatt felt the hair on his neck stand up. The thick shielding belowground might have been good for particle experiments, but it was terrible for situational awareness in the battlespace. He wheeled around to Bell.

"Is the server room close?"

"Yes, it's just down the hall."

"Go get your data *now*," he barked. He switched back to the comm. "Kenny, bring the Jackal—"

A sharp whine screamed in his ear, and the signal went out.

26

Chris Thompson didn't have much to occupy his time with while he waited his turn with Doctor Kenta. He contented himself with watching Epione's sensor wand scan the new occupant who had moved full-time into the med bay.

So, this is the survivor, he thought. He looked well enough. Rumor had it the trooper had been in bad shape not that long ago—malnourished, oxygen-deprived, post-traumatic stress. Chris could barely imagine the despair of floating alone for a month in a pressure sleeve inside a dead spacecraft. Now, Sergeant Jameson lay conscious in Chris's old patient bed with multiple intravenous lines pumping vitamins and fluids into his arm, coordinating how to keep him on the narrow road to recovery.

But what gave Chris unease were the two pinprick pupils that remained fixed inside the survivor's irises.

"Very good, Sergeant," Kenta said. She swiped her tablet as she reviewed the vital signs coming in from Epione. "I think we'll get you back on your feet yet."

The trooper typed something on his own tablet and showed it to her.

Kenta read the message. "No, I don't think you'll be going back to active duty. Let's just do our jobs, and we'll see what happens."

Jameson's face fell, but he nodded and let the tablet drop to his chest.

Active duty? Chris thought.

"Now, Sergeant, I want you to rest. If you need anything, let Epione know. I'll check on you in a bit."

The trooper nodded again. His gaze drifted wistfully to the ceiling.

Kenta turned away and gave a little start at seeing Chris. Her face looked as though she had forgotten they had an appointment.

"Still here, doc."

"Ah, my Mister Difficult." She sighed. "Give me a minute and we'll see how you're progressing."

"Sure thing, Doc."

Kenta stepped through the hatch into the main berth. Chris crossed his arms, trying to stave off the discomfort of being left alone next to this oddity of a trooper with constricted eyes.

Sergeant Jameson swiveled his head and looked at him.

Chris stiffened. He had been in this position before, faced with an unnerving gaze that opened a torrent of golden sparks. Once, it had felt like heaven. Every other time it hurt like hell. Maybe that was because he now shot at the individual as quickly as possible.

It took a second for him to realize that he sensed nothing. No sparks. No voices. He might as well have been looking at the wall.

The trooper tapped on his tablet. A moment later he tilted it so Chris could see.

WHY ARE YOU STARING AT ME?

Chris blinked. "What?"

Jameson pointed at Chris, made a V with his fingers and gestured toward his eyes, then tapped his own chest. He followed it with an open palm that did an adequate job to punctuate the question.

Chris didn't know what to say. He gaped at this man and his constricted eyes who messaged through passing notes. This whole thing was just weird.

The trooper scowled, clearly annoyed. He typed some more and held the tablet back up.

NO ROMANCE HERE, PAL.

Despite himself, Chris felt a laugh escape. "I'm not checking you out. Not my type."

He peered more closely at the trooper in the bed. The eyes were wrong, but he certainly seemed aware and alert. Chris didn't detect any sign of the vacuous gaze universally worn by the constricted colonists on Juliet.

This thread warranted some pulling.

"I'm Chris Thompson. You?"

Tapping. JAMESON.

"How do you feel, Jameson?" Chris said. "You feel okay?"

A moment of hesitation before the trooper's fingers moved over his tablet.

IT'S HARD TO SEE VERY FAR. CAN'T FOCUS ON THINGS.

"Makes sense, because of your eyes, I guess."

The trooper cocked his head as if he didn't understand.

"Why are you writing instead of talking?" Chris asked.

Another puzzled expression. Jameson's eyes drifted to his lap as he became lost in thought. He almost seemed disoriented by the question, as if Chris had just pointed out his shoes were on the wrong feet.

Was it the sedatives? Chris knew firsthand that Kenta had top-shelf stuff in the pharmacy that could send you to another world. But part of him sensed the confusion came from somewhere else. Jameson was missing a sort of awareness about his condition, unable to assess his loss of speech or the fact that his irises no longer focused correctly.

Did Jameson have constriction? It seemed likely given the eyes. But nothing else was matching up. Nothing.

"Do you remember being rescued?"

Snapping awake from his private reverie, Jameson glanced at Chris. He thought for a moment before shaking his head.

"How about before, on the carrier?" Chris asked. "What's the last thing you do remember?"

SITTING IN ENLIST BERTH.

"That's it? Were you doing anything? Maybe watching a vid?"

Jameson's face slackened as he slipped back into his memory. His fingers slid over the tablet in jerky, uncertain taps.

READING.

BUNKMATE CAME IN.

He frowned, searching. As he typed, he paused between each line to show Chris before continuing.

FELT HAPPY.

GLITTER.

SONG.

Chris watched as the trooper's entire demeanor changed. Jameson's lids grew heavy and his head began to sway as if listening to some silent music. The tablet began to slip out of his fingers. For a moment, the faintest of smiles seemed to cross his lips, reminding Chris of some schoolboy who was perhaps reminiscing about his first kiss.

It could be the drugs, he thought.

No. That's not what this is. He's remembering.

Abruptly, Jameson's entire demeanor changed. His eyes popped open and his body jerked upright in a sudden burst of exertion. He glanced frantically around the berth and locked on Chris in abject panic.

"Whoa, take it easy—"

A sudden thrash nearly yanked the IV line clear of his arm.

Chris dove across the patient bed. Jameson convulsed in the throes of outright hysteria, thrashing his arms in wild arcs and fumbling his tablet onto the deck. Chris tried to slap his palm across the IV port while he held the trooper down. If he didn't do something, Jameson was going to hurt himself.

"Kenta, need you now!" he shouted.

Jameson was staring at him, his constricted eyes filled with terror. He kept working his mouth as if he were trying to speak. Nothing was coming out.

Footsteps clattered on the deck behind Chris. Doctor Kenta appeared next to him and tried to elbow him aside, but as soon as she did so, Jameson rallied with a particularly violent spasm.

"Hold him down!" she said.

Chris was finding that direction hard to follow. Panic always brought adrenaline, and he was no stranger to what that could translate to in terms of physical strength. He clutched the edge of the patient bed and held on, his face hovering mere centimeters from Jameson's.

Kenta was grappling with the trooper's arm. "Epione, I need five hundred milligrams of methohexital immediately."

The ethereal response echoed from the room speakers. "Understood. Readying application."

The trooper's mouth continued to voice his silent panic. *Oh, oh, oh.*

No, that wasn't it. It was a word. Chris scrutinized Jameson's lips, sound or no. Not *oh*. Something else?

Cold, cold, cold, cold.

Epione's voice breathed across the berth. "Administering methohexital, five hundred milligrams."

To Chris's surprise, no robot arm whirred out of the ceiling to maneuver with a syringe. Jameson's terror ebbed almost immediately. A dazed look entered his eyes as he sank into the bed. Chris realized belatedly that the drug had been administered through his IV.

Kenta quickly restrained Jameson's arms and legs with the bed's microgravity straps. She turned to Chris. "What happened?"

"We were just talking. I asked questions, he typed."

"Did something set him off?"

Chris shook his head. "I asked him what the last thing was that he remembered. Before being rescued."

"And?"

"I think he was trying to say 'cold.'"

"Cold," she repeated. The physician drew a deep breath. "Explosive decompression? Rapid evac would create a chilling effect."

Chris suddenly felt horrible. He hadn't considered what he might dredge up with his questionings. "Oh, no. I'm sorry—"

"He seems to be okay for the moment," Kenta said, cutting him off. "That sedative will keep him out for about ten minutes. Let's just let him wake up, and after that leave him alone for a bit."

"Yeah, okay."

"Now, do you want to see if we can taper your meds, or not?"

"Yeah."

"Come with me, then. I'll take care of it in the other room."

Kenta stepped toward the hatch. Before he moved to follow, Chris turned one last time toward the man sleeping on the bed. His eyes were closed, his youthful face slackened. He couldn't have been older than his mid-twenties. Chris wondered if he had a wife, girlfriend, maybe a baby at home. He wondered if anyone knew that a normal life wasn't going to be in the cards for him.

Just like Annika.

A sudden, overwhelming sense of sorrow enveloped him. He felt his throat begin to tighten.

It wasn't fair. These people deserved better. Even Wyatt would be hard-pressed to use his old-fashioned idea of some all-powerful supreme being to put a spin on the pain and suffering these people were going through.

There's not a God to save us, he thought. *There's only us.*

There's only me.

He patted Jameson on the arm. Then he wheeled around and marched after Kenta.

27

Los Cuernos
Juliet, Alpha Centauri A
07 April 2272

Corridors flew by in a blur as Wyatt stormed through the building, helmet on, safety off. He slowed his pace once he reached the lobby. From the doorway to the administrative offices, he could see how the glass exterior walls had been blown out to leave thousands of glittering shards on the ground. A canopy of oily smoke writhed against an inactive sprinkler system along the ceiling. Wyatt proceeded forward carefully, boots crunching on glass, the infrared camera of his helmet piercing the billowing clouds.

He stepped around an overturned sofa and spied the bodies of two teenagers, dead from the nerve gas attack long before. The pressure wave that had shattered the lobby had blown them together into an awkward embrace against the reception table. Wyatt gave them a hard look. He wondered if they had even realized what was happening to them as their muscles convulsed and asphyxiated them to death.

A harsh whine cut through the air outside before suddenly disappearing.

Wyatt crouched by a kiosk near the outside door and scanned the lawn. Smoke was billowing from the charred hulk of their Jackal, now a useless lump of metal twisted into abstract art. He didn't see any sign of Kenny. But a few moments later the whine returned, echoing overhead against the carbon-fiber structure of the nearby buildings.

One of those Ibex drones, Wyatt thought. He recognized the pitch of the engines, etched in his mind from his first visit to Venice. It was flying very low in its search between buildings.

"LT," a low voice said on the comm.

Wyatt turned to see Laramie creeping up behind him. She stopped behind a table and hunched down, alone and carrying her Vector in front of her.

"Where are the others?" he asked.

"Back in the hall."

He ran his eyes over the wreckage again. He didn't see a body anywhere. Did Kenny make it to cover? "Battle Two, this is One, over."

He listened carefully to the comm. No response.

"Kenny?" he said again. "Do you copy?"

Sharp static burst in his ear. It sounded like a connected channel. But no one spoke on the other end.

Another jet whine flashed across the courtyard, this time joined with a strange echo that indicated another set of engines. Wyatt's skin turned cold. He looked back at Laramie.

"There's more than one," she said, hearing the same thing.

"My guess is they're working in pairs. One with a bomb payload, one flying cover."

"How can you be sure?"

Wyatt felt his lips twist into a mirthless smile. "Because otherwise, people like Chris would shoot them down."

The noise of the drone jets momentarily faded.

"Okay, I'm going to find a way out of here. Stand by to move." He turned toward her one last time. "Remember, stay in cover. We're not wearing sealed clothing, and we won't outrun nerve gas."

The blank faceplate of her core helmet stared back at him and said nothing. She didn't need to.

The courtyard outside offered minimal concealment, so Wyatt's attention fixated on a small rest area smack in the middle of the open lawn. A pair of park benches shaded by a bamboo pergola looked like they might provide a small bit of concealment from anything buzzing overhead. Beyond the benches, Wyatt could see the gatehouse-style structures marking the entrance to the courtyard. Numerous shops and restaurants of the town itself lay on just the other side of the road.

The engine whine remained distant as the drones flew out of sight.

Wyatt pushed off hard and sprinted at full speed toward one of the benches. He felt the heat from the burning Jackal warming his limbs as he sailed past it, his legs pumping against the ground, until a few seconds later when he crashed into the rest area. He pressed his body against the backrest or a bench and stole a quick glance above. The sky remained clear.

Now he swiveled toward the gatehouse entry. A flagpole with a blue-and-green pennant fluttered in the breeze, displaying the colors of a university that now existed only on paper. If he could get there without being spotted, it would be easy to duck into the alleyways of the buildings on the other side of the road.

He pushed off again. This time, the run did not feel so effortless. Lactic acid pooled in his thighs as the heavy gravity caught up to him, a slumbering monster slowly coming awake. The thud of the hard ground reverberated through his legs while his ears filled with the sound of his own breathing. He wondered if his heart might explode before he even made it halfway to the gatehouse, which seemed like it was moving away with every step.

Lumbering. Staggering.

Wyatt crashed his body into a hard carbon-fiber wall and shuffled to a stop. Great gulps of air filled his lungs and ears.

Still no sign of Ibex drones.

Still no sign of Kenny.

"Laramie?" he called on the comm.

"Here, LT."

"You saw the route I took. Send Bell and Annika next. Stop at the benches, then wait for my go before running the rest of the way to the entrance."

"On it."

His breathing was starting to ease as he waited. No one exited from the lobby.

"Laramie, do you copy?"

"Affirmative, LT," she replied. Distraction laced her voice.

"What's going on over there?"

A pause. "Annika won't go with Bell. She doesn't want anything to do with him."

"Send him by himself, then. You provide cover with me. Hurry!"

A moment later, a lone, lanky figure charged toward the park bench while clutching a large cylinder to his chest. Dr. Bell reached the pergola and tumbled to the ground. Wyatt gave him a few moments to catch his breath and then waved him to advance. The doctor sprinted again, slower this time, and eventually came crashing against the building wall behind Wyatt. He clung to the cylinder as if it were a life ring in the middle of the ocean.

"What the hell is that?" Wyatt asked, pointing.

Bell was gulping air after his run. "The ... AI core."

The experimental data. Wyatt didn't know why he expected the storage node to be smaller. The cylinder looked like it weighed twenty kilos.

He turned his attention back to the lawn. "Laramie, you're up."

Seconds passed. No one exited the lobby.

Wyatt covered the sky with his Vector. He was getting nervous. Drones didn't just take out an enemy vehicle and leave. They would be coming back as part of their search pattern. And the town of Los Cuernos just wasn't that big, esteemed academic university or not.

"Laramie? Where are you?"

The comm channel hissed again, just like before when Wyatt had tried to contact Kenny. He barely noticed, his concentration falling entirely on Laramie as she finally emerged from the shattered lobby. He could tell something was off. She was clutching something across her chest as she ran, just as Bell had done, but this was larger and more awkwardly shaped. It was slowing her down considerably.

Annika.

Of course. Anni wasn't in any shape to run, not after that crazy ordeal in the neuro lab. Someone had to carry her. Wyatt cursed his own stupidity at not accounting for the obvious. He had to remember he wasn't dealing with just able-bodied—

The whine of jet engines thundered overhead.

Wyatt saw an Ibex patrol drone sweep lazily around the corner of the building next to him. For a moment, the drone proceeded on a straight line as it scanned the ground in front of it. Then it suddenly veered left. Toward Laramie.

"Run!" he shouted.

In his mind he saw a high-powered laser weapon scorch the air, melting a hole through the figures dashing across the lawn. He imagined their hearts pounding in their chests as their bodies fueled a desperate run. Then he realized it was himself running, the sensations coming from his own body, his legs carrying him at a sharp angle away from Laramie. He was aiming his Vector at the drone. And then he was snapping off shots as he hoped to God to draw fire away from the figures caught in the open.

The orange targeting reticle in his HUD blinked red. The Ibex banked once again, this time toward the source of incoming laser fire that its onboard AI determined to be the greater threat.

Wyatt broke into a full-out run. A carbon fiber building sat just twenty meters ahead of him. Two seconds, that was all he needed. But his body felt so sluggish moving through the heavy gravity, it was as if the soil was grasping his boots to hold him fast. And he knew he was racing an optical targeting system that received its data at the speed of light...

Heat.

He blinked, disoriented. All around him lay thousands of shards of broken glass. In front of him, what was left of a shop door hung from a single hinge, its frame twisted into melted filament by a high-powered laser. The laser he had only just narrowly avoided.

The rectangle representing the drone on his HUD blinked red again. It was taking fire, and not from him. Wyatt crawled back to the shattered door and understood why the shots from the Ibex hadn't connected.

While Annika ran, Laramie was taking cover behind one of the gatehouse buildings and shooting at the drone. Wyatt could see the thin lines of invisible light shining brightly in his helmet's UV-band, a deadly spray targeting the outboard engines. Every third shot or so bit a chunk out of the airfoils.

The Ibex reacted by gaining altitude and moving toward Laramie's position. Even though it wasn't a military drone lobbing rockets down from five thousand meters, it remained a deadly adversary. And it was about to wipe out his staff sergeant.

"Laramie, displace!"

Wyatt sighted his Vector until his helmet computer locked on the airframe, then unleashed a flurry of trigger pulls at the drone. Wyatt could see a magnified view through his neural stub as his shots bit holes in the drone. The Ibex veered upward in response and cut short its track of Laramie. It stopped fifty meters above the street, reoriented its body toward his position, and burned the air with multiple laser blasts aimed at the shop. Wyatt barely recognized the sound of his own voice screaming as he flattened himself against the floor.

The drone stopped. It remained in place, its engines filling the street with a nerve-racking echo.

Waiting for its ground attack partner to show up.

They were running out of time. They had to get out of here.

"Kenny, do you copy?" Wyatt tried again. "Can you hear me?"

No reply. Just the hiss of an open channel.

He switched to the channel used for the Javelin. "Savage Echo, Savage Echo, this is Battle One. Do you copy?"

Teo's voice came through a bit too loudly into Wyatt's ear. "*Copy you, Battle One. Been trying to reach you.*"

Wyatt cursed again at the price of being underground. "Teo, our Jackal is destroyed and Kenny is MIA. We need air support ASAP."

"*I am inbound, ETA is six minutes. I also have a fix on Kenny, Lieutenant.*"

"He's alive?" Wyatt said. His heart surged with the knowledge that his trooper hadn't been blown to hell.

"Yes sir, about a hundred meters south of your position. His comm is out, but I have him on short band." A pause. "Lieutenant, you have two more bogeys inbound. Any LZ in your vicinity is going to be too hot. But I have an idea if you can get down to the river."

"Copy that. We'll stay in cover until you get close, then make a push to the water."

"Roger. See you soon."

Wyatt switched back to Laramie. "Did you copy that, Staff Sergeant?"

"Aye," she replied, still panting. "I told Bell we're staying put, but he says we need to get scarce. The other drones—he says there's nerve gas coming."

Any relief Wyatt felt vanished in an instant. If only they still had their wheels, they could be buttoned up in a sealed cabin and headed out of town at a hundred and forty kilometers per hour. But the Jackal burned brightly on the lawn, with plumes of black smoke swirling into the sky.

Wyatt's mind worked furiously to think of a way out. He turned back to the building where the others were holed up. The structure appeared to be one long edifice, divided like row houses into connecting partitions. Perhaps there was a way to use that to their advantage and displace without exposing themselves to fire?

He glanced back at the sky. The Ibex orbited patiently in a slow circle over the lawn, as if anticipating the opportunity to add bodies to those littered in the street.

"Laramie. Can you move between storefronts? Are there any interior doors?"

The breathing on the other end had softened, but Laramie's voice still carried the weight of a full-on sprint. "No, but there are fire exits. I think they dump into an alley, away from the street."

"Okay." He eyed the drone. "I want you to displace and head back the way we came. Use that alley and stay out of sight. I'll cover you and figure out how to regroup."

"Aye, LT."

"Move out."

Wyatt peered again through the window. The Ibex had begun a broad sweep of the courtyard to look for any more prey. Dust swirled from the street as the jet engine wash blasted the ground. So far, it didn't seem to be engaging.

"We're out the back," Laramie said. "Heading down the alley."

Alone in the smashed store, Wyatt surveyed his surroundings. He had to work out an extraction route himself. The main entrance opened to the street being watched by the dronc. All the windows faced the same direction except for the ones oriented toward the lawn of the research lab, which was just as bad. The corpse of a young man in fashionable clothes was sprawled out near an interior wall, an ominous sign for what may lay in store for him if he didn't figure something out.

He looked hard again at the body. The dead man was on his chest with arms outstretched, as if he had been running toward something in the back.

This building had to have a fire door too, didn't it?

Before he had a chance to find out, the Ibex outside dipped a wing and started to swing toward the alley to where Laramie and the others had moved.

"Laramie, inbound on your six!" Wyatt yelled. He moved to the doorway, raised his Vector, and started firing again.

28

As they entered the alley, Laramie winced at the scent of trash mixed with the sickly-sweet stench of death. It was only six or seven meters wide and barely enough room for a garbage collector to navigate between the dumpsters. Several bodies lay slumped against the walls. She tried hard not to think of the people who were now rotting in the sun, their lives cut short just days before by the insanity of the government.

Both directions seemed clear. The whine of the drone's engines warbled somewhere in the distance.

She waved at the others. "Stay close to me."

Laramie moved ahead with her Vector held close to her chest. Behind her, Annika remained practically attached to her hip. Dr. Bell remained a few wary steps back.

"I feel like a rat in a tunnel," Bell said. "Locked doors and no access. There's no way out."

"Well, keep moving or it won't matter."

They scurried forward and followed the bend in the alley. Laramie recalled the street they had taken on their way in, how it had veered toward the lab. They were following the same angle but in the other direction. She thought their route was tracking back the way they came. They were making progress.

She had barely made the corner when she saw it. Another Ibex, far in the distance, but perfectly lined up with the bend.

"Back," she yelled. "Back!"

Her mind knew it would be too late. If the drones had any sort of peer-to-peer network, what one saw would be relayed to the other.

On cue, the comm crackled with Wyatt's voice. "Laramie, inbound on your six!"

Laramie reacted without thinking. She aimed her Vector at the nearest fire door and gave two quick pulls of the trigger. A sharp *snap-snap* punched a figure eight-shaped hole in the latch.

A vicious kick sent the door flying inward. "Come on, move!" she yelled, her fist closing on a wad of Annika's clothes.

The dark interior enveloped them. Laramie stumbled forward until a hard counter jabbed her in her gut. Some sort of metallic contraption rattled at the impact.

Bell rushed inside behind Annika and slammed the door shut. "I saw bulges on that drone. It has a nerve gas payload."

"Can we shelter against it in here?"

"Did you forget everything I told you earlier? Did you miss the bodies?"

Annika let out an audible whine.

Laramie cursed.

She pushed Annika roughly through the dim outline of an interior door. They stumbled into a deserted but otherwise intact café. Directly in front of them, big picture windows flanked a set of glass double doors. The rest of the interior had jaunty orange walls with framed posters hung around the perimeter.

One poster caught Laramie's eye, a painting of a man and woman strolling arm in arm in front of a big metal tower. Even with adrenaline coursing through her system, with imminent death lurking outside, her brain detoured to come up with the name of the tower. Wyatt had shared lots of pictures from Earth, and the metal structure with its wide, vaguely pyramidal base seemed familiar.

The waffle tower. That was it.

"Laramie, do you read?" came a faint voice over the comm.

"LT?"

"Get out of the building, now, now!"

She stared out the windows at open grass. No cover whatsoever. But she wasn't going to argue; she trusted Wyatt with her life.

"Outside!" she ordered. "Down to the riverbank!"

The doctor froze in the doorway. "Where?"

"River!" she yelled, and shoved him through the doorway.

Laramie ran, half pushing, half dragging the others. The wind pressed against them as they loped across the grass. When Annika fell behind, Laramie stopped to scoop her up once more before continuing her run. Behind them, a series of sharp crackles reverberated from the alley behind the café. Laramie thought it sounded like firecrackers.

"Faster!" Bell shrieked.

The uneven ground sloped downward toward the river's edge. For a moment, Laramie felt the horror of what might happen if a rock or pothole caused a bad step. If any of them went down, they might not get back up in time.

Her eyes caught a glimpse of a weathered boathouse along the waterfront. It wasn't much, but it would be better than nothing if it obscured the targeting optics of the drones. She yelled at Bell to head toward the structure, desperately ignoring that its isolation might mark it as the location of their last stand.

Another harsh whine sounded behind them. Jet engines in the open.

They reached the boathouse. Bell dove through the open doorway and tumbled inside, followed by Laramie barreling in behind him. A second later, the sharp hiss of an energy weapon hitting carbon fiber filled the air, and splatters of molten material flew toward the water.

"We're at the river," Laramie shouted on the comm. "Tell me there's a plan, LT."

"The ride out is coming your way," came the reply.

"Is Teo landing on the water?"

"Not exactly."

The drone engines were getting louder.

Laramie motioned for Bell and Annika to get behind her and lie flat. She shouldered her Vector and peered out the door of the shed, waiting in case the Ibex decided to maneuver over the water. It knew they were inside. It probably wouldn't care about blowing away such a low-value building. But if she could get off just a couple shots, at least she'd feel good about going down fighting in her last moments on her home planet.

The Ibex moved into view. It was flying low over the river—so low in fact that the jet wash ripped the surface into a storm of fog and mist. Laramie's CORE helmet optics cut through the spray well enough for her to notice that there wasn't any ground ordnance mounted to the belly. This was the escort, not the nerve gas bomber.

She aimed for the nose. Her threat computer bracketed the weapon pod in an orange square.

The turret swiveled toward her.

Before she could pull the trigger, a blur of motion disrupted her sighting. Something large and fast zoomed directly in front of the drone. As it cut away, the Ibex dipped its wing in a sudden dodge to avoid the collision.

A hydrofoil? Who was ...?

In an instant, she grasped what was happening. "Yeah, Kenny!"

She didn't know if an AI could get pissed off, but the Ibex did its best imitation. The drone accelerated hard after the sport boat. Kenny swerved wide across the expanse of the river, shifting from one foil to the other as he banked to throw off the aim of the Ibex. The drone chased him along the surface of the river. But each attempt to shoot him just vaporized water in distant puffs of mist.

Now the hydrofoil was racing toward a small island shrouded in bamboo. Kenny put it into a wide turn and disappeared around the back side of the island.

"Friendly coming in!" yelled a voice from the other side of the shed.

Laramie jumped as Wyatt dove through the doorway at full speed. He promptly tripped over Jack Bell and sent both of them flat onto their stomachs.

"Where have you been?" Laramie said. She grabbed his hand and helped him up.

"Had to ditch the drone back at the buildings."

Dread crept back into her. She'd forgotten about the Ibex with the nerve gas. "How many are there?"

"Four. Teo's tangling with one. He can't slow down to land."

"Then what's the plan?"

Wyatt pointed out to the river. "Our boy there."

Laramie turned to look again. A glint in the distance was quickly turning into something approaching them very rapidly. She didn't see anything in the sky overhead.

As the hydrofoil neared, Kenny throttled back the engine to something less than terminal velocity and settled the sleek hull down into the water. Laramie thought it looked more like a spacecraft than a boat. The waves caused by its approach slapped against the seawall as Wyatt dashed out the door to grab the railing.

Laramie pulled Bell up by the collar. "Come on, *Doctor*. We're leaving."

"Don't start," he said. He shrugged his utilities free and kept his death grip on the data storage cylinder from the lab.

Annika, on the other hand, was sobbing uncontrollably. Laramie scooped her up in her arms and squeezed her tight. "Hold it together, Anni."

The tears were tumbling out. Annika's eyes locked on Laramie's in near hysteria.

"Anni, you can do this. I believe in you."

Wyatt's voice bellowed from the water. "Now!"

Laramie stormed outside. An instant later she stepped onto a wide, wedge-shaped deck that bobbed in the disturbed water. Kenny gunned the engine the moment she was aboard. She almost lost her footing.

"Bogey at five o'clock," Wyatt was calling out. "Coming in fast."

Kenny crouched down. "Hang on!"

Laramie released Annika but kept a tight grasp on her wrist as she desperately searched for something to steady herself. The gee forces from the boat's acceleration made it difficult. Each time the hull bounced, spray washed over the gunwale and reminded her that they were no longer on solid footing.

Another hard bump slammed her knees to the deck. Then the hydrofoil lifted out of the water. The ride turned unsettlingly smooth, but the wind screamed through the cockpit with such a howl that Laramie wondered if it might somehow grab the underside of the boat and flip it over.

Crack.

Everyone winced as a barrel-shaped container suddenly exploded at the aft end of the hydrofoil. Metal fragments and orange shards of the inflatable life raft scattered into the air behind them. Laramie lifted her head just enough to see the scorch marks extending toward the cockpit, the fingerprints of some ghostly specter that had reached out but just come up short.

"Count?" Kenny yelled.

"Five ... six ..." Wyatt said in return.

Laramie understood. It wasn't just about driving fast, it was about timing the dodges. Kenny was trying to keep track of how long before the drone's capacitors recharged for another shot. She found herself with a newfound appreciation for Lance Corporal Kenny O'Leary, well beyond the fact that he had managed to survive an armored Jackal getting blown to bits right next to him.

A glint in the sky caught her eye. Laramie made a chopping motion with her arm toward it. "New bogey, twelve o'clock!"

"I see it," Kenny said.

"Why are they so low?"

Bell shouted at her over the wind noise. "They're police drones. They're programmed to pursue fugitives, not blow away things."

"Could have fooled me!"

In the distance, the second Ibex was skimming the water surface and closing toward them. The glare of the sun off the water made identification difficult. But Laramie was pretty sure she could make out the bulges of bomb pylons on the underside of the airframe.

"Eleven ... twelve ..." Wyatt continued.

"In three!" Kenny said. "Everybody grab something!"

Laramie thought she knew what was coming—a sharp bank, a reckless dodge, a slam against the cockpit wall at a hundred and forty knots. She tightened her grip on a nearby handle. Annika, however, seemed to be slow on the uptake. Laramie watched as the girl sprawled flat in the middle of the cockpit, not realizing that in moments she would be flung sideways by a ruthless evasive maneuver.

Her instincts took over. Laramie let go of her own handle and snatched a nearby rope. In a single stride, she lunged at Annika and thrust the line into her tiny hands.

"Now!" came the call from the controls.

The boat turned hard.

The world revolved on all axes as the hydrofoil spilled its lift and dunked the far railing into the water.   Laramie saw her companions brace themselves in the heavy gravity. But not her. She barely realized that her feet were no longer in contact with the deck.

Floating.

A whirling sensation filled her stomach. Then her body crashed into the river with the force of running head-on into a concrete wall.

29

"Man overboard!" Bell yelled.

"What?"

Wyatt tried to look over his shoulder but found himself pinned by the turn. As his mind raced to catch up with the words, he realized in horror that they had lost someone out of the boat.

Laramie.

"Turn around!" he yelled at Kenny.

The hydrofoil kept a steep bank for a few more seconds before leveling out. Kenny now had them running away from the new drone and back toward their first pursuer, but their velocity dipped and the hull slapped against the water. A stiff wind blew into their faces and made it seem as if they weren't even moving forward at all.

"I need to get speed back up before we get burned," Kenny said.

"Copy," Wyatt said, but he couldn't find the head bobbing among the whitecaps. He turned toward Bell. "You still got eyes on?"

The doctor pointed at an open patch of water several hundred meters away. "She's there. I see her!"

Wyatt squinted against the wind. Now he found her, a tiny dot bobbing up and down between swells. He made a quick mental note of a tall copse of bamboo near the shore to use as a landmark.

The hull finally rose above the surface. Kenny steered back and forth in a wide, erratic S-pattern as he slowly reoriented them back toward Laramie. A sense of alarm began to grow in Wyatt's head as he realized they would be moving far too fast to pick up a swimmer.

"We need to slow down!" he said.

Kenny kept his eyes forward and did not turn around. "Not till that drone takes its next shot."

Kenny's maneuvering had now oriented the first Ibex on their seven o'clock. Wyatt hadn't been counting and didn't have a clear idea of how much longer the drone's capacitors needed to charge. Perhaps he didn't want to know. At such a close range, the turret would easily burn them into a molten pile of slag.

"Turning!" Kenny said.

The hydrofoil banked hard left, toward the first drone. Wyatt wrapped his fingers around the railing as his momentum shifted and his feet nearly lifted off the deck. A sudden increase in the air temperature behind them signaled a near miss of deadly laser fire.

The hydrofoil started to pick up speed as it turned in a tight radius.

"Count for me!" Kenny yelled.

Wyatt started the mental rundown again. Sixteen seconds until the next barrage. Sixteen seconds to get Laramie back onboard.

He scanned the water again for the copse of bamboo. He found it, but it didn't help him spot Laramie's head in the water.

"Where is she?" he called over to Bell.

"She's diving under!"

"Where?"

Bell chopped his arm in a different direction. "The other drone!"

Wyatt's heart fell into his stomach. Sure enough, the second Ibex—the one he had worked so hard to distract earlier, among the buildings—was lurking over the location he had last seen Laramie. Bomb pylons studded the wings instead of a laser turret on the nose.

They were accelerating again. Kenny had the throttle levers all the way down and was hunched against the wheel like the racer he had once been.

"How long?"

"Eight!" Wyatt yelled back.

The hull lifted and Kenny put them into a wide turn that arced toward Laramie. Wyatt couldn't take his eyes off the second drone. The Ibex swept in a lazy circle over the water, knowing its prey couldn't stay submerged forever. Meanwhile, their hydrofoil was coming in very fast because of the drone now close on their tail.

He realized there was no way anyone could possibly grab an outstretched arm to pull Laramie on board—the boat would either fly past her or kill her. And if they cut the throttle, they would be a sitting duck for the next barrage.

Maybe we don't have to slow down?

Wyatt scanned the open cockpit. His eyes fell on a bundle of nylon rope, conjuring up images of the safety lines used to keep troopers from accidentally drifting away in zero gee.

"Kenny, maintain speed and bearing toward the staff sergeant! Full blast!"

"Aye."

Wyatt made his way to the stern. It only took a moment for him to reach the largest bundle of rope and tug the end loose. He threw it out behind the hydrofoil, where it quickly unfurled into a tow line fifty meters long. It trailed in the water like the tail of a giant rat.

He switched on his comm. "Laramie, if you can hear me, we are approaching your position. I threw a tow line out behind the hydrofoil. Grab it as we pass. Over?"

Wyatt prayed to God that his transmission made it to her. The bone-induction earpieces worked well even submerged, and she could still click an acknowledgment. But that was assuming her helmet hadn't flown off when she hit the water at a hundred klicks per hour.

Their bow was pointed almost directly at the ground-attack Ibex above her position. The wind blew at their backs. If ever that was an omen for good fortune, Wyatt hoped it was today.

The seconds drew out forever. As they approached, Wyatt couldn't help but notice how everything seemed exceptionally crisp and detailed. The bamboo on shore popped in a brilliant green, the water churned in a fierce blue-gray. He saw the vibrant orange of the rank insignia on the back of Kenny's helmet. On the Ibex, Wyatt could even see the cluster bomb magazines beneath the wing pylons, despite the spray of water kicked up by the jet wash.

Then time seemed to collapse all at once. The hydrofoil screamed past the Ibex's position, causing it to veer off almost as if it were a startled animal. A staccato rain of bomblets scattered into the air as it gained altitude. Wyatt knew each projectile would release an invisible cloud of gas that could end their lives as soon as they hit the water. But the hydrofoil cruised swiftly through the target area without slowing down.

Wyatt peered aft. Because of the chop, the hydrofoil blades trailed a fine mist of water into the air that made it difficult to spot the tow line. He worried about what he would find once he did. Such a crazy idea, tossing a rope into the water. How could he expect Laramie to just grab on? Her arms would get yanked out of their sockets. And even if she managed to hold on, the pounding against the water would surely bludgeon her loose like someone trying to slap dirt off a shoe.

The line suddenly whipped against the gunwale and lost all slack. Wyatt stared for a moment as his brain worked to understand what it meant.

"Turning!"

The hydrofoil banked hard to starboard, and the world turned sideways as the hull sank back against the water. Wyatt caught a glimpse of Dr. Bell holding Annika tightly. The little girl wore a mask of hysteria.

A massive *crack* from the bow made them all flinch.

Smoke tinged with burned plastic permeated the air around him. Wyatt tried to shut it out and focus on what he was doing. He hauled in the tow line, hand over hand, tugging against the weight that he hoped meant Laramie clinging to the end. His arms began to burn. His back muscles felt like they might give out. But all he could do was tell himself that the next pull might be the one that got his squad mate back aboard.

The boat was back up on the hydrofoils now. Indistinct shouting about flames and smoke carried intermittently between the howls of wind.

Wyatt gave another great heave on the rope and the entire line went slack.

Oh no.

A wave of panic flushed through him.

No. Two hands reached over the stern deck and grabbed the railing.

Wyatt seized one of them and managed a last yank. A spray of water and one Laramie McCoy slid into the cockpit on top of him. Her helmet was gone. So was her ARC vest, probably ditched so the weight didn't drag her to the bottom of the river.

Thank you, God.

"You all right?" he shouted.

Laramie managed a dull nod.   Then she coughed out a lungful of river.

The relief Wyatt felt only lasted a moment. He looked off the stern and saw both Ibex drones in pursuit.   And based on that last shot, Wyatt presumed the targeting AIs were getting smarter about Kenny's evasion tactics.

He switched his comm to reach the Javelin. "Savage Echo, we need that extraction. Where are you?"

"I'm thirty seconds from the river," crackled the reply. *"I have eyes on your position."*

"Can you take out these drones?"

"Negative," Teo replied.   *"Turret's damaged—had a tangle on the way here. Any of your bogeys have rockets?"*

"I think they used what they had on the Jackal."

"Copy that.   Maintain your speed and bearing. I'll make this easy on you."

Easy? Wyatt was almost afraid to guess what that meant. Pilots like Teo regularly traded in the ridiculous.

The hydrofoil started into the beginnings of another S-shaped evasion pattern. Kenny yelled at them over the noise of the engines. "Another blast coming. Everybody down!"

Laramie was still hacking up water. Wyatt pushed her flat and tried to scan the sky through the smoke. He could barely even see Kenny, hunched over the steering wheel just two meters away. But the drones chasing them remained clearly visible a hundred meters off their stern.

Kenny threw the boat into a bank. A second later, an explosion shattered one of the jet turbines mounted alongside the hull. Wyatt saw a rain of engine fragments pelting the river before he lost sight of them in the smoke.

Another sharp whine filled the air around them. It took Wyatt a moment to recognize the pitch as different from the remaining hydrofoil engine.

"*Dropping ramp*," Teo said on the comm.

Everything suddenly became darker. Wyatt looked up and saw the broad profile of the Javelin ten meters off the bow, blocking the late-afternoon sun with its wedge-shaped airframe. Even in silhouette, numerous holes were visible in the fuselage from rounds of laser fire. Wyatt prayed that the aerospace engineers behind its design made it tough enough to reach orbit again.

The hydrofoil, on the other hand, was succumbing to its mortal wounds. Kenny struggled to steer in a straight line with only the port jet turbine functional. And in doing so, a teeth-grinding shudder was quickly killing their forward velocity.

The cargo ramp on the Javelin hinged downward, extending so low toward the surface of the river that the lower edge sent spray into the maelstrom of jet wash. Kenny gunned their remaining engine and lurched the hydrofoil forward. The bow of the hydrofoil jabbed into the empty space of the cargo bay, but the hull threatened to settle back into the water any second.

"Jump now!" Kenny shouted.

Wyatt grabbed Laramie by the collar and gave her a shove. She reacted so slowly that he wasn't sure she'd even get off the boat. But she started crawling toward the bow under her own power, giving Wyatt enough room to move on to Bell and Annika. "Both of you, come on!"

Cacophony reigned around them. Even through his CORE helmet, Wyatt could hear the thunderous whine of the Javelin's swivel-mount engines, the wind blowing laterally across the deck, the effort of the remaining hydrofoil turbine as it fought to propel the shattered boat through the water. Smoke and spray obscured everything. Wyatt pulled Annika against his side and dragged her and the doctor forward. He almost lost his footing as the boat bobbed up and down.

They reached the bow, positioned just over the edge of the Javelin's outstretched cargo ramp. Laramie had managed to make it onboard and stood with her arms outstretched.

"Annika," Wyatt yelled. "You need to jump. Okay?"

The girl didn't wait. She pushed off without any hesitation despite the terror on her face.

Wyatt motioned for Bell to do the same. Then it was just Wyatt and Kenny.

The hydrofoil was settling into the water as they continued to lose velocity. Jagged holes in the hull gulped in the river water and widened the gap. They were out of time.

"Kenny—"

"Get off, I'm right behind you, Lieutenant!"

Wyatt scrambled and his artificial leg slipped. His knee went down hard into the deck, flooding his brain with agony at the point where his prosthetic melded into flesh.

He forced himself forward. He had to. He reached the point of the bow, then drew his foot up to the edge of the gunwale and propelled himself off into nothing.

Time slowed. Wyatt felt his senses become hyperaware, recognizing the tiniest details of weightlessness, the water droplets against his helmet, the video feed from his camera sending the spray right to his optic nerve. He saw the edge of the cargo ramp so close to the water that it would be submerged if it went any lower.

He was floating through space, tumbling away without a lifeline.

He didn't think he was going to make it.

But then everything rushed back to normal speed in a massive catch-up. The cargo ramp slammed into his body and knocked the breath from his lungs. Boots appeared in front of his face as hands dragged him away from the water.

Shouting filled the comm. "Come on, Kenny!"

He barely felt the vibration as another body jumped aboard. Then Wyatt's weight suddenly increased twofold as his stomach sank into his feet. He clutched at the tie-down fittings in the deck plates as the cargo ramp closed behind him.

30

Chris thought naval food should have tasted better. If you were going to spend months deployed on a claustrophobic spacecraft, sitting on the lap of your closest friend while waiting for the next boarding drill, there needed to be some kind of morale booster. Apparently, chow had not received that certification.

The trooper in front of him moved forward, and it was Chris's turn to slide up to the dispensing counter. He watched the cook's mate fill the molded sections of his tray with a sort of pudding from two separate hoses. One looked brown and chunky, the other smooth and green. A gloved hand slapped two tortillas on top with a loud *thunk*.

"What's this supposed to be?" he asked.

The cook's mate was already reaching for the next tray. "Barbecue chipped beef."

"Is that the green one?"

The mate threw him a look. "No. Those are beans."

Clearly, no one had ever accused this guy of having a sense of humor. Chris dipped his nose toward the alleged dinner but couldn't smell anything. He felt angry for a moment. Then he let it go. Maybe he was coming out ahead.

By the time he sat down next to Finn, Chris knew he wouldn't be touching the *chipped beef.* He pushed his tray onto the grippy tabletop that kept things from floating away when not under acceleration.

"I think I'm going to starve to death," he said.

Finn had a mouthful going and studied him behind silent eyes. A moment later he washed it down with a drink bulb. "You're not going to eat it?"

"Oh, I'll eat it. It just sucks."

"It's not that bad. Nothing a little hot sauce doesn't fix."

Chris took a bite of his tortilla and held up the remnant. "Thank goodness for these, at least."

"Those? Those taste funky."

"They're tortillas."

Finn shook his head. "María made her own. I know what they taste like, and these are *not* tortillas."

A silence descended between them. His friend rarely brought up his wife. When he did, things would get quiet as Finn slipped into some private memory before Firebreak.

Chris changed the subject. "Well, from what I'm told, you've got to have tortillas in zero gee. It keeps the food bits from floating all over." He dipped his spork into Finn's chipped beef, then pasted a glob on the flat dough. It stuck fast.

"Hey. Eat your own."

Chris let his eyes wander around the enlisted mess. RESIT troopers sat in crowded clumps, eating and talking and otherwise filling the compartment with noise. One group near the serving line was dominated by a trooper telling a loud story full of wild gesticulations. The troopers around him punctuated the gaps with lewd comments. Another cluster of crewmen appeared to have just gotten off their shift and still wore the purple tunics of the power plant teams.

But a trio of men sitting by themselves caught Chris's interest over the others.

"See those guys over there?" he said, pointing with his chin.

Finn turned to look, his sleeve making a *snick* sound as he pulled it from the grip-tight table.

"Blond crewcut and friends?"

"Yeah. From the Fast Scout. The ones that pulled guns on Wyatt."

Finn adjusted his body so that he could stare unimpeded. Subtlety wasn't one of the Marine's strong points.

Chris thought back to the briefing documents Wyatt shared from Beck's interrogation. The Fast Scout was *Needle*. Four crew. The skipper of the spacecraft was an officer and wouldn't be here in the enlisted mess. Of the others, Chris failed to recall any significant details. He thought the blond one's name was Zum.

All three men were young, perhaps mid-twenties. Each had the slight build of someone working years in zero gee. They kept to themselves as they dined, but Chris noticed they didn't actually seem to be eating anything. They just pushed food around on their trays as their eyes traveled around the compartment, resting every few moments on different groups of troopers.

"Not a very friendly bunch," Finn observed.

"Yeah. They're not acting like people who got rescued. Something's off."

Finn took another mouthful, but his eyes didn't leave the Fast Scout crew.

Chris watched how they interacted with each other. Zum's attention seemed to be on the power plant crew the next table over. Every few moments he would make a comment to his companions. One of them nodded and typed on a tablet.

A burst of laughter pierced the air from the unruly troopers near the serving line. One voice carried a little louder than the others. It reminded Chris of a donkey braying.

"How can they not be annoyed by those knuckleheads?" Finn asked.

"They're focused." Chris watched the guy typing. "They're making notes about the engineering guys."

"Is that what they're doing?"

"Looks like it to me."

Zum leaned back and stretched, momentarily disrupting his attention from the men in purple. His eyes wandered across the mess until he noticed Chris watching him. A bland expression fell over his face. He lowered his arms, speaking softly to his companions and staring back at the Marine.

"Something's not right," Finn said.

"Definitely."

The Fast Scout crew deliberated for a few seconds before all three of them stood up to leave. One picked up his tray and started toward the dish return. A moment later, a loud crash echoed through the mess hall as he dropped everything onto the deck.

"Hey!"

Chris didn't need much time to recognize Gavin's hulking figure walking past the Dagger crew member.

The Texan shot them a distasteful look. "Watch where you're going, jackass."

"You did that on purpose!"

"You should have kept to your side."

The spacer pawed at some brown and green paste now smeared on his utilities. Zum stood up, followed by his companion. Chris glimpsed something shiny disappearing into one of their palms. A knife?

"Finn," he warned.

"I see it."

Clearly angry, the Dagger crew member shoved Gavin from behind.

Gavin moved quickly despite his size. He grabbed the man by the throat and hauled him close. Zum and the other spacer leaped at him. From the other side, Chris saw Carlos and Rahsaan abandon their table and rush to head them off.

Zum reached the scuffle first and threw a punch at Gavin's side. The big staff sergeant seemed to be expecting it. He blocked it with his elbow before swinging the spacer around by the neck like a human shield. His other fist caught Zum square in the face.

By this point, the entire mess hall was beginning to take notice. Troopers were standing at their tables. The boisterous storyteller had broken off his monologue. But Chris was only vaguely aware of them as he sprang from his bench toward the spacer coming up behind Gavin.

Chris threw a block just as the man's wrist started to come up. A knife clattered to the deck.

The two men fell sideways against one of the hard metal tables. An arc of pain shot through Chris's still-healing broken arm. But he managed a quick elbow to the neck and sent the Dagger crewman down hard to the deck.

To his left, Gavin stood in the middle of a tangle with Zum, Carlos, Rahsaan, and the third Dagger spacer. The Texan seemed to be pushing the entire scrum toward the bulkhead.

"Let go of him!"

"You shot at my lieutenant!"

The thud of body blows.

"*Unnh.*"

More grunting and cursing.

Chris recovered enough to grab Zum's collar with both hands and give him a hard yank. Zum managed to keep a tenuous grip on Gavin's uniform, but the sudden jerk whipped his face backward and left a cloud of bloody perspiration floating momentarily in the air.

"*Stand down!*" roared a voice behind them.

The entire compartment froze.

Heavy footsteps echoed off the deck plating. Chris looked to his right and saw the stout figure of Havoc Company First Sergeant Hardy Sullivan approaching the scuffle. He didn't think he could find a word for the displeasure on the face of the top enlisted man aboard *Vigorous*.

"Everybody takes one step back, right now." The first sergeant spoke as if he could command clouds to rain.

The troopers let go of one another. None of their faces expressed any regret.

Sullivan was built like a tank—barrel chest, no neck, and a vein that Laramie had described as popping out of his forehead when he was irritated. Currently that vein was on full display. His eyes blazed into each spacer as he sized up the situation.

He came to Chris and his face darkened. How could a senior non-com not only allow such jackassery to take place in the mess hall, but actively jump into the middle of it?

Chris threw a glance at the deck.

Sullivan's gaze followed. When he saw the knife, his face turned even redder. "I see."

"Yes, First Sergeant."

Sullivan turned his attention to the Dagger spacers. Zum had a broken nose that painted a triangle of blood across the lower half of his face. The other Dagger spacers hadn't fared much better. The one with the food all over him clutched his arm as if it had been fractured. Amazingly, Gavin's only injury appeared to be that he was breathing hard.

"Sergeant Mills!" Sullivan bellowed.

Another trooper marched up. Scars from a long-ago shrapnel wound disrupted an otherwise thick head of black hair. "Aye, First Sergeant?"

Sullivan glared at the three Dagger men. "Take these men to med bay and get those wounds cleaned up. Then escort them to the brig."

"Aye, aye."

Mills snapped his fingers and two more RESIT troopers moved alongside him. Chris startled when he saw the escorts had sidearms at their waists.

"Hostile battlespace protocol," Sullivan explained, seeing his reaction. He looked the master sergeant up and down. "You should get that arm looked at as well, Master Sergeant."

"I'll be okay."

"No." Sullivan's tone softened along with his volume. "You want to be ready for when there's a real fight. Go with Mills to med bay."

Chris let out a sigh. This wasn't what he wanted to be dealing with right now. Getting caught up in a rumble didn't help him build confidence in Beck to send him back to Juliet.

Then again, neither did injuries. He frowned at the thought of not being part of Wyatt's team.

"Med bay," Sullivan repeated.

"Aye."

He turned around and almost walked directly into Finn. He didn't seem to even have a scratch.

"You all right, Top?"

"Yeah." Chris jerked his head toward Gavin. "If the first sergeant leaves anything left of these guys, beat some sense into them."

"Will do. I'll catch up with you after."

With that, Chris joined the procession and followed Sergeant Mills out of the enlisted mess.

31

As they marched through the corridors, Chris wondered how Laramie would react when she heard her troopers had been in a fight in the mess.

Chris blamed the Dagger crew. He saw their shady behavior, the sucker punch one of them took, the attempt at a makeshift weapon. If it had been up to him, he would have gladly helped Gavin wipe their "guests" across the deck like dog shit off a boot.

But he also knew Laramie didn't think the same way he did. She didn't judge things using the same scorecard. When she'd gotten confused on the maglev train, she had taken more potshots at him and his Marines than at the guard stations actually shooting at her. When she disobeyed his directions at the health department, it resulted in one of his men killed and one of hers badly injured. Even when that freaking *death drone* punched through the hull of their freighter, she was sticking to failing tactics that would have led to their collective demise if Finn hadn't somehow inexplicably produced one last explosive charge.

Chris could absolutely picture Laramie chewing out her own team and placing the blame on them for this little altercation. It wasn't right, but he could hear it in his brain.

Yet who stepped up to protect Anni?
Sigh.
Not Wyatt. He had a mission to run.

Not Bell. Chris didn't trust that guy outside of punching range.

It was Laramie. She looked him in the eye and promised she would keep Anni safe.

And, inexplicably, Chris had believed her.

"Turn left, Dagger," Mills told the spacer crew.

The corridor ended in a T-intersection at a large white hatch painted with a red cross. The spacers took their sweet time making their way toward it. Chief Zum kept frowning at the guy who tried to stick Gavin with the knife. They each continued their little glances as the sick bay doors slid open on their tracks.

Doctor Kenta was handing a small pill dispenser to a trooper and giving him instructions on how to take them. "Twice a day, with food, for ten days. And make sure you finish it this time, so I don't have to see you *again*—" Her gaze lifted to the sudden influx of bloody faces in her compartment.

Sergeant Mills cleared his throat. "Doctor, we had a scuffle in the enlisted mess. Can you clean up these boys so there's less blood in the brig?"

Kenta blinked. "There was a fight?"

"Yes, Doctor."

Her eyes slid over to Chris and an eyebrow went up.

Chris pointed a lone finger at Zum's back.

She sighed in apparent disbelief. "All right, just a minute," she said, and turned back to the first trooper. "*Ten days*. Got it?"

"Yes, ma'am."

"Now, out. And *you*," she said, pointing to the adjoining compartment hatch, "*you* don't need to be in here. Get."

Chris followed her gesture and saw Corporal Jameson standing in the opening, his pinprick eyes filled with curiosity.

"Get!" Kenta repeated.

Jameson disappeared around the bulkhead. Distracted by the exiting trooper, two of the Dagger spacers didn't see him. But Zum did. He watched the empty doorway with intensity.

Kenta assessed Zum's broken nose and maneuvered him toward a patient bed. His gaze didn't leave the spot where Jameson had stood a moment before. Kenta didn't seem to notice. "Sergeant Mills?"

"Yes, Doctor."

"My nurse is off her shift and I'm not calling her back for this."

"Yes, ma'am. What do you need?"

"Put each person on a bed until I get to them." She pulled on some exam gloves.

"Have a seat, boys," Mills ordered.

While the security troopers zip-tied the three spacers to the folding beds, Kenta began with Chris. The disapproval on her face spoke volumes.

"Always my Mister Difficult," she said.

"I aim to please."

Probing fingers on his wounded arm made him sit up with discomfort. "I don't like the feel of that," she said.

He winced again at another squeeze. "Neither do I."

"Yours may take the most time." The doctor positioned his arm in his lap as if she expected him to keep it that way. "Sit tight. We'll get to you last."

Kenta moved to the spacer sitting next to Zum. He had taken a blow to the neck, now swollen to the size of a balloon. He seemed to be having trouble staying awake.

Chris sighed. He glanced around the room and caught Mills's eye. The sergeant just shrugged at him.

"I need to use the head," Chris said.

"Go ahead. You're not the one under arrest."

"Yeah."

He cradled his arm and slid off the edge of the patient bed. He only managed two steps toward the patient toilet before Kenta spoke over her shoulder. "You'll have to use the troop lavatory. Ours has a maintenance ticket open."

"Great."

Mills gave him a look that said *welcome to RESIT*.

Truth be told, Chris didn't really want to sit around with the Dagger guys. He opened the hatch and stepped into the corridor. As the door closed, he glanced back and got a final glimpse of Zum staring down one of his prisoners.

A minute later Chris was standing over a small toilet, thankful that he didn't have to use the strange, zero-gee attachments stowed on the wall. His arm hurt. It made him pissed. He was trying to get back into the fight, not extend his recovery. He remembered the block that sent shards of pain to his elbow. The tingling was still there. All he could do was hope it was temporary and reflect on how it could have been much worse.

A dinner knife.

He finished up, scowling in the mirror as he washed his hands and wondering how much time he'd cost himself by getting involved. Freaking RESIT. Why was he even here? He needed to be back on Juliet. He needed to be in the fight.

Good and pissed off, profanities echoing inside his skull, Chris exited into the corridor and made his way back to the med bay. His steps echoed off the decking as he stewed in his thoughts. His arm was just bruised, that was all. The bone growth was solid, stronger than the original, and he'd be back behind the trigger despite all these idiots who zinged around space for a living.

He took a deep breath as he gripped the latch and swung the door open.

The med bay was empty. No Doctor Kenta. No Sergeant Mills. No spacers with swollen necks or broken noses.

"Hello?" he said.

The hatches leading to the adjacent medical compartments were closed. He thought of Corporal Jameson peeking around the bulkhead. The hatch had been open then.

A broken flex cuff lay on the deck near one of the beds.

Danger.

Adrenaline dumped into his system like fireworks. Chris stepped across the med bay threshold and listened, felt, sensed. He didn't hear any noises except the hiss of the ventilation system. Everything lay still and deserted.

He slid quietly to the hatch on the right, a breaching stack of one. *Slow is smooth*, he told himself. *Smooth is fast. Slow is fast.* Slow meant fewer mistakes. Mistakes cost you time—or worse.

He slid the dividing door open.

At first, he didn't realize what he was looking at. A shape in RESIT utilities slumped in the corner, a deep red gash creasing his bare neck. Then recognition crashed home in a single moment that wrapped anger and dread into a single braid. Sergeant Mills sat in a pool of blood, his hand flopped next to an empty pistol holder.

To the left, another trooper lay sideways with his throat slit in a similar fashion to Mills. Three more bodies lay jumbled in a heap in the center of the berth. One of them wore a white lab coat.

"Kenta!"

Chris dove forward. The doctor was on top of the pile, flopped backward with her arms sprawled out. He raised her head and peered into glassy eyes, cursing and howling inside, feeling her neck for a pulse despite knowing it was a waste of time. The meaty, dark circle burned through her sternum provided unnecessary punctuation.

"Doc. No ..."

Beneath her corpse lay Corporal Jameson. The latter had been shot once in each eye and now stared at the ceiling with a pair of blackened holes dominating his face.

One of the Dagger spacers was sprawled face-down underneath Jameson, a dark stain of fluid oozing onto the deck from a hole in the side of his head. Mills must have gotten a last shot off. There was no sign of Chief Zum. No sign of his other crewman.

The room spun. Chris found himself standing over the comm call button while his mind served up the right three-digit code.

The speaker clicked. "Armory—"

"This is Thompson ... I need a Security Alert Team to med bay *now* ... armed intruders and fatalities ..." he cursed again.

A twinge of urgency entered the comm voice. "I'm calling the Master at Arms. Is the med bay secure?"

Chris stepped away and tugged open a storage compartment labeled First Aid. His hands fumbled through the contents until he found a portable technician kit. It only took a few seconds to unzip it and inventory the contents, and another second more to pull out a pair of large utility shears. A weapon.

"Master Sergeant Thompson, are you there?" the comm said.

Chris rushed back into the main compartment. Mills. Jameson. *Kenta*. Good people. Fury boiled through him. If he hadn't hit the latrine, would the Dagger spacers still have been able to overpower them? Or would Chris just be dead too?

He burst into the corridor. Empty.

Where did they go?

Keep your head, Chris. Think.

While a spacecraft like *Vigorous* teemed with traffic, it still undoubtedly had places to hide. But it wasn't like Zum and his buddies could just go back to their bunks and pretend nothing happened. The security team would hunt them down and smoke check their asses.

So where could they go? How could they escape their handiwork?

There was only one answer that made sense.

Chris sprinted down the corridor, ducking through hatches in a desperate rush aft. He dodged through an airtight bulkhead hatch and nearly bowled over an ensign who was standing completely absorbed in her neural stub. Her tablet went skittering across the deck as he caught her from falling.

"Hey! What the—"

"Did they come this way?" Chris said.

"Huh?" The ensign blinked rapidly as she tried to shift her focus back to normal vision.

"*The Dagger crew!*" Chris shouted.

Her eyes went wide, trapped between confusion and fear.

"Thompson!" boomed a voice from the corridor behind them.

Chris turned and almost let the ensign drop. Four armed troopers wearing ARC vests trotted toward them, including a sergeant wearing a CORE helmet painted deep red.

"Hong?" Chris said. He recognized the voice of the Master at Arms from his time in the brig. That might not be a good thing, he realized.

"Release the ensign."

Chris did so immediately. The young officer stumbled back before sliding toward the safety of the security team.

One of the troopers eyed the shears in Chris's hand and raised his Vector. Chris realized he needed to get the story out quickly before it was too late.

"The flight crew from the Fast Scout," Chris said. "From Dagger Team. I was with them in med bay. When I stepped out to use the head, they jumped Sergeant Mills and killed everyone inside."

At the mention of murder, the ensign put a hand up to her mouth.

"There's no place for them to go after pulling a move like that," he continued. He heard his own voice break with a twang of emotion. "They've got to be headed for their spacecraft."

The Master at Arms stood in the corridor, his reaction masked by the solid faceplate of his helmet. He didn't budge.

"Hong. *I* called in the security alert."

A bead of sweat trickled down the small of Chris's back. This was bad. They were wasting precious time, and there was no way he could just turn and leave in front of an armed security team. Hong would throw his troublesome ass back in the brig in an instant.

The sergeant switched on his comm. "Armory, this is SAT One. Give me the location of the Fast Scout crew."

Chris watched in silence as Hong listened to something only his team could hear. "No, med bay's trashed. Thompson's in corridor H-six." Another pause. Two of the troopers exchanged a helmeted glance.

Hong cursed. Chris let out the breath he was holding.

"Where are they?" Chris said.

"Not where they're supposed to be. Come on."

The five of them pushed down the corridor toward the main interchange while Hong barked orders into the comm. "I need SAT Two to External Docking ASAP. Be advised, targets are armed and dangerous. Secure all vital compartments and have crew avoid contact."

They were running quickly now. Chris tried to work out how long he had been out of med bay, how much of a head start Zum and his buddy might have. He guessed no more than two or three minutes. That would feel like an eternity dashing down the stairs to the aft levels.

They reached the main interchange between decks and Chris went for the stairs. To his surprise, Sergeant Hong stopped him by the elbow. One of the other troopers waved a security card in front of an electronic sensor. The door lights turned amber as the elevator prioritized its travel to arrive at their deck.

"I didn't know you could do that," Chris said.

"Security override."

The lift doors parted and disgorged a pair of confused crewmen expecting a different level. Hong ushered them aside with the tenderness of a bulldozer. The five of them stormed into the elevator, and a trooper punched the destination on the touchscreen.

As the crowded lift whirred to life, Chris found himself face-to-face with the master at arms. The glare of the deep red CORE helmet practically dared him to do something stupid. Chris knew his mouth got him into trouble and that he had been in rare form after Beck locked him up for insubordination. He had given Sergeant First Class Hong the brunt of it. Part of him was amazed that he hadn't been whipped to a pulp right then and there.

"Thank you," Chris said.

The red CORE helmet didn't move. "Don't make me regret this, Thompson."

A chime bleeped at each deck that passed by. Chris felt his heart beating madly. All he could think about were the faces of those back in med bay. Kenta had dedicated her life to healing people. Mills was just doing his job. Jameson ... damn. The guy had managed to survive a catastrophe aboard his spacecraft, then got hit with some variant of constriction. Somehow he had still been holding it together. And Zum and his mates had killed them all.

Just like they would try to kill Annika if they ever saw her.

His heartbeat accelerated even more.

Hong was listening to the comm again. "Echols is missing," he said.

Chris shook his head. "They're trying to get away."

The lift slowed down as it arrived at the External Docking level, the deck just above the hangar bay. Sergeant Hong shouldered his Vector with surprising dexterity in the crowded space.

"Team, stack on me," he said. "Thompson, stay back."

The doors parted and the Security Alert Team swept onto the landing.

"Clear left."

"Clear right."

"Casualty on the deck," came another callout.

Chris peeked out. The landing had several hatches leading to corridors that extended radially outward like spokes on a wheel. Large stenciled letters identified each one. Hatch C was wide open. An older crewman with a shaved head sat crumpled next to it, two blackened scorch holes gracing his belly.

"Secure the area," Hong said. "SAT Two, what is your location?"

One of the security team knelt and placed his fingers against the crewman's neck. "He's alive. His pulse is weak."

Hong appeared preoccupied with the comm. "Copy that, Two, we are moving up on your six to Docking Boom C." He turned around to address his squad. "SAT Two beat us here. Targets are already onboard their vessel. Aiden, see if you can stabilize that crewman. The rest of you, come with me."

Chris started to follow. The sergeant held up his hand as his two other troopers disappeared into the docking boom. "Not you, Thompson."

"Hong, those bastards just murdered—"

"No."

One of the troopers spoke from further down the corridor. "Sergeant, we can't get the airlock open."

"Tell Gene to bring up the cutting torch—"

A thunderous boom filled Chris's ears, and the world shattered.

***

Wind. An eternity of wind.

The only reason Chris realized he was tumbling was because his body smashed abruptly into the edge of an open hatch. Red emergency lighting bathed the compartment. Somewhere in his brain, a distant instinct urged him to find a handhold, any handhold. A cacophony shrieked all around him as if trying to announce the end of the world.

His body slid off some surface and tumbled some more.

Then, almost as quickly as it had begun, the tornado around him suddenly abated. Chris found he could barely breathe. It felt like he was sitting on top of a tall mountain, the meager oxygen drawn into his lungs far from sufficient to sustain life.

His head was spinning. Thoughts came slowly, as if he were pushing through a wall of fog to find something on the other side. Somewhere in the distance, an unintelligible sound repeated over and over, the words indistinct but urgent. "*Ull-ee, ull-ee.*"

He pushed himself up on all fours.

A distant hiss grew louder. Like flooding, but not quite the same. The world spun in a bath of red light, dispelled only by the glimmer of a white porthole at the end of the corridor.

His breaths seemed barely able to fill his lungs. But it was getting easier. Thicker. Louder. His thoughts seemed to be solidifying in concert with each gasp.

What ... the hell?

Chris stifled a yawn.

A speaker rang out with an automated voice. *"Hull breach. Hull breach."*

He looked around. Sergeant Hong had somehow remained standing. The master at arms staggered over to his man who had been treating the casualty and picked up the trooper's helmet. A deep gash in the trooper's forehead matched a glistening mark on the metal bulkhead nearby.

Chris forced himself into a standing position and wobbled his way to a small porthole next to corridor C. What he saw outside didn't make sense.

Instead of a normal docking boom, he saw a metal and plastic stump abruptly truncated by a clean line, as if a surgeon's scalpel had made an incision clear across a patient's limb. Debris tumbled in a haphazard formation through clouds of venting gas. The Fast Scout, docked only moments before, had now displaced a hundred meters away and was oriented away from *Vigorous,* its reactionless drives pointed back toward the boom as if giving a final farewell salute.

Hong pushed next to him and peered out the porthole.

"I had men in the corridor," he said.

The air pressure had still not returned to a normal level, and Chris felt woozy. "What happened? Did they use explosives?"

The master at arms squinted out the glass. "Laser fire. Precision shot."

"From Zum's ship?"

"No."

Hong pointed at a section of the starfield. In the distance, the glimmer of reflected light caught Chris's eye. Another vessel was moving in an intercept trajectory toward the Fast Scout. It was too far away to get a good look, but Chris swore it had the same profile as the spacecraft that had tried to kill *Kumano Lily*.

32

Wyatt felt safe. Sara lay on top, her weight pressing against him, their bodies sinking into the bed as if the mattress might form a protective cocoon. Clothes or not, he relished her body as it smothered him. She stroked his hair with her fingertips and traced gentle circles across his scalp. When she breathed, he could feel her abdomen slide outside of his.

Her fingers brushed down his body and massaged his forearms.

It should have felt nice. It did feel nice.

Wyatt opened his eyes. Her face hovered just centimeters from his own. He could taste her breath.

He tried to kiss her but she turned away.

"Is something wrong, Sara?"

A knot formed in his stomach, an iron ingot that started to sink deeper into his belly as if under the attraction of a giant, unseen magnet. Sara's fingers continued their sweep along his sides, creating the illusion of more hands than just two. Was someone with her?

He searched her face for answers. Her smile hardened.

"Sara?"

It was getting more difficult to inhale. Multiple hands squeezed his limbs, their tendrils tightening around his body and squeezing him like some unseen demon.

"Sara?"

The light was fading. Sara was fading. Her body floated above him in a pale facsimile of the woman with whom he had gone to bed. But her face remained solid, staring at him, smiling, crying.

He tried to embrace her but his arms weighed a thousand tons.

"Don't leave me."

Her eyes said to him *you're the one who's leaving.*

Wyatt couldn't breathe. The grip around his torso squeezed harder. He felt his fists balling up, panic erupting from his stomach. Sara was floating away, but his body was being crushed. Oh God. What was he doing? What had he done?

"Sara?"

No...

***

Wyatt opened his eyes. It took a moment to figure out where he was.

The bridge of *Sawtooth* arched around him. A glance at his body confirmed the presence of a grav couch, the soft whir of the peristaltic mechanisms filling his ears as they pushed circulation through his arms and legs. Above his head, ruggedized holo monitors glared back at him with the byzantine telemetry of astronavigation

Of course. Teo had picked them up from the river. They left the drones behind at Los Cuernos and recovered their ascent booster hidden safely away from the town. Then a bumpy ride back into orbit had set them up for their rendezvous with Otto and the Fast Attack.

Wyatt blinked away the afterimages of his dream. He couldn't remember details, just the emotion and overwhelming sense of loss. The cost of happiness for the sake of a career.

A conversation on the intership comm caught Wyatt's attention. It sounded like Otto was talking to someone in Engineering. "Copy that. Bring power plant up to eighty. We'll charge capacitors in ten minutes."

"Aye, aye, powering up. Will advise on charge start."

Wyatt tried to raise his head against the heavy acceleration. He found he couldn't, so he rolled it sideways until his eyes rested on the captain's couch next to him.

"Morning," Wyatt said. "Anybody put the coffee on?"

Absorbed in his telemetry, Otto ignored him. The comm squawked with the voice from Engineering. "Power is at eighty and clean."

"Very well. Be advised, we'll evac the cabin in five minutes."

"Aye, sir."

Evac the cabin?

Wyatt felt like he was missing something. The weight of acceleration suddenly seemed more urgent in purpose.

"Everything okay?" he asked.

"New orders. Taking a detour for a little interdiction." Otto remained focused on his holo monitors, looking away only to do an occasional calculation on his computer.

Something was definitely going on. "Skipper, I'd appreciate a little insight. Our mission had a very tight window for completion."

Otto tapped on his tablet for another ten seconds before rolling his head over and giving Wyatt his attention. "You know the Scout spacecraft we picked up?"

"Yeah, I led the boarding team."

"Ah. Well, it sounds like the crew decided not to stay."

"What do you mean?"

"I don't have many details—I just get told what I need to do my job. But another spacecraft came along and cut them free. A certain Fast Attack that's an old mate of yours."

"*Razor?*" The word sounded fantastical to Wyatt's own ears as he said it.

"Aye."

"How is that even possible, to get anywhere near a RESIT task force?"

A wry smile crept over Otto's face. "That's what we do, Lieutenant. We sneak up and shoot you before you know we're there."

The peristaltic fingers of the grav couch suddenly felt like shards of broken glass. His skin went cold.

The whole premise seemed unbelievable. Wyatt remembered the elaborate debrief to Beck, Laramie's gut feeling around details that didn't seem to line up. Had Echols and his crew been playing them this whole time? Why? A jumble of questions vied for consideration in the fog of the newly awake.

Otto had turned back to his holo monitors and was adjusting one of them with a small joystick in his armrest. Wyatt cleared his throat to get his attention. "So, what do we do?" he asked.

"What we do is we get dressed for the big dance. Fun, aye?"

Wyatt wanted to ask more questions but was forced to shelve them as *Sawtooth* prepared for the upcoming interdiction. Otto reduced acceleration just long enough for the crew to don pressure sleeves and helmets. When they resumed four gees, he gave the order to depressurize the cabin. Sound became eerily distant as the atmosphere evacuated to the high-pressure tanks deep within the hull. Other battle preparations consumed everyone's attention as the crew readied for a confrontation with armed vessels making a mad dash of an escape.

The knot in Wyatt's stomach grew. The vast majority of his spaceborne experience involved stationary vessels. Inspections, rescues, even forced boarding occurred at low relative velocities. He'd never really thought about the Fast Attack strikes that sometimes immobilized a spacecraft beforehand.

Yet somehow, to be onboard the *bridge* of a Fast Attack felt exhilarating. And terrifying. It wasn't that long ago that Wyatt experienced a taste of an attack ship's lethality. His eyes traveled across the bridge and marveled at the sheer destructive power around him, bottled up for the use of half a dozen human beings.

The navigation screens showed their prey as two orange icons labeled *Rack-1* and *Rack-2* with floating text, both designations usually reserved for RESIT assets. To Wyatt, both seemed to maintain a steady acceleration that was widening their orbital arc around Alpha A. *Sawtooth* was coming up behind them along another arc that obliquely crossed their trajectory a few degrees ahead of their current position.

"How are we able to catch them?" Wyatt asked. "Can't they go as fast as us?"

A moment passed while Otto adjusted some readouts and studied more telemetry. "They can. But they're not."

"Why not?"

Otto ignored him. "Getty, switch to red."

"Aye, sir," said the helmsman, barely visible in the confines of his acceleration chair. Red light suddenly bathed the interior, banishing the white to a place far away.

"Distance to contacts?"

"One-one-seven kilometers."

"Very well. Weapons, get me a targeting view."

The tactical telemetry on one of the screens disappeared, replaced by a camera feed. A tiny spec of light appeared just off-center in the field of blackness.

"Zoom in on Rack One."

A quick succession of distortions warped the monitor. Wyatt felt his eyes narrow as the stern end of the Fast Scout came into focus.

"I have good optics," the weapons officer said.

Otto studied the screen. "Get me a lock on the drive pylon."

"Aye, sir."

A red bracket blinked on the screen. Wyatt watched as it wandered across *Needle* until it settled on a strut that supported one of the drive nacelles.

"Othello, Othello," the weapons officer called out. Wyatt watched a nearby readout illuminate with the letters OTL, Optical Target Lock.

Otto spoke in a low voice over the comm. "It depends on where you're going."

It took a moment for Wyatt to realize the skipper was talking to him. "What?"

"Your question. Why they aren't using more acceleration." He adjusted some more readouts on the screen, his voice distant, still focused on his pursuit. "Orbital mechanics are funny. Sometimes going slower gets you to your destination faster. It just depends on where you're going."

"So, you think they're not just running away? They're headed somewhere specific?"

"Maybe. But it won't matter in a minute."

The bracket on the monitor began to flash before blinking into a bright orange. "Range to Rack One is nine-zero," a voice said.

"Copy, nine-zero."

The image of the Fast Scout continued to enlarge until someone reduced the zoom magnification. Wyatt realized his hands were balled into fists again. He forced himself to relax, something that was all but impossible under the crush of heavy acceleration.

"Getty, watch your drift," Otto said. His voice held an unnatural calm, as if he were a surgeon performing a delicate medical procedure. "Keep us in their blind spot."

"Aye, sir," the helmsman replied.

The bridge remained silent as the spacecraft continued to close.

Wyatt could feel the sweat clinging to his skin inside his pressure sleeve. He did his best to ignore it. Instead, he focused his attention on the holo monitor showing the Fast Scout. It seemed incredible that their prey hadn't seen them yet. Then again, how did Earth sometimes not see a meteor until days before it hit the atmosphere? It all depended on location and relative movement, something that Otto seemed to be well in command of right now.

"Range is seven-zero," said the helmsman.

Otto spoke in a loud, clear voice. "Are capacitors charged?"

"Capacitors charged and ready."

"Weapons, fire on yellow."

"Aye, sir, preparing to fire." A pause. "Thirty seconds to yellow."

The targeting bracket on the screen remained a steady orange. Wyatt knew the color corresponded to different range intervals, but it still seemed surreal to watch them change. *Sawtooth* was trying to get close enough to ensure it could take out the engines with accuracy and not obliterate the entire spacecraft.

"Twenty seconds."

The bracket started to flash. The label next to it said sixty-eight kilometers.

"Fifteen—"

Wyatt watched as the bracket suddenly stopped flashing. But it hadn't changed colors to yellow, and the image of *Needle* was suddenly diminishing in size. He glanced at the number floating nearby and saw it rapidly increasing.

"Rack One is bugging out," the helmsman said.

"What?"

"Range is eighty ... *six gees*—"

"I've lost optical lock."

"... ninety klicks ... range is red."

"Should I still fire, Captain?"

Wyatt glanced around in confusion as multiple voices relayed information. Otto had been so careful about not being noticed. How had they been spotted? And did Wyatt hear correctly that *Needle* was now accelerating away at six gees? He didn't think spacecraft could go that fast under their own power, and it seemed terribly sudden for a planetary slingshot.

"Rack One is at one-zero-zero."

"I still have red, am I cleared to fire?"

Otto's voice cut through the air like a knife. "Where is Rack Two?"

Sudden silence. Wyatt worked to remember that there had been a second spacecraft. One with a far deadlier trade than a reconnaissance vessel.

"I have Rack Two. She's rounded on us."

33

Fear shook Wyatt's body despite the heavy push of the engines pinning him against his chair. *Razor* had nearly killed him twice before. He prayed to God that the third time was no charm.

"Rack Two range is five-zero klicks with eight gees negative closure," Getty said, his words at a rapid clip.

"Change trajectory for intercept. Maintain acceleration."

"We are now on intercept."

"Weapons, target their turret. You're cleared hot." Otto's voice remained calm and precise, a stark contrast to the tension Wyatt felt sitting helplessly on his grav couch.

The weapons officer replied with a similar monotone. "Aye."

The tactical monitor changed to the sleek silhouette of a Fast Attack pointed right at them. Wyatt understood the general sense of the tactical situation. While the two spacecraft were still fifty thousand meters apart, it would take only thirty seconds to close that entire distance under constant acceleration at four gees apiece. The absurdity of the physics involved struck him with peculiar discomfort.

"Othello, Othello," the weapons officer said. "Firing."

An odd, low hum that hurt Wyatt's teeth vibrated through the spacecraft. On the monitor, the yellow bracket spun clockwise in conjunction with a brief flash on *Razor's* hull.

"Hit—"

"Vampire, Vampire," the helmsman called out. "Multiple drone launches, designate Rack Three through Rack Six."

"Hard evasive."

Wyatt caught his breath as *Sawtooth* seemed to point straight up and find another burst of acceleration. What blood remained in his brain pieced together an ominous conclusion: they had just drained the massive capacitors powering the laser turret at the same time that *Razor* launched four boarding drones at them. *Four.* It would be impossible for *Sawtooth* to recharge in time and shoot each of them out of the sky. His mind filled with the sudden horror of a killer robot drone tearing through the bridge.

"Weapons, retarget on three through six," Otto said, his voice ice. "How long until you can pulse?"

"Six seconds..."

"Lock on and stand by."

"Locking on."

Wyatt's own panting filled his ears as the tactical screen tracked the four inbound bogeys. They would hit in a matter of seconds. Then the drones would burrow through *Sawtooth's* hull in their mission to kill everyone aboard. Wyatt wanted to somehow take over command, to tell Otto to cut acceleration so they could climb out of the grav couches and at least arm themselves for one hopeless last stand. But he was not the captain. And Otto was clearly preoccupied with whatever his alternative strategy seemed to be.

"Two seconds," the weapons officer continued. "One."

Otto didn't hesitate. "Burn 'em."

The same hum as before buzzed through the cabin, but this time it only lasted a fraction of a second. One of the target markers bracketing an inbound drone rotated around what now looked more like a smudge than a bright speck of light.

"Scratch one," the weapons officer said.

"Hit the next one."

For what seemed like forever, nothing happened. Wyatt glanced at the time indicator on his telemetry screen and watched as the seconds seemed to sprint ahead.

"Firing."

Another short hum. Another bracket twirling.

"Scratch two."

Wyatt struggled to understand. Somehow Otto was firing their main weapon with a shorter recharge cycle. Even with years serving in RESIT, he had only ever seen big, solid-state systems fire in the all-or-nothing way that kept space battles brutal and brief. Never had he considered that a Fast Attack could fire quicker, lower-powered bursts to pick off smaller targets.

The helmsman's voice rang out through the comm. "Ten seconds to impact."

"Cut engines," Otto ordered. "Change course to two-seven-zero by zero and stand by."

"Aye, sir."

The sudden absence of the crush against Wyatt's body produced massive disorientation. His insides sloshed forward at a different rate than the rest of him.

"Six seconds."

"Getty, stand by," Otto said.

On the monitor, the two drones were moments away. Wyatt thought the timing was working out to where they would probably shoot one more. There would be no way to get both.

"Impact in four ..." the helmsman said.

"Firing." A low hum. "Scratch three."

"Full accel, now!" Otto barked.

It was like being launched out of a cannon. The crush returned, and Wyatt could feel his body squish against the gel matrix of the grav couch. The tactical view on the holo monitor now displayed a mess of lines and parabolas that were undecipherable to a simple trooper. But the visual feed was another story. Wyatt saw the final drone delivery vehicle just off to *Sawtooth's* port side. It chased them at an uncomfortably close distance against a sea of blackness, the conical tip of the shape charge sniffing them out like the nose of some nightmare monster.

A cloud of white gas appeared behind the delivery vehicle. Wyatt knew it must be the final thruster burn meant to send the drone through the hull. He wished he had his Vector, not that it would make a difference.

The drone charged at them on the monitor.

The hull rang with a metallic *clank*.

And then the drone bounced off.

Wyatt watched in disbelief as the delivery vehicle started to fall away, its last propellant proving insufficient to keep pace.

"Clear of Rack Six," Getty said.

"What's the damage?"

"Nothing registered."

"Right work, mate. Where is *Razor*?"

"Continuing on an evasion course, max accel. They're withdrawing."

"Aye." Otto sighed audibly. "Getty, ease accel down to two-five."

The anvil on Wyatt's chest lightened. A faint tingling in his face made him realize he hadn't been breathing, and he immediately took a gulp of air like a fish yanked from the water.

"What just happened?" Wyatt asked.

"They've got their dirty tricks, we've got ours," Otto said. He glanced over at Wyatt. "We maneuvered so that last drone came in too shallow. It couldn't adjust quick enough and skipped off the hull when the penetrator fired."

Wyatt stared at the monitor, dumbfounded. "That was ... that was incredible."

"Not the word I'd have chosen." He pointed at the tactical monitor. Two orange triangles, each with text designating them as Rack-1 and Rack-2, pushed relentlessly toward the edges of the screen along separate arcs. "Our prey is escaping."

"Can't we go after them?"

"The angles are all wrong now. We had just that one shot to intersect their orbit. We'll have to get them next time."

"You mean, we blew it," Wyatt said.

"Nah. We didn't blow anything. That FA was just better than us today."

"What do you mean?"

Otto turned toward him, the chagrin clearly on display through his visor. "That skipper on *Razor*? He knew I was going to shoot first. He took it on the chin anyway because he'd already planned to fire his drones. And he knew that would distract us enough so that both of them could get away.

"In this business, you learn to be cautious when your opponent's a step ahead."

34

Crushed for days by heavy acceleration. Targeted by drones *again*. Laramie couldn't wait to get out of the claustrophobic deathtrap otherwise known as a Fast Attack.

By the time she was sitting in the hold of the Javelin to ferry back over to *Vigorous*, Laramie felt positively giddy. The horror of Los Cuernos faded to a dull ache as her body rejoiced in freefall, her muscles relaxed, and her mind wandered to places it rarely had the time to go to.

Across from her, Annika's loose hair danced in the microgravity. The strands snaked through an endless succession of shapes that reminded Laramie of growing up on the ranch, stealing away to watch the cloud formations shift from one exotic animal to the next. Dragons gave way to horses. Maybe an elephant or snail. Laramie had never seen any of those in real life, only in the picture books that lived in her dad's study back on the ranch. Relics from her grandparents when they emigrated from Earth. Now, instead of clouds, Laramie watched Annika's hair. The girl had a thick mane, Laramie gave her that. The mystery of what shape might come next captivated her attention as they maneuvered through an endless series of thruster bursts.

Annika watched her back. Occasionally their eyes would meet and trigger a little smile.

But just as Laramie's father would invariably catch his idle children and send them back to their chores, the timetables of RESIT decided that it was time to return to the present.

"Docking in one minute," Teo said over the comm.

Another shared glance. Another smile.

"Almost there," Laramie said. "Ready to see Uncle Chris?"

Annika gave a weary nod. This time the smile reached her eyes.

The hull shuddered as they began a steady deceleration. Annika's hair fell limp. Then a docking clamp clattered overhead and the vibration of the Javelin's engines died away. New shudders and tremors signaled the journey through the first vehicle pressure lock, then the second. The distant whir of heavy machinery became louder outside the hull and gave away that they were now in atmosphere. A few moments later, their movement ceased as their vehicle nestled into its designated stall for maintenance and refueling.

The cargo ramp opened and a crew chief climbed aboard to start the turnaround process. Laramie unbuckled her straps and helped Annika with hers. The little girl darted toward the ramp before suddenly pulling up like she had been yanked by an invisible leash. She turned to Laramie, her face pleading for permission to leave. She knew by now that lots of dangerous moving parts lived in the hangar bay.

Wyatt's voice carried over from the front of the cargo bay. "Go ahead and take her down, Staff Sergeant."

Laramie turned to see the lieutenant tugging open storage lockers, an officer left to clean out the gear while the noncom went to play. The scene struck her as entirely backwards. "Really, LT?"

"Really." A tiny smirk turned up the corner of Wyatt's mouth. "Maybe I still feel bad you went swimming."

"The swimming was nice, except for the death drones overhead."

"No kidding. Tell that to Kenny's boat."

She gave him a nod and turned to leave. Annika had already seized on Wyatt's comments and bounded down the ramp. Now she stood enveloped by the arms of a large Marine kneeling on the deck.

"Still in one piece, like you asked," Laramie said. "She's a brave kid."

Chris stood. Annika dangled around his neck, refusing to let go.

"Yeah, she is," he said. He cocked his head around Anni's mane of hair. "How did it go?"

How did it go ...

Such a simple question. The answer should have been, too. They made it to the university. Jack Bell scanned Anni. They observed firsthand how the little girl could seemingly push away someone with constriction. They made it back alive. By objective measures, their mission was a success.

Thousands of corpses in the street.

Priceless lives cut short forever.

My home.

The aftermath of the nerve gas attack filled her mind. Limbs pointed in grotesque poses from their last convulsions. Jaws dropped open in vain attempts to breathe. Innocent people murdered by a government they themselves had elected. A complete betrayal masked by the guise of serving the public good.

Her expression must have reflected what she was thinking, because Chris put Annika down and stepped close—very close, his face centimeters from hers, concern sweeping over him. She felt his hand on her arm.

"You okay?"

Laramie blinked. Her nose was running. Part of her raged at the atrocities she had seen, demanding retribution swift and sure. But something deeper down squirmed with a different emotion. Thoughts of being back home, a little girl no older than Anni, acting tough on the ranch but being secretly afraid of hoppers and karks and the noises at night that dragged off livestock. She felt small.   Weak.   Powerless and in need of protection.

No.

She was a RESIT staff sergeant, for God's sake. She couldn't do this.

Her body went ramrod straight. "I'm fine. It's all fine."

"Laramie, I'm just—"

"Whatever you want to know, you can hear it after the debrief," she said.   She stepped to the side and marched toward the lockers, wiping her cheeks with the back of her hand before anyone saw.

***

The day didn't get much better.   The hangar deck officer insisted on a particularly thorough decontamination that routed Laramie and the ground team through full-bore radiation, scrubdown, and extra Di-X tablets that upset her stomach even without the additional dose.   Bell griped and provoked with indiscriminate ease and wouldn't let anyone near his precious AI core with the data from the experiment.   And after all the effort to go to Juliet and back, Major Beck didn't even hold a debrief with the team.   He asked Wyatt to give him a five-minute summary, and the two disappeared into his office.

So when Wyatt reappeared near the junior officers' quarters, Laramie was ready to pounce.

"How did it go, LT?"

Wyatt blinked. "Good morning, Captain."

"Don't give me that. How did it go?"

"It was short. He asked me about the insertion, what Bell did, did we get the data. I told him we were successful. He said everything else could go in the written report."

"That's it?" Laramie could feel the heat radiating from her own skin. "What about all those dead people?"

Wyatt had both hands up in a calming gesture. "He knows, Laramie. But I think he's deprioritizing it—"

"*Deprioritizing it?*"

"—because we're going into action later today. *Stop* it, Laramie."

She made herself take a breath. Jeez, she had to get a grip.

Wyatt apparently took her efforts as a brain short circuit, because he quickly slid into deeper explanation. "Yes, deprioritizing. I didn't say dismissing. He's as horrified as we are, Laramie. But in case you hadn't noticed since we've been back, Bering is going to pop open in a couple hours. We're going to go through it. And if someone's waiting on the other side, they might very well be working with Echols and Zum."

Echols. Even more reason to see red. Those bastards murdered her crewmates. *Murdered.* Mills, Doc Kenta. Hong's security team. She'd never heard of such a thing on a troop carrier.

The most someone typically got out of line was cutting too loose on shore leave and getting tossed in the brig for some extra time to sober up and think about it, headache and all. Once in a blue moon there might be a fight, the culmination of months of stress, close quarters, and limited privacy. But the injuries were limited to one's pride and a few bruises.

She wished Gavin had been able to finish the job on those guys. Then Kenta would still be alive, along with half a dozen troopers. Even Corporal Jameson with his pinprick eyes.

Which is what set them off, of course.

Damn.

"They were feeling us out," she said.

"Yeah."

God, what a struggle it was to compartmentalize. Thousands—no, tens of thousands—exterminated like insects back home, and she had to pack it up and stow it away for later, just like Beck. Her heart screamed in agony like a prisoner beating his fists against the bars.

Wyatt put his hand on her shoulder. "Look, Laramie. This isn't done. We've got Annika. We've got Bell. He's got his data. We're going to figure this out. We're going to contain this disease and we're going to bring every criminal behind every killing to justice. Kaz is good for it. Beck is good for it. So am I, I swear to God."

Laramie managed a weak smile. "I know."

He clasped her other shoulder and made as if to respond, but his face pinched off abruptly. "Did you just say I was right?"

"I deny that characterization."

"Good, back to normal." Wyatt jerked his head down the corridor. "Let's get our gear and our teams in order. I think you're exactly right— Echols was a plant. And that gives me a bad feeling about what we're going to find out in just a couple hours."

35

While Beck and his officers handled prep for the RESIT troopers, Kate Kazimira had no shortage of tasks to ensure her carrier group was ready for whatever was coming their way. The good news was her crew had ample practice. Skippering *Vigorous* for the past two years provided plenty of time for officers to know her style. She drilled them hard on competence and precision, but most of all, ownership. When someone made a mistake, it was vitally important to recover and adapt. When equipment failed, survival might hinge on creative workarounds. Such was the life of a troop carrier skipper to ensure that culture.

She was standing comfortably in her tiny ready room off the bridge, reading her tablet as the magnetic soles of her boots held her to the deck. The zero gee felt distracting for some reason. Normal operations kept *Vigorous* in transit and under constant acceleration, but right now they remained on station next to Bering Gate. The engines were throttled to zero. Kate had to force herself to overcome the feeling of vulnerability and concentrate on the words in her last log entry. If disaster struck, it was her duty to record the current situation for others to recover and understand. Ideally, no one would ever need to read it other than herself.

Her personal comm chirped. Kate somehow knew that her hope had just slipped away.

"Kazimira."

The voice of her XO rang a bit too loudly in her ear. "Captain, we have a development. Bering Gate is powering up."

Kate's fingers froze on her tablet. "That's two hours early."

"Aye, ma'am."

So it began. "Sound general quarters. I'm on my way."

Kate closed her log and slipped the tablet into a nearby locker. Then she rocked her feet so that her boots detached from the deck. A quick push sent her toward the hatch and the whir of electric motors sliding the door open.

The bridge on the other side hummed with the tense anxiety of pre-conflict preparation. Her XO had already ordered the interior light switched to red.

"Captain on the bridge," a voice rang out.

"At ease." Kate pushed off toward her command chair. "Pete, give me the details."

Her XO looked at her from the chair next to hers. His cool tone didn't match his eyes. "The boot sequence started out of the blue. T-minus four minutes until the quantum tunnel forms. Our guests must not have been able to wait."

Kate grabbed her armrest and rotated herself into the padded cushions of her seat. From there, it only took seconds to pull her body through the chair's five-point harness. On the main holo monitor, a 3D graphical representation of the local battlespace showed a blue chevron representing *Vigorous* in the middle of the screen. *Piranha*, their destroyer escort, kept station off their port side. Bering Gate sat some one thousand klicks away in the same orbital plane. All of them sped through the void at the constant velocity afforded by one of Alpha Centauri A's Lagrange points.

"Do we still have contact with *Sawtooth*?" she asked.

"Negative. They're hiding."

"Good. Let's hope that's insurance we don't need."

The XO glanced at her again. "I kind of have a feeling we will."

"Me too."

She spent a minute mentally reviewing their game plan. Their task force was small—a carrier, a destroyer, and a Fast Attack interceptor—but they had enough teeth to control almost any normal situational encounter. Up until recently, their biggest question was what they would find on the other side of Bering. But the actions of the Fast Scout crew and now the early activation of the gate signaled they might have to pivot to a more defensive mindset. The quantum gate wasn't offering them a red carpet.

Smugglers, pirates, and Oscars didn't play by the rules. They threw curve balls and thought up unexpected tactics. *Vigorous* needed smart and observant crew to find a way to win anyway. After many engagements, Kate had every confidence that those around her fit the bill.

Yet in her entire career, she had never had to test those skills against her own colleagues.

"Marley, I want to know as soon as that gate is open," Kate said.

"Aye, ma'am."

More readiness updates came in. "Ma'am, Major Beck reports all troopers are at damage-control stations."

"Reactor is standing by and ready for maneuvers."

"*Piranha* reports weapons ready."

"Negative contacts on the screen."

As she slipped into the cadence, Kate found herself beginning to relax. The status checks formed a mantra of preparedness and unity. It focused her crew. It focused her. She was in command of a RESIT task force, the best-trained personnel using top-of-the-line assets. They were well equipped to deal with any threat the universe could throw at them.

And she had an insurance policy. Her eyes flitted to the secondary holo monitor at the front of the bridge. A magnified visual feed showed Bering Gate hanging against the starfield, its station lights blinking in a repeating pattern of three quick flashes. Her Fast Attack interceptor was lurking out there somewhere. Otto. He was their trump card in case whatever happened came down to who got in the first blow.

"Bering Gate is open," the radio operator said.

The volume of chatter died down in an instant. On the monitor, the position lights around the hoop of the quantum gate ceased flashing and remained steady as the only visual cue that anything had changed. There was no cacophony of flame, no shimmering in the starfield to indicate that a quantum tunnel had just blinked into existence.

"New contact emerging from Bering now."

Kate watched in silence as the bow of an unknown vessel slid through the gate. The profile slowly resolved itself to show the dual hoop drives mounted on either side of the aft end.

A RESIT Pompey-class destroyer, just like *Piranha*. Used both to defend and annihilate.

"Mark the contact," she said.

"Designating new contact Rack One," replied the weapons officer.

She studied the three-dimensional image displayed in the holo monitor. "Who is it?" she asked.

"Unknown, ma'am. They're not broadcasting a transponder signal."

"Marley, zoom in on Rack One," Kazimira said. "Show me a visual on the forward quarter."

"Aye, ma'am."

The image shifted. Kate squinted and was just able to make out the registration number and the name *Claymore.*

"That's the destroyer escort for *Alexander*," her XO said. "Returning to the scene of the crime?"

Kazimira shook her head. "That's Bill Drexel's command."

"You know him?"

"Yeah, from the Academy. He was two years behind me. He's a good man."

"Hmm." Peter sat motionless except for his right hand rubbing its fingers together. "Maybe you should give him a hail—"

"New contact from Bering," Marley called out.

All eyes went back to the array of holo monitors, where a new screen was zeroing in on the quantum tunnel. To Kate's dismay, a second vessel slid in ominous silence through the gate. It possessed an uncomfortably similar profile to the first.

"What the hell?" Peter muttered.

She turned to the radio operator. "Mark second contact and get me an ID, please."

Marley held a short conversation with the Threat AI before answering. "No transponder signal on Rack Two," she said. "Scanning the bow. No other identification visible."

"Not even a registration number?"

"No, ma'am."

Kazimira watched as the holo monitor showed the two warships spreading apart. Each took a position in front of the quantum gate.

"Are they moving to close?" she asked.

The weapons officer replied in monotone. "Affirmative. One-half-gee negative closure."

"What do you think, Captain?" Peter asked.

"I think if they wanted to kill us, they would have ambushed us. You know, let us go through the gate first instead of tipping their hand."

"Possibly." The XO stared at the vessels on the holo monitor as if trying to divine their intentions. "Or maybe it's more important to keep us from seeing what's on the other side."

Kate stroked her chin. "Are they still closing?"

"Yes ma'am. Same bearing and acceleration."

Taking their time, it seemed. "Marley, hail both ships."

"Aye, captain." A moment later, the radio operator shook her head. "They're not acknowledging our hail."

"Is the channel open?"

"Yes, ma'am."

"Patch it to me."

"You're on."

Kate spoke to the images of the spacecraft on the holo monitor. "To USIC *Claymore* and unidentified RESIT vessel, this is *Vigorous* Actual. Halt your approach and declare your intentions. Acknowledge."

Several moments passed in silence.

"Marley, switch to tight-beam and raise *Claymore* by itself."

"Done. You're on, ma'am."

"Calling USIC *Claymore*. Bill, it's Kate Kazimira. Been a long time. Think you could let me in on what's going on here?"

The spacecraft continued to grow on the holo monitor. One of the bridge crew adjusted the zoom so that he could keep them on the same display. Another screen showed the telemetry of all assets on the board. The two Dagger destroyers maintained constant bearing and decreasing range.

"No reply, ma'am," Marley said.

Kate shifted in her chair. Despite the five-point harness, her body felt loose in the zero gee.

This wasn't a good place to be. *Claymore* likely had a standard weapon load—two twelve-megawatt laser turrets, eight Pilum-B kinetic torpedoes like the kind used to hull UISC *Alexander*. It was fair to assume the unknown destroyer carried the same. The Dagger vessels would outgun *Piranha* and *Sawtooth* four turrets to three, plus the ability to throw projectile weaponry.

The key to this fight was going to be *Vigorous*.

Carriers weren't intended to be used in engagements—that's what the smaller, more maneuverable assets were for. But her vessel brought speed to close quickly and enough bulk to absorb punches. Just as importantly, she could add another laser turret to the fight. Energy weapons took time to recharge, and having an extra set of capacitors could make all the difference.

"Ever been in a ship-to-ship engagement, Pete?" she asked.

The XO nodded. "Yes. Against Oscars."

"And what's the key to winning?"

"Hit first and protect your weapons."

The destroyers slowly closed on the holo monitor.

"Well, now you get to try it with a troop carrier."

Peter turned and gave her a long look.

"Helm," she said, "set your course for the gate. Ahead point-five gee."

"Aye, point-five," the helmsman acknowledged.

Her XO shuffled in his chair, though whether he was trying to get comfortable with the new acceleration or the impending action wasn't clear. "We should have *Piranha* move wide, to be ready for a flanking shot," he said.

"Do it. Just tell Wexler not to get too far ahead of us."

"On it."

Kate took a deep breath. She knew this could be a dreadful mistake.

But there wasn't any point of being in system if they didn't advance their mission. A RESIT troop carrier would be a formidable vessel, designed for force projection and control over the battlespace. She intended to use that capacity.

Waiting to challenge that intention were two of the deadliest spacecraft class ever built.

36

The call to general quarters caused troopers and crew to drop everything cold. Wyatt met up with Laramie and the rest of his squad suiting up in pressure sleeves just outside the enlisted berth. From there, bodies flowed through corridors like water. Captain Chappelle joined them in the armory and fed them snippets of chatter from the bridge as they issued vests and weapons. Then they were off again to their damage-control station near the stern of the carrier, marching in a steady cadence to klaxon blasts and flashing red strobes.

This time, Wyatt actually had a full unit. His replacements came in the form of two former Marines who had just been cleared for duty.

"So, let me get this straight," Chris said as Battle Squad rode down the cargo lift toward Propulsion. "We're facing two of your own destroyers?"

"Yeah," Wyatt said.

"I don't suppose Zum and Echols pissed them off, too?"

"Yeah, don't think so."

"Just as well. They'd have to get in line."

Chappelle overheard them from the front of the loading gate. "Only one of the vessels is RESIT," he said.

Wyatt and Chris looked at each other. "What do you mean?" Wyatt asked.

"One of them doesn't have a name or hull number. The bridge can't figure out who they are. It's completely dark."

Chris started laughing. "Surprise."

Laramie's helmet turned and fixed Chris with an eyeless glare. "You think this is funny?"

"How many times do I have to tell you people? The enemy can do whatever the hell they want."

"Shut up, all of you," Chappelle said.

The lift stopped. The loading gate opened, and Wyatt and the rest of his team trotted out into a familiar corridor of storage lockers near the Propulsion section. But something was happening that made it difficult to walk. Wyatt had to lean to the right to maintain his balance.

"We're maneuvering," Chappelle called out. "Everyone, hold tight."

The press of sudden acceleration quickly created a disorienting effect. Wyatt was now leaning against the corridor wall. Or was it the floor? Either way, *Vigorous* was turning hard. Around him, curses and insults filled the air as troopers inadvertently tumbled on top of one another.

"What's happening?" Chris asked.

"Hard evasive."

"Why?"

Now the carrier was accelerating forward. More troopers slumped to the deck as they felt the weight of two-plus gees pull their limbs downward.

Wyatt wondered what the hell was going on. Here they were, trapped inside a massive tin can, blind as a bat and deaf as a doorpost. Were they under fire? Were they trying to escape? Death could be wrapping its arms around them that very moment, ready to crush *Vigorous* into a mass of scrap metal, and there was nothing they could do to change it. Maybe it was better that he didn't know what was going on.

Chris pushed himself up on his elbows and turned to Wyatt. "Typical day at the office for you guys?"

"Captain, is there anything you can tell us?" Laramie asked.

"*Vigorous* is engaging."

Wyatt blinked twice. What?

Laramie apparently had the same reaction. "We're taking the *carrier* into a fight?"

"Yeah," Chappelle said, his voice betraying his own bewilderment. "Kazimira must have ... Jesus Christ."

Everyone waited for an explanation. The captain listened in silence.

"Sir?" Wyatt prompted.

"Two destroyers just shot torpedoes at each other."

Everyone sat dumbfounded on the deck. RESIT spacecraft were actually engaging each other. The situation felt surreal, as if a child had made up the situation and was acting it out with plastic toys.

Underneath them, the acceleration of *Vigorous* seemed to climb above two gees with increased urgency.

"Did they hit, sir?" someone asked.

Chappelle didn't respond. Wyatt realized his platoon leader was probably struggling to parse through the bridge audio himself.

"Yes," he said, his words cold. "I think we hit them near their power plant. Not sure about *Piranha*, though. They got it forward of the pressure doors. Near the bridge."

Wyatt realized his hands were clasped in front of his helmet as if to pray. Kinetic torpedoes were designed to penetrate and then break apart, using their energy to destroy a target from the inside. They were a last-ditch option for extreme circumstances. He remembered seeing the devastation from a torpedo strike against *Alexander* during their recovery operation. If one had hit *Piranha*, a much smaller vessel, it wouldn't matter how deep the skipper and his crew were inside the protective hull.

Chappelle continued the play-by-play, giving Wyatt the feel of an old-time radio broadcast where the announcer acted as the only conduit into the action. "Rack Two is firing. There. It just took out both turrets on *Piranha*." He paused. "I think *Piranha's* dead in the water."

A collective pall settled over the platoon in the corridor. A trooper cursed nearby. Wyatt gritted his teeth in frustration at not being able to fight back.

The lights in the corridor dimmed.

"Are we taking laser fire?" another voice worried.

Chappelle waved his arm for quiet. "No, we're firing. *Vigorous* is firing."

Heads turned and looked at each other through the eyeless faceplates of CORE helmets. Troop carriers never closed with another spacecraft. It was the job of other vessels, built for stealth and speed and trading punches, to neutralize other ships and secure the battlespace. Nonetheless, an energy seemed to fill the platoon; at least they were fighting back.

"It's a hit." Chappelle pumped his fist. "*Direct* hit on Rack Two's turret."

Loud cheers thundered through the comm.

"*Sawtooth's* in the fight now. They just traded shots with *Claymore*—Rack One. Rack Two is closing, too." He listened intently. His silence drew out into an uncomfortably long tail.

"What's happening now, sir?"

"Something's not right."

"Sir?" said a corporal.

"Rack Two is firing again, but their capacitors should still be recharging. They shouldn't be able to do that."

Chris's words echoed unbidden in Wyatt's mind. *The enemy can do whatever the hell they want.*

"My God, they're firing *again*," Chappelle muttered. "Oh, no."

The concerned trooper spoke for all of them. "Sir?"

No answer. That wasn't good.

They remained in silence for what seemed like forever. The lights in the corridor dimmed a second time as *Vigorous* shot again, but this time their platoon leader didn't give them any explanation about the target or the result. Wyatt could feel the anxiety pushing toward despair. Worse, there was nothing he could do about it. He was lying helpless inside a massive spacecraft, pressed against the deck by heavy acceleration that felt both excessive and insufficient. He closed his eyes, and his mind wandered to the only place he had left—his faith, and a plea to God to let him make a difference.

Chappelle's head popped up over the spray of troopers and barked out in the voice of command. "First Platoon, listen up! New orders. We are heading to the hangar immediately. Get your gear squared away for Javelin operations. On the double!"

Troopers struggled to stand back up in the heavy gee. Wyatt clicked on the tactical display inside his helmet and saw sixteen blue chevrons representing the troopers in the corridor. Chappelle and Gunnery Sergeant Fujiyama each had a star over their indicator for Acid, the platoon's command element. First squad under

Wyatt was Battle, while Lieutenant Korbett had Chemo Squad. Two green chevrons labeled Chris and Finn as non-RESIT friendlies attached to their unit. Everyone except the green were lining up into two orderly columns.

"Chris—get in a line unless you want to get trampled."

The Marine ungraciously bulled his way in front of a Chemo trooper, pushing the whole stack backward.

"Let's move, *now*!" Fujiyama thundered.

Back to the lift. Wyatt felt a few sideways accelerations as they marched, but by and large he got the impression that *Vigorous* was heading very deliberately toward a specific destination. What that was, he would have to wait to find out.

The lift stopped back at the hangar level and disgorged them through the loading gate. Lines painted on the deck indicated where troopers were to remain, lest they participate in a close encounter with a forklift or Javelin crane.

"What are we doing?" Chris asked him. "Abandoning ship?"

Wyatt shook his head. "We're launching our Javelins."

"And we're doing that why?"

"Later."

Wyatt saw Chappelle standing to the side and arguing with the hangar operations officer in charge. His platoon leader was pissed about something. Wyatt couldn't hear the quarrel, but the uncharacteristic anger in Chappelle's arm gestures could only indicate bad things.

His platoon leader pointed at the Javelins and then to the charging stations for the powered BHEAST suits. The OIC shook his head, motioning emphatically for the squads to board. Chappelle stepped forward until his helmet was just centimeters from the OIC's and pointed again at the charging stations.

Oh. Wyatt drew a sharp breath.

He opened a private channel to Laramie. "We're doing a forced boarding."

"What?"

"It's got to be. Chappelle wants to load the heavies, but there's no time to get them onboard."

"A forced boarding," Laramie repeated, as if the words were a foreign language. "Against a RESIT destroyer."

"Yeah, I think so."

"There's no way, LT, not without those suits."

"Hence why he's pissed."

Chappelle abruptly turned and marched back toward the platoon. His anger radiated even through his pressure sleeve. "First Platoon, move to board! Bay Three!"

Laramie and Wyatt traded glances through their CORE helmet cameras. Wyatt motioned for his squad to follow him across the hangar deck.

As they trotted past Bay One, he couldn't help but look over at Teo's Javelin. The vehicle was clearly out of commission. Toolboxes and safety tape cordoned off the area while a crane suspended the vehicle two meters above the deck. Missing panels seemed just to accentuate the numerous holes in the fuselage. Teo wasn't anywhere to be seen. It seemed like an ignoble end for such a talented pilot not to take them out on what very well might be their last flight.

The squad quickly formed up next to Chemo Squad near Javelin Three. Chris figured out his place this time, standing next to Laramie as the squad's other senior sergeant. Gavin grabbed Finn's shoulder and helped position him in the correct place. The two men gave each other a fist bump. Wyatt wondered what that was all about as he assumed his station at the front.

Wyatt's platoon channel chirped a second before Chappelle came over the comm. "Squad leaders, you copy?"

"Yes, sir."

"Listen up," the captain said, his voice still laced with fury. "We are going to board *Claymore*. *Vigorous* is going to shield us from enemy fire so that we can get close. Then it's up to us. Our objective is to take the bridge and control of their remaining turret.

"Everyone needs to be crisp on this one, people. We won't have BHEAST suits. Understood?"

"Aye, aye."

Chappelle gave the signal for the troopers to board and led First Platoon up the ramp. Wyatt came next, followed by a mass of fully loaded troopers rustling their way through safety harnesses and four-point buckles. Numerous cargo boxes lay strapped to the deck, making a sort of half-height wall that split the cargo bay lengthwise in two. By the time Chemo Squad started to board, nearly every trooper smacked their equipment into the stack of crates.

"What's with all this junk?" Laramie said.

Wyatt strapped himself into a sling chair in front of one of the boxes and read the yellow stencil on the side. "They're emergency rations."

"Rations? Not ammo?"

The implication hit him with crystal clarity. "In case there's not a *Vigorous* to come back to."

37

Gunny Fujiyama boarded last, inspecting everyone's gear as he made his way to the seat opposite the captain. He flashed a thumbs up to the crew chief. The chief hit a button and the cargo ramp started to close with a sharp hydraulic whine.

It took Chappelle less than five seconds to patch his squad leaders into the Javelin's sensor suite. The left half of Wyatt's vision crackled as the neural stub switched away from the helmet cam. Now an opaque rectangle appeared between him and the trooper across the cargo bay. Since they had not yet launched from the hangar, the visual came from *Vigorous* herself rather than the Javelin. He could see Bering Gate, off-center and alone against a field of black.

An orange data tag highlighted the position where *Piranha* and *Claymore* had tangled. Wyatt squinted. He didn't have any control over the data feed, and all he could make out were two tiny reflections. Another tag indicated Rack Two, the unnamed warship they couldn't otherwise identify, moving ominously at the bottom of the screen.

Wyatt watched the camera view zoom in on the unnamed destroyer, filling the edges of the visual feed with data and threat information. He ignored the telemetry and focused on the chunks of wreckage catching bits of reflected sunlight.

"What's all that floating behind it?" he asked.

"I think it's what's left of *Sawtooth*," Chappelle said, his voice flat. "Total mismatch."

"My God."

Wyatt's stomach twisted into a knot. He had been sitting next to Otto only yesterday. Despite Laramie's quips about him being crazy, the skipper and his crew had proven their level of competence in trading blows with *Razor*. Now they were gone, eight human beings who lost their lives fighting against their own service in a battle that shouldn't be happening.

Wyatt tried to bow his head in a quick prayer. The neural stub made it impossible to concentrate through the overstimulation of a continuous feed that streamed past closed eyelids.

Chappelle spoke again, his words taking on a more ominous tone. "Rack Two is closing on *Vigorous*."

Wyatt noticed a gentle acceleration tugging his body sideways. The carrier was maneuvering again.

"Weapon launch," Chappelle said.

The chatter in the Javelin went completely silent.

Vigorous lurched forward into a full two gees. Wyatt fought to keep his head upright as the sudden additional weight drew him sideways. On the visual feed, a small bright speck accelerated away from Rack Two and out of the image frame.

"Do destroyers have boarding drones?" one of the troopers asked.

"No," Chappelle said. He was studying the holo monitor from his platoon-leader station. "There's a second launch now. Two torpedoes inbound."

Major Beck's voice crackled over the platoon channel, drowning out the chatter of brevity codes and terse orders behind him on the bridge. "*All platoons, this is* Vigorous *Actual. Move to launch chute and deploy immediately. I repeat, deploy immediately, acknowledge.*"

"Acid copies, wilco," Chappelle said.

Wyatt's teeth chattered as the four engines powered up and vibrated the hull. He felt a new sensation of movement as the docking clamp loaded them into the launch port. Technically all that needed to happen from there was for the clamp to release them. Then the Javelin would float through the port and get a little extra boost from the drive hoops. But these were combat conditions, and another flare of throttle telegraphed the pilot's intentions of immediate maneuvers once they were outside the carrier.

A carrier about to be torpedoed.

A voice from the bridge called out the range and time to impact. "Pilum One contact in forty seconds. Pilum Two contact in fifty-three seconds."

"Can't we just shoot those things down?" someone asked.

"Cut the babble," Chappelle barked. "Brace for launch, it's going to be heavy."

Every trooper gripped their harness. Wyatt found himself dwelling on the question lingering in the air, thinking back to the old Earth vids where anti-aircraft guns threw up a wall of flak. They could use a couple of those defensive weapons right now. But laser fire had been the standard spaceborne weapon for a century. You couldn't shoot down beams of light. And to Wyatt's knowledge, no one had ever fired a RESIT torpedo at their own spacecraft before.

"Launching in five," said the pilot. "Four. Three."

A troop carrier had two high-speed docking ports oriented aft. Each one could spit out a Javelin in about five minutes if they really hustled. The missiles would hit—or not—before all the Javelins even got into the launch clamp.

"Two. One."

Wyatt closed his eyes and wondered if theirs was about to become their lifeboat.

His stomach lurched as the clamp released them. The momentary lack of acceleration from *Vigorous* was quickly replaced by a sudden burn of the four engines in the opposite direction. Wyatt gripped his harness even tighter as they quickly transitioned past the drive hoops of the carrier and banked hard to port. With no instructions other than to get out as fast as possible, he couldn't help but wonder if Beck and Kazimira had already written off their chances.

The pilot's voice spilled over from the flight deck. "This is Judo Outlaw, we are clear of *Vigorous* and matching heading of two-seven-six by six-zero by one-four-four. ETA to intercept is six minutes."

A flash of light in Wyatt's eye indicated the neural stub had cut over to the Javelin's sensor package. He really wished it hadn't. They were flying alongside *Vigorous*, using the troop carrier as a shield against hostile fire from Rack One and Rack Two. But it also meant they could no longer see their enemy from the Javelin's vantage point. The hull of the massive spacecraft blotted out the sky.

"What's happening, Captain?" Wyatt asked.

Chappelle leaned through the flight deck hatch. "Can you switch it back?"

A moment later, the visual signal changed. Wyatt almost started to breathe a sigh of relief, except the torpedoes were rapidly approaching the camera.

One of the tiny points of light snuffed out.

"Scratch Pilum One," Chappelle said.

Wyatt wanted to rejoice. He wished he could. But his gut told him that Otto's little trick of cycling his laser wasn't an option here. For one thing, a torpedo was faster, armored, and dense. For another, the carrier gunnery crew wasn't Otto.

Chappelle cleared his throat. "Impact in ten."

They watched the speck of light get closer. Out of the corner of his eye, Wyatt saw Chappelle physically brace himself.

Then it happened. A puff of gas vented from the broadside of *Vigorous*, followed immediately by a plume of orange fire.

"Hit amidships on *Vigorous*."

A secondary explosion blew pieces of debris through the hull around the initial penetration, followed by a larger rush that reminded Wyatt of the wind blowing snow off the top of a mountain. He squinted, trying to figure out which compartment had been struck.

The hangar. That much gas venting, it had to be. That impact had probably killed whoever had been queueing up to launch out the docking port. At least one more platoon of troopers. Wyatt realized he was clenching his teeth hard, seething in anger at this murderous attack.

"Who's left, Captain?" Laramie asked. "Anybody at all to support the carrier?"

Chappelle's voice carried a heavy weight. "*Sawtooth* is gone. *Piranha's* not maneuvering or firing. It's just *Vigorous* unless we can even things out."

Wyatt wanted to yell at the top of his lungs. He felt so helpless. The redness in his face, the tightness in his throat threatened to overcome the environmental controls in his personal pressure sleeve.

A new voice intoned on the radio like a death announcement. "... *pire, Vampire. Designate Pilum Three and Pilum Four.*"

God, please.

Wyatt looked at Chappelle, a child turning to a parent, hoping to be imbued with some imperceptible magic of a way out. To his surprise, his captain had already swiveled around to face him.

"Time to intercept *Claymore* is two minutes. It's up to us. Get ready."

38

On Approach, USIC *Claymore*
Alpha Centauri A
10 April 2272

The Javelin's interior lighting switched to red. A symphony of clicks and snaps surrounded Wyatt as troopers readied their Vectors and recalibrated their helmet targeting interfaces. Then the gentle rattle of the air vents began to fade as compressors removed the cabin atmosphere in preparation for hard vacuum.

Wyatt went through the rote motions too. The video feed showing the two additional torpedoes closing on their carrier made it difficult to pay attention. A quick glance at his squad down the line revealed similar tension underneath the layers of pressure sleeves and combat equipment.

An emotionless voice came from the flight deck comm as the pilot maneuvered. "*Vigorous*, this is Judo Outlaw, we are matching target trajectory. ETA thirty seconds."

Any reply from the bridge of the carrier was quickly drowned out by Gunny Fujiyama. "Troopers, sound off," he ordered.

Each person counted down to indicate readiness. One platoon, two squads of eight, led by a command element of the captain and first sergeant. The first series of voices sequenced through the comm, followed by Wyatt's counterpart. "Chemo is ready."

The process repeated for Wyatt's squad. "Battle ready."

"Acid is ready," Chappelle said, referring to his command element.

"Roger," the pilot said. "Stand by."

A last glimpse of the camera feed showed *Vigorous* sliding away from the Javelin, the knobs and domes of various sensors acting as a sort of measuring stick as they shrunk on his heads-up display. Most of the hull still looked smooth and undamaged. But Wyatt knew the other side was bleeding atmosphere and debris and probably body parts through multiple breaches. He hoped the engineers who had designed the carrier had built it strong enough to last a bit longer.

"Rear door opening in three, two, one."

A low thrum vibrated through the hull as the actuator motors split open the rear of the cabin. A bright swath of white flooded the interior. Wyatt peered outside and saw the unmistakable sight of *Claymore,* marked Rack One on his heads-up display. Its side hangar doors looked cold and hard under the intense glare of the Javelin's floodlights. It would be the one place in the armored hull that their breaching charges would be able to penetrate.

"Confirmed, we are next to hangar access on the starboard side of the target," the pilot said.

Staff Sergeant Washington from Chemo Squad gave the order to fire the harpoon. A moment later, a metal bolt with a trailing steel cable flashed from the deck-mounted gun.

"Hit," the gunner said. "Turning on the winch. I have good tension."

"Breach team, go!" the staff sergeant said.

Two troopers slid down the harpoon cable until they reached the exterior hull of the destroyer. Wyatt watched them detach from the line and deploy magnetic anchors with tethers to allow them to move clear. It took a few moments to unfold and arrange four breaching charges into a rough square, about two meters across on the hangar door.

"They're too slow," a voice said on Battle's squad channel.

Wyatt turned to see Chris and Finn critiquing the breaching team. The master sergeant was leaning toward Finn and pointing at the charges. "You'd have that lit by now."

"I don't know," Finn said. "It's a big hole."

"But with two of them, they should be faster."

Finn sounded uncertain. "Give 'em a break. It's zero gee."

The breach team moved back toward the harpoon line. "Charges set."

The Javelin maneuvered laterally so that the cargo doors were positioned adjacent to the breaching area. Now the harpoon line stretched at an angle out the rear door. For all the technology advances that made space travel possible, certain parts—like tearing a hole through a hull—seemed decidedly low tech.

"All squads, prepare to drop," Gunny Fujiyama said.

The troopers near the rear door hooked their safety tethers to the harpoon line.

"Fire in the hole!"

The charges detonated. Wyatt's helmet camera automatically dimmed at the sudden flash, but he could still see the sudden outgassing of atmosphere and whatever claptrap hadn't been secured inside the berth. It took only seconds. Then it was over, with a new hole neatly punched through the hull of the hostile destroyer.

Laramie leaned toward Wyatt. "Something's not right, LT. They didn't evac the cabin atmosphere?"

She was right. Any RESIT vessel smaller than a troop carrier would suck oxygen into armored holding tanks during a fight. It wouldn't do for a collision or hostile fire to vent such a precious resource.

Right now, though, he didn't have time to dwell on it. A line of troopers were forming up in front of him and attaching carabiners to the harpoon line.

"We have good entry," said one of the breachers.

Fujiyama gave the order in a gravelly voice. "Drop."

Bodies cascaded from the Javelin. Each trooper ziplined to the hull and planted magnetic boot soles against the metal before detaching their carabiner. By the time Wyatt brought up the rear of Battle Squad, calls of "clear" were coming from the other side of the breach.

Wyatt swung through the hole. He quickly found himself at one end of *Claymore's* small but versatile hangar. Storage boxes and pallets of smaller crates were locked into the deck latching system lining the perimeter. The center of the floor was dominated by a pair of sliding doors that allowed direct access to the storage deck below. Above it, a powered cargo clamp hung from the ceiling, ready to unload cargo containers filled with supplies for deep-space operations.

Without having to worry about entrenched defenders—explosive decompression typically took care of that—the forward elements had already moved alongside the interior compartment hatch. Carlos and Kenny were covering the threshold with their weapons. Wyatt realized that once they went through the hatch, there wouldn't be enough room to leverage the manpower of two squads at the same time. Battle would have to take point. Chemo would remain in reserve.

So far, Chris and Finn were doing an admirable job of maneuvering themselves through freefall. The pair moved into the stack to the side behind Laramie, squatting down and holding themselves in place against the bulkhead with their mag boots like they had been taught. Finn's voice had a hint of breathlessness as he spoke into the comm. "How many hostiles are there?"

"About twenty crew," Wyatt said.

"Can they fight?"

"They're trained to repel boarders, if that's what you mean."

The Marine didn't reply. Instead he patted the chem mags around his belt as if counting inventory.

Chappelle and Gunny Fujiyama slipped in behind Wyatt. Fujiyama didn't waste time in barking out more orders. "Secure the hole and stand by to advance."

Two troopers from Chemo had already unfurled a roll of heavy breach cloth and had drawn it across the opening. A third took a portable impact driver and shot a series of rivets around the perimeter. When they forced open the next berth, the atmosphere would blow into their current compartment and equalize across the larger volume. The cloth would press against the hole and keep it from rushing into space. More importantly, it would allow the boarding team to avoid an explosive decompression every single time they advanced into the next compartment.

Wyatt moved away from the breach to form up with Laramie near the hatch. "Ready?" he asked.

She stole a glance at him through the eyeless faceplate of her helmet. "Never thought we'd be storming a RESIT destroyer."

"Me neither."

"Let's agree not to get shot," she added.

"Copy that."

Behind them, a final, faint vibration reverberated through the hull. "Cloth in place," the riveter said.

Chappelle delivered their orders. "Battle, open the hatch. We need to take the bridge."

"Do it, Carlos," Wyatt said.

Carlos hit the release button. As the hatch door slid open, a faint roar slowly became more audible as atmosphere vented in from the other side. Wyatt looked over his shoulder and saw the breach cloth press against their entry point as it captured the outgassing.

They didn't need fancy instrument readings to anticipate equalized pressure. Carlos and Kenny swept through the hatch with their Vectors raised, followed by Laramie and Finn to round out the first fire team.

"Stairwell clear down," Carlos said.

"Clear up," Kenny echoed.

"Battle, on me," Wyatt said. He pushed through the hatch.

The squad floated into a rectangular landing that connected to the primary interior stairwell. A pair of wide ship's ladder-type staircases extended at sharp angles into the deck and ceiling. Like most spacecraft, a Pompey-class destroyer relied on constant acceleration from its reactionless drives to create artificial gravity for its occupants. "Up" led toward the bow. "Down" was aft. But with its drive system out of commission, microgravity ruled the day. Wyatt's brain had to work overtime to fight the vertigo and disorienting spatial alignments. It was as if he were cave diving into the murk of the cabin, the confusing angles and conflicting cues threatening to trap him in a dead end. A momentary slip in attentiveness could easily put him in the wrong place to take cover in a firefight.

"Stack up on the down ladder," Wyatt said. "The next level is the storage deck. It's going to be tight quarters. Ready?"

Multiple aye, ayes.

"Go."

Rahsaan covered the stairs leading up so that Kenny could join Carlos on point. The unit flowed downward through the microgravity like a single organism, moving to the distant chime of a general quarters alarm bleating through the thin air. When Wyatt got to the next landing, the stairs ended. Everyone stacked up properly on the next hatch and Carlos held his hand over the door release.

"Open it," Wyatt said.

The hatch slid noiselessly into the bulkhead.

Carlos and the first fire team swept inside. Wyatt waited a beat and then followed with his

Vector held up to his shoulder and his finger on the trigger. A long corridor stretched across the diameter of the destroyer. A row of potable water tanks crowded the left side, while waste tanks and trash storage lined the right for eventual processing by the spacecraft's organic reclamation system. The warm red light of the alert status bathed the compartment and the closed hatch at the other end.

As Wyatt followed his troopers, he felt the hair on his neck stand. There was remarkably little cover provided by the narrow nooks between the tanks and compartments.

"This is a damn killing zone," Chris intoned, his voice low.

"Quiet," Wyatt said. But the truth was he agreed completely. How he wished they had those power suits.

He motioned for his squad to press themselves as tightly as they could against the sides of the corridor. He clicked on the comm. "Battle One to Acid One."

"Copy, Battle."

"We're at the storage deck. The main corridor stretches maybe thirty meters to the other side of the pressure hull. There's no cover at all."

"Understood. Keep pressing forward."

Wyatt sighed in resignation. He knew Chappelle didn't have any real choice. They had to get to the bridge, and this was the path that fate had set before them.

As if to punctuate that inevitability, a low thrum vibrated through the deck plates into their mag boots. The laser turret was firing again—at *Vigorous*, at *Piranha*, at their brothers and sisters. Every minute of delay meant more death.

"Battle Squad, spread out at five meters and move forward," Wyatt ordered. *"Stay sharp."*

Carlos pressed ahead on the left. Kenny trailed a few meters behind him. Laramie and Finn spread to the right and held their Vectors high.

When Carlos reached the halfway mark, the far hatch opened.

39

USIC *Claymore*
Alpha Centauri A
10 April 2272

"Contact—"

Wyatt heard a loud *pop*. The blue chevron representing Carlos in his heads-up display began to flash as the corridor descended into chaos.

"Contact front!" Kenny yelled.

Everything happened at once. The single snap blossomed into a cacophony of laser fire as Kenny, Laramie, and Finn let loose with everything they had. Whoever was guarding the hatch did the same. Wyatt dove to the deck and tried to keep from rebounding in the zero gee, while Chris dragged Rahsaan behind the lip of a gray water tank that was too small for the both of them.

"Carlos!" Wyatt called out. "You with us?"

A strained voice wheezed, "Son of a *bitch!*"

"Get some cover!"

A grunt came back in reply. Up ahead, Wyatt could see his trooper somehow manipulating his body in the microgravity to stay flat against the deck.

Thank God for ARC vests, Wyatt thought. The vaporizing of an ablative gel puck had caused the pop. The blowback might have rebroken Carlos's ribs, but it was better than a hole burned clean through his guts.

Wyatt needed to get some return fire on the defenders. He called Laramie on the comm. "Shoot at the hatch! Open fire!"

"I'm totally pinned, LT—" The comm drowned in gunfire.

"Hang in there!"

"Hanging in."

The chem mag exhaust from the shooting had created a remarkable amount of smoke in the confined corridor. Wyatt remained pressed flat against the floor decking. He couldn't get a marked target with his helmet computer. The incoming laser fire, on the other hand, was chewing bits of metal from the storage containers and twirling them through the microgravity.

Another loud *pop*. Another cry of pain on the comm.

Wyatt switched to the platoon channel. "Acid, this is Battle, we are in contact on the storage deck and pinned down, I repeat, we are completely pinned down. We need support ASAP, do you copy?"

The reply from Chappelle came almost instantly. "Coming up behind, Battle. Friendlies behind."

"Copy."

The *snap-snap-snap* of laser fire suddenly abated by one less weapon. Kenny wasn't shooting anymore. A moment of panic swelled through Wyatt's stomach. Maybe he was just reloading? God knew his squad was burning through chem mags, trying to keep enough suppressing fire going so that they didn't get annihilated. Wyatt struggled to get his Vector pointed toward the targets his helmet urged him to take out.

A new voice came over the comm. "Fire in the hole!"

Movement barely visible through the fog. A pair of cylinders, each no larger than an apple, sailed toward the far hatch.

The first made it through. The second struck the bulkhead and spun madly as it ricocheted back toward them.

Oh, no—

He instinctively looked away just as the grenades exploded. Wyatt's camera plunged into blackness as soon as the concussive charge hit him, the overpressure momentarily squeezing him like an elephant rolling over his back.

Behind him, a voice was shouting. "Chemo, go, go!"

The *snap* of laser fire intensified until it became one with the universe around him.

Trapped in a confined space, under hostile fire and unable to see, it would have been easy to panic. Wyatt forced his lungs to take a steadying breath. He reached toward his helmet and fumbled for the power switch, his fingers taking far too long to find the button on the underside of his chin. He pressed and held it in.

Come on, please don't be dead. Please...

The firing stopped.

Wyatt's limbs were practically vibrating with adrenaline. Was his team still alive? Or was the next shot about to drill him in the middle of his helmet?

A moment later, the boot sequence of his helmet computer flashed on his heads-up display. The tactical display came back online. Wyatt saw blue chevrons from Chemo Squad had taken up positions in the hatch behind him, covering the corridor with their Vectors. Then the camera twisted back to life to reveal Laramie, Kenny, and the others inching along the deck. Finn was holding on to a support brace near a water tank, a novice struggling in the microgravity.

"Clear!" a trooper from Chemo said. "Corpsman up, got casualties!"

Carlos was twisting awkwardly up ahead. Wyatt pulled himself toward the trooper and clutched at his shoulders. "How bad?"

"I'll live, Lieut—" The reply came as little more than a hiss through clenched teeth.

Wyatt patted him down and found an entire gel puck missing right in the center. The force of ablating an eight-megajoule blast had probably cracked his sternum.

"You can't get a break, can you?" He slapped Carlos on the side of the helmet. "Move to reserve in the back."

"I'm ... can fight ..."

"That's an order," Wyatt said, and turned toward the hatch.

The landing on the far end of the storage deck looked like a hit-and-run accident. Six bodies floated in a corridor marked by chem exhaust and floating debris. Four of the figures were destroyer crew, judging by the orange uniforms under their ARC vests. The concussion grenade that cleared the hatch had done its job and disoriented them enough for Chemo to storm their position.

The remaining two casualties belonged to Chemo. One trooper had a laser hole melted through his faceplate and was beyond hope. The other floated in the neutral position, unconscious, his squad mate trying to tie a tourniquet around the stump of his left arm. Dribbles of red spheroids swarmed around the pair like insects in the summertime.

Wyatt scanned the area around him until he found Korbett, his counterpart from Chemo. The other squad lieutenant had a scorch mark running diagonally across the top of his CORE helmet.

Wyatt floated over and slapped him on the shoulder. "Thanks," he said.

"Yeah. You good?"

"Good. Sent Carlos to the back. We've got seven."

"I've got five."

"All right."

Wyatt saw Chappelle over by the stairwell that descended to the next deck. He followed the captain's gaze and realized the corridor would only be wide enough for one fire team at a time.

"We're going to leapfrog," Chappelle announced, working out the tactics. "Battle will go first, take up position, then Chemo. If we glide into another ambush, the covering team throws grenades and we repeat what we just did." He looked at his squad leaders. "Good?"

"Good," Wyatt and Korbett said in unison.

Another low-level hum vibrated through the metal around them. *Claymore* was firing its turret again.

Chappelle's voice darkened as he shouldered his weapon again. "We've got to get to the bridge."

"Aye, Captain," Wyatt replied. "Battle's got the lead. Moving to the crew deck."

He motioned to Laramie to go.

The troopers floated effortlessly through the microgravity as they descended the stairwell. For a moment, Wyatt wondered what was happening outside. If *Claymore* was still shooting, it meant *Vigorous* was still in the fight. He suspected that could only last so long. The weaponry of their opponents could whittle down a mass as large as a troop carrier if given enough time.

They had to get control of *Claymore's* turret. They had to even the odds.

They reached the bottom landing and stopped in front of a powered sliding hatch. A peek through the porthole glass revealed a row of four crew berths that formed a hallway behind the hatch. Each berth had an airtight hinged door that Wyatt thought wouldn't be out of place on a submarine. At the far end of the berths, the corridor turned to the right into what he presumed would be the enlisted living area. He didn't see any signs of crew.

Wyatt punched the open button on the hatch. Nothing happened. The Chemo fire team moved up from behind and took positions on the other side.

Wyatt pushed back from the door. "Gavin—open it."

"Aye, Lieutenant."

The big Texan snapped off an access panel to reveal the hatch motor. It only took a moment for him to disengage the clutch before he slid the hatch into the bulkhead.

Wyatt didn't need to give the order to move. His stack of troopers slid into the corridor, orienting themselves effortlessly to check corners as they floated ahead. Finn and Chris even seemed to be keeping pace now that they had a few corridors under their belt. They all floated as close to the left side of the passage as possible. Behind them, the troopers from Chemo aimed their Vectors down the right, covering the approach and ready to shoot at the first sign of a threat.

The hallway ran about ten meters long. Wyatt peered into one of the berths and saw the typical

RESIT bunks with storage and equipment lockers. All four were deserted. He wondered which room belonged to the men they had just killed. The thought made him angry that they had been put in this position at all.

They reached the end of the corridor. His squad moved to one side while the Chemo troopers floated into a neat, single-file stack against the ceiling, ready to propel themselves forward.

Laramie peeked around the corner.

"What do you see?" Wyatt asked.

"Common room," Laramie said. "Couch in the center. A bunch of storage boxes stacked around it. Hatch and stairs on the far side."

"Looks empty," Kenny added, floating just below her.

Wyatt frowned. He didn't believe that for a second. "Grenades—pass 'em up."

Hands from the back of the stack passed two of them up to Kenny and Laramie.

"Everybody, grab hold of something," Wyatt said. "Korbett, you ready?"

"Chemo's ready."

He gave the order. The cylinders went sailing.

The two detonations ripped through the air. Wyatt's helmet display warped as a hurricane gale smashed through the confined space. With a pressure sleeve that protected against external vacuum but not overpressure squeezing inward, he couldn't shake the impression of another elephant backing into him and rocking its buttocks to satisfy some itch hidden in its ass.

"Chemo team, go!" Korbett ordered.

Five troopers flowed into the common room, weapons covering every nook like a laser-equipped hedgehog.   Battle Squad pointed seven more Vectors across the compartment.

In his gut, Wyatt knew there would be an ambush.   His platoon was storming an enemy vessel, and the interior layout would only present so many defensive chokepoints for the defenders to leverage.

But even when it came, Wyatt still felt a moment of surprise when he spotted one of the shooters with a bare head, aiming at their troopers with just an optical sight.

Multiple volleys of *snap-snap-snap* arced across the room.   One Chemo trooper got off a single shot before a laser blast burned his shoulder. Another took a hit in his stomach. And Wyatt was still aiming his Vector when he saw the shot that took down Korbett.

40

Strained voices yelled *contact front* as if there were some question where the fire had come from. Laramie and Kenny started shooting. Wyatt joined in a split second later and caught a quick glimpse of a hostile defender with black hair ducking behind the couch.

"Get to cover!" someone yelled into the comm.

Staff Sergeant Washington was one of the few who seemed to have made it without getting shot. He huddled behind a large table built into the deck, but still managed to stretch out a long arm to tug Korbett to cover. The unconscious, helpless lieutenant floated at such an agonizingly slow rate that Wyatt was certain he was going to get shot again.

Wyatt poured on the suppressing fire. It seemed to be working. But he counted at least four shooters holed up behind the storage crates in what was now obvious to him as a reinforced position.

He stopped to change chem mags. Chappelle smacked him on the back to get his attention.

"We can't shoot through those boxes. We need more grenades."

"Aye, Captain."

The problem was they were running out of grenades. RESIT usually assigned drones or BHEAST troopers to assault prepared defenses. The platoon had neither. A quick inventory with

Wyatt's squad managed to scrounge up a solitary device.

"Washington, Korbett, you guys still with me?" Wyatt said on the comm.

"Still here," the staff sergeant said, his voice strained. "Korbett's down."

"Got any poppers left?"

"Got one."

"I've got one too. Throw on three. Then we're coming in to reinforce your position, so check your fire."

"Copy that."

Wyatt slapped Laramie's shoulder. "Ready, Staff Sergeant?"

"Ready," she said.

"Ready," Kenny repeated.

"One. Two. Three!"

He pulled the pin. A gentle toss sent the device on a flat arc toward the hostiles. Washington's flew out a bit too hard, gliding past the fortified position and twirling off the far bulkhead.

Wyatt pulled back behind the corner.

The grenades detonated with two quick, deafening *whumps*. The hair on his skin stood on end an instant before a hurricane blew into the corridor and squeezed the air out of him.

"Go!" he yelled.

Laramie and her team surged forward, shooting at the storage boxes as they moved. Wyatt, Chris, and Finn added to the suppressing fire from the corner.

It was a decent plan. It should have worked.

The far hatch opened on the other side of the common room.

Wyatt's brain raced to adjust. More hostiles. The grenades might have stunned the defenders behind the storage boxes, but anyone in the far corridor would be shielded from the concussion. Just like Battle had been.

A barrage of fire from the newly opened hatch seemed to ignite the air of the common room.

Laramie's team scattered like a school of fish spooked by a predator. Gavin took a laser shot in his shoulder. A second hit him in the chest and sent him tumbling into Kenny with a grunt. Next to him, another blast vaporized a puck from Laramie's vest and propelled her to the deck with a sizzle of gas. She bounced hard and tumbled out of view.

"Contact from the corridor!" Wyatt said. "Put fire on that hatch!"

The interior buzzed with another low-level hum. The destroyer's turret firing again.

Wyatt didn't have a single target marked on his heads-up display. He fired anyway. The fusillade of gunfire ripped through the living quarters like a fireworks stand ablaze. Countless little impact holes began to cover the furniture inside the compartment. Bits of debris spiraled through the microgravity and mixed with the exhaust clouds of chemical lasers.

The trigger on his Vector froze, and Wyatt released the empty chem mag. Just as he inserted another into the housing, he saw the head of a defender pop up from behind the storage boxes to take advantage of the dip in fire. The crewman sent a series of badly aimed shots dangerously close to Gavin.

This was bad. Wyatt's teammates were clinging to exposed surfaces inside a killing zone. As he resumed his suppressing fire, he knew he needed to assault that position behind the storage boxes. It didn't matter how dangerous it was. They were running out of time...

A voice growled at him from behind. "Wyatt, make a hole."

He felt a presence looming closer to him. Wyatt turned to see a large metal door inexplicably floating in the corridor, with Chris and a trooper from Chemo manhandling it into a horizontal position.

"What the—what's this?"

"It's a hatch door," Chris said.

"From where?"

Chris gave him a look. "From a hatch."

Wyatt stared at the metal hatch to one of the crew berths, both hinges melted into slag by point-blank laser fire. The Marine with the black CORE police helmet guided it to the edge of the common room.

A shield.

Chris didn't mince words. "Finn! Stack up behind this, you first, then Wyatt, then me. We push through freefall, clear out the bunker first. Then the hall. Got it?"

"Oorah!" Finn said.

Wyatt got it, too.

It only took a moment to reorient the makeshift shield and clear the bend in the corridor. Then the three men pressed tightly behind the edges. Each held their Vector at their sides. Wyatt realized with a start that Finn was left-handed.

"Ready?" Chris asked.

Without waiting for an answer, he jabbed his boots against the bulkhead and pushed into the common room. Voices joined into a sudden roar of aggression. To his surprise, Wyatt's was one of them.

A momentary lull broke the gunfire as the defenders tried to figure out what was happening. Then a new torrent of *snap-snap-snap* electrified the air. Tiny chunks of pulverized metal broke free of their improvised shield and tumbled behind them like the tail of a comet. But none of the laser blasts were getting through the door, and their mobile cover was gliding closer to the prepared position.

Time seemed to stop. Lines of invisible light burned oxygen into ozone as they floated. Wyatt couldn't see the shots, couldn't smell them, couldn't really even hear them through the din of noise, but he could sense them nonetheless. Troopers trying to kill troopers in a twisted perversion of circumstance. He forced his mind to focus, his body position to remain still so he didn't cause any unwanted rotation, his trigger finger to relax so that he got in the first shot.

The deck plates moved like a silent conveyor belt below them.

Almost there.

The storage crates.

The edge of the couch.

He saw a trooper wearing an emergency respirator pointing a Vector at him.

Wyatt shot reflexively, his Vector kicking against his armpit. The trooper's neck split open in a sudden black gash that spewed a stream of red against the nearby cushions. Wyatt caught a glimpse of surprise on the trooper's face before he quickly slid into unconsciousness.

A chorus of chemical laser fire filled the air around him. Their improvised shield quickly took on an uncontrollable spin from Chris and Finn's Vector shots, and Wyatt felt the bodies of the Marines separating from his. He caught a glimpse of another defender shooting desperately at something out of sight and brought his Vector around for another burst.

Snap.

Wyatt hit the trooper in his right arm, just below the protection of his ARC vest. A chunk of flesh popped out like meat falling off a barbecue spit. The trooper convulsed as Wyatt sent another shot into the middle of his oxygen mask. His rebreather disintegrated and left a black ring of charred plastic and metal around the dark hole that remained.

"Corridor!" Chris growled. "More hostiles!"

Their hatch door rotated uncontrollably now. Wyatt pushed free and swung into the fortified nest of storage boxes. A quick hold on one of the couch mounting legs let him reorient himself so he could take aim at the far corridor.

He didn't shoot. He couldn't. Gavin's hulking form lunged toward the two troopers in the corridor.

The defenders must have been startled by the sudden charge of a giant man in zero gee, because neither of them fired at him. By the time they recovered, it was too late. A massive hand grabbed one trooper and slammed him against the other, pinning both of their weapons into an unusable position. Then Wyatt saw the flash of a Ka-Bar blade. Two seconds, two savage thrusts. Gavin let loose a primal growl as he made brutal short work of the hostiles.

The sounds of killing finally ceased.

Suddenly feeling naked and vulnerable, Wyatt swung his Vector around the compartment and scanned for any remaining threats. All he saw were the remaining troopers of First Platoon emerging from cover.

"Clear middle," Chris said, his voice ragged.

Another voice echoed the call. "Clear left."

"Clear right."

The smoke swirling around them had taken on a red tinge from the blood and gore. Wyatt tried not to dwell on how those contaminants had once been living persons. He pulled himself over the edge of the couch and floated toward the far hatch.

Staff Sergeant Washington moved among the wounded troopers with his corpsman in tow. One body pirouetted in the microgravity like a ballerina cast into a sustained dance pose.

Wyatt called him on the comm. "Washington, who do we have left?"

"Just me and Wicz." His voice sounded sullen, a dull anger lacing his words.

Wyatt struggled to push down the guilt that suddenly welled up inside him. It could have just as easily been Battle's turn in the rotation to leapfrog into the common room. Then his squad would have been the one slaughtered, with him instead of Korbett floating tentatively between life and death.

Chappelle was floating near the exit corridor where Gavin had dispatched the last defenders. "Rally on me," he said.

Only a few bodies moved to stack up. Gavin hovered in front of the hatch and covered the last stairwell to the bridge with a Vector from a dead trooper. Laramie made her way over with an unusual sluggishness. Kenny seemed more or less okay. And then Chris appeared, a large patch of maroon staining the pressure sleeve around his shoulder.

No one else.

Wyatt gave a quick scan of the compartment. Rahsaan's face scrunched up in pain as he tried to self-administer first aid to the bloody hole in his side. Finn was bare-headed and blinking hard, calling to the corpsman that he couldn't see. Nearby, his helmet floated in the microgravity with a hole melted partially through the faceplate.

Chappelle's face was hidden behind his CORE helmet, but his tone communicated the determination all the same. "Troopers, listen up. I know we've got casualties. But we need to get control of the bridge, and we need to do it right *now*. Otherwise, *Vigorous* is dead and us with it. Copy that?"

Numerous aye, ayes filled the channel.

"Next deck is the bridge," he continued. "That hatch is going to be reinforced. We'll use a breaching charge, blow it off its tracks, and clear the room." Chappelle turned to Wyatt. "Lieutenant, your team takes point. The rest of you line up behind.

"We have one more deck. We *must* take that bridge."

"Yes, sir."

Wyatt drew a deep breath. This very well could be the end of them all. If that was the case, he supposed it didn't matter if he bought it first. At least he'd go down with his best friends at his side.

"Let's move," Chappelle said.

The platoon slid through the opening and floated down the next stairwell. They were deep inside the hull now, well protected from the laser fire streaking through the vacuum outside. Strobing emergency lights seemed to make the walls press inward, as if the vessel itself were constricting the corridors to resist their advance. Wyatt swept his Vector over sealed storage lockers and cargo netting as he moved. Whoever remained of the crew were apparently holed up behind the *Claymore's* final strongpoint.

At the bottom of the stairs, an armored bulkhead surrounded a solitary powered hatch door. Wyatt saw the vertical yellow stripe that confirmed that the bridge was behind it. He floated to the side as the ad-hoc fire teams stacked up behind him and Laramie. Gavin floated up with a breaching charge in his hands.

Including Washington and Captain Chappelle, they had seven troopers left out of the original eighteen in the whole platoon. If the bridge crew had fortified their position like the other two strongpoints, Wyatt doubted it would be enough.

Chappelle didn't need to give any orders because the fire teams knew what to do. Gavin pushed over to the hatch and slapped the breaching charge onto the door. In just a few seconds, they would storm the bridge with weapons blazing.

In just a few seconds, it would be over. One way or the other.

But before Gavin had a chance to trigger the fuse, the hatch abruptly slid open on its own.

41

Laramie was having trouble understanding why the breeching charge didn't blow. Her thoughts remained fuzzy and her ears kept ringing, the aftermath of too many grenades, too many chem mags, too many pucks now vaporized on her ARC vest. But the hatch to the bridge opened anyway, and she did what she had been trained to do. Flow in, turn left, clear the room.

The destroyer had a different bridge layout than Otto's Fast Attack. Instead of four grav couches arranged two by two, this room consisted of a central captain's chair behind a wide, arc-shaped console for the different station personnel. The console seemed like an easily defensible strongpoint for combatants to use for cover, ducking to avoid enemy fire while letting loose at whoever entered the hatch.

When Laramie saw the targets just standing there, she almost squeezed her trigger and burned them down.

They had their hands up.

All of them.

Unbelievable.

"No one move!" Chappelle barked. "Keep your hands where we can see them or we will fire!"

The bridge crew all wore pressure sleeves, but they carried a blue tint that was different than the uniforms they had in Proxima. Rebreather masks with clear faceplates covered their heads. Laramie knew instantly these were people who channeled destruction through computer console, not up close and personal. They were crew. Not troopers.

A man with a yellow horizontal stripe across the chest of his pressure sleeve turned toward Chappelle. "My crew and I surrender," he said.

"Yeah? We'll see if I don't accept that. Where's the weapons station?"

The captain nodded toward a set of controls on the computer console.

"Get flex cuffs on 'em," Chappelle ordered. "Wyatt, over here with me."

Gavin and Staff Sergeant Washington moved up and immediately secured the prisoners. Kenny and Chris covered the far hatch leading to engineering, while Wyatt joined Chappelle at a bank of electronic controls with a dedicated holo monitor. Laramie suddenly found herself with nothing to do. She eyeballed their captives and thought about how unfortunate it was that she hadn't *accidentally* shot one of them.

"*Vigorous*, this is Acid One," Chappelle said. "We have control of the bridge on Rack One. I repeat, we have control of the bridge."

He was talking on the command channel reserved for platoon leadership, so Laramie couldn't hear the response from whoever might still be alive on their carrier. Chappelle directed Wyatt over to one of the other stations. A moment later, the large holo monitor at the front of the bridge changed views from a tactical plot to the visual feed of a troop carrier on fire.

"My God," Kenny said.

Laramie wasn't sure if she should start shooting or just curl up and cry. Kazimira had somehow kept her engines intact, but the rest of *Vigorous* was an absolute mess. Streams of gas and boiling liquid trailed from the hull as the carrier maneuvered in a tight circle with Rack Two. Laramie caught a glimpse of a massive gash from a torpedo hit just forward of the power plants. The damage slipped out of view as the spacecraft turned in its arc, continuing its dangerous dance with its opponent.

Gavin leaned toward her and lowered his voice. "What's the skipper trying to do, circling like that?"

"She's trying to ram him," a voice said behind them.

Laramie jerked around to see the man with the striped pressure sleeve listening to their conversation. A quick glance showed the word *Drexel* beneath a captain's insignia.

Anger flushed through her. Who did this guy think he was? He didn't deserve an opinion after, what—how many people had he just murdered with his destroyer? "Shut up with your crazy talk."

The captain stared back at her, his face expressionless through his emergency mask.

Chappelle remained completely absorbed in his comm by the console. "Affirmative, *Vigorous*. I have weapons control. Stand by. Targeting Rack Two's turret per your command."

"You should take out the hoop drives," the *Claymore* captain said.

Multiple heads swiveled around.

"No one's asking for your advice," Chappelle growled.

"An armored turret is a tough shot," the captain continued. "If you take out their propulsion, they can't get away. You can carve them up as you please after that."

Laramie frowned. Why would they listen to the commander of an enemy ship? And why was he even talking? She should just elbow this fool in the face.

She snuck a sidelong glance at Gavin. She couldn't see his expression through the CORE helmet, but the slight swivel of his head indicated he was thinking the same thing.

Chappelle turned back to the console. He spoke without looking. "Staff Sergeant McCoy, if the *Claymore* captain speaks again, shut him up."

At least that felt satisfying. "Aye, aye."

Captain Drexel didn't seem fazed by the threat. His eyes moved carefully about the bridge at the different troopers, gauging each of them. He remained silent.

"Acid One has the turret online," Chappelle said on the comm. "I have optical lock on Rack Two turret." A pause. "Affirmative, standing by."

The two spacecraft on the holo monitor continued to round on each other, one a destroyer with an arsenal of deadly weapons, the other a troop carrier with enough mass to take the punishment. Laramie watched what seemed like a slow-motion ballet where any mistake could lead to a lethal strike.

"Firing in three. Two. One. Firing."

The now-familiar hum vibrated through the deck plates. On the bridge screen, a quick flash of light near Rack Two was the only visual indication that a seven-megawatt laser had connected with its target.

"Hit," Chappelle reported. He swiped through one of the control panels in a clumsy attempt to ascertain the result.

Every set of eyes on the bridge seemed to be watching the holo monitor. At first it didn't seem like anything had happened. Then Rack Two began to divert itself from its previous trajectory, arcing into a long slide that oriented its bow toward the screen.

"You didn't hit the mark," Drexel said in a deadpan voice. "They'll be closing with us now. To take us out."

Chappelle didn't so much as glance at the *Claymore* captain, but an edge crept into his voice as he worked the comm channel. "*Vigorous*, standing by for orders."

"What's the status of their weapons?" Wyatt asked. He was looking directly at Drexel.

The captain turned his head. "One turret operational."

"Torpedoes?"

Drexel's lips moved into a tight line that bordered on a smile. "None left."

Rack Two slipped lower on the holo monitor. *Vigorous* continued its chase, but a gap had opened between the two vessels due to differences in maneuverability.

"You'll want to reorient the *Claymore* before he takes his shot," Drexel said. "Our turret is wide open."

Even though he was floating effortlessly in zero gee, Chappelle looked anything but relaxed. He seemed to be staring a hole through the weapons console as he waited for new instructions from *Vigorous*. But whatever was going on, *Vigorous* seemed busy trying to figure out their own actions.

"Clock's ticking," Drexel said.

Chappelle stiffened, then drew his Ka-Bar from the sheath on his vest. Laramie felt the blood drain from her face. She watched as her platoon leader pushed off toward the captain and grabbed him by the front of his pressure sleeve.

"Tell your helmsman to fly this thing for us. And by God, if you try anything, I will gut you like a fish."

Drexel didn't seem fazed in the least. He turned his head to the officer next to him.

"Lieutenant Farr, please follow this man's instructions related to ship navigation."

"Aye, sir." The helmsman raised his wrists and presented the flex cuffs binding them together. "I'll need my hands."

A quick flip of the knife and the prisoner was free. He quickly glided over to a different console and grabbed a pair of joysticks on either side of the grav couch.

The compartment around them immediately rotated on the ship's long axis. Laramie watched with amazement as the helmsman seemed to guide the ship and strap himself in at the same time. It gave Laramie a wrenching sense of vertigo as she tried to keep covering the prisoners with her Vector.

The bridge shook suddenly before plunging into darkness, with only the glow of the instrument panels providing illumination. Somewhere far away, a metallic grating sound echoed through the hull like a child shaking a can of rocks.

"What happened?" Chappelle yelled.

"They fired on us," Drexel said.

A harsh white emergency light came to life and revealed their platoon leader fumbling through the consoles. "I don't ... how do you get a damage report? We need to shoot them."

"My crew can do it for you," Drexel said.

Chappelle's voice seethed with anger. He grabbed the captain's pressure sleeve and yanked him close. "You murdered my men."

"We defended our vessel. That doesn't mean we all need to die, now that you control it."

"Rack Two's maneuvering. I think they're trying to get a better shot," Wyatt warned.

Chappelle's other fist still gripped his Ka-Bar. For a moment, Laramie thought he might follow through on his earlier threat about what would happen if the captain spoke again.

"You shoot the turret," he said. "Not the engines. The *turret*."

"Very well."

Chappelle sliced the plastic cuffs from Drexel's wrists. The Claymore captain pointed to his weapons officer and a second later he was free as well. The pair moved effortlessly toward the console next to Wyatt.

"Excuse me, Lieutenant."

Wyatt backed away. He raised his Vector and trained it on Drexel as if expecting some last-minute trickery to send them to their deaths.

Laramie couldn't believe what was happening. Hadn't they just captured these guys? These traitors who had been putting heavy laser fire on their troop carrier, who had been shooting at her friends in the corridors? And now they were giving them control of their vessel back. The universe felt like it had been turned upside down and flipped inside out.

The captain studied the holo monitor. "He's waiting for us, Farr. He wants us to reorient and take aim. Then he'll shoot before we can lock."

"Yes, sir," the helmsman said.

"How long until our capacitors are at full charge?"

"Nineteen seconds."

Drexel turned to the weapons officer. "Can you thread that needle?"

"Aye."

Laramie frowned inside her helmet. Watching the spacer crew operate their tools of destruction seemed a world away from the visceral combat of a trooper. Their voices remained dull, monotone, almost as if they were chatting about different paint colors. It was hard to reconcile with the fact that their actions over the next several seconds could determine the fate of hundreds of people.

Her heart raced madly, reminding her of the fragility of human life in the vacuum of deep space.

A bright green bracket appeared around Rack Two on the holo monitor. A second later, the weapons officer cracked his neck with an audible *click*. A prize fighter about to enter the ring.

"Ten seconds to charge," the helmsman said.

"Lieutenant Farr, stand by to come about on my mark."

"Aye, Captain."

The black hull of the unnamed RESIT destroyer slid closer on the monitor, lurking like a predator readying to strike.

"Six. Five."

"Stand by," Drexel said. He leaned down until his face was next to the weapons officer's ear. "Weapons free, Keat. Don't miss."

The gunner didn't make any acknowledgment.

Farr kept counting down as if it were some sort of religious mantra. "Four. Three. Two—"

Every trooper from Battle and Chemo Squads grabbed the nearest handhold.

"Now," Drexel said.

The bridge rotated again. Laramie watched in fascination as a green reticle appeared inside the bracket transposed on top of Rack Two, right around where she imagined the destroyer's turret was located. No sooner had it appeared than that all-too-familiar hum vibrated through the deck plates.

Drexel straightened up and peered intently at the holo monitor.

"What happened?" Chappelle growled.

The bridge remained silent for a moment. Then Captain Drexel patted the weapons officer on the shoulder.

"*What happened?*" Chappelle said louder.

Drexel turned around. "Have we been shot, Captain?"

"No?"

"That's right. Because we got him first. Which should be obvious, given that we got a shot off at all."

Laramie let all the air out of her lungs at once. She hadn't realized she'd been holding her breath.

"That destroyer is now combat ineffective," Drexel continued. He glanced back at the holo monitor. "No energy weapons, no torpedoes. See? He's already turning back toward Bering Gate. Once he's through, I'm pretty sure the quantum tunnel will close rather dramatically."

"So, it's over?" Chappelle said.

"Yes, it's over."

Their platoon leader relaxed his grip on his weapon and motioned toward Gavin. "Secure the gunner's hands before he blasts our troop carrier again."

The big Texan slid toward the weapons console. The weapons officer raised his wrists without comment.

"Captain Drexel, from this point forward I am in command of this vessel," Chappelle said. "You will direct your helmsman to follow my instructions and maneuver us toward the troop carrier. Upon transfer to *Vigorous*, you and your crew will be placed under arrest."

The commander of the *Claymore* shook his head.

"No. What you're going to do is take me directly to Captain Kazimira. She and I have some things to discuss."

42

As Rack Two retreated into the night, *Vigorous* pulled back to lick its wounds. *Sawtooth* was gone, their Fast Attack obliterated by laser fire and a single torpedo. Their destroyer *Piranha* had survived, but with a ruptured power plant, it would need to be towed to a fleet yard for extensive repair. *Claymore* had come out the best in the exchange. The enemy vessel had a working turret, and the chief engineer thought that with enough time he'd be able to repair the damage to the drive hoop and restore propulsion—assuming he wasn't locked up in the brig.

Then there was *Vigorous* herself.

Laramie got her first real glimpse of the damage as they flew back while aboard the Javelin. Two torpedoes had savaged the carrier's forward port side and ripped massive gouges through the hull. A third had struck near the hangar section at the aft end of the carrier. Other parts of the hull had large chunks missing, including the part that normally held the main sensor array. The starboard side had long, black scorch marks stretching diagonally across the exterior, reminding Laramie of whip lashes she had seen as a child on a wild steer at the county fair.

Her eyes went to the hangar. She wondered if any other Javelins had made it out. Of those who didn't, how many troopers had perished queuing up for the next launch? The burning in her throat stoked the fires of her emotions, a tug-of-war between fury and grief.

The hangar doors were damaged and forced their Javelin pilot to find an intact docking boom closer amidships. Laramie and the walking dead of First Platoon listened for the resounding *clack* of the locking collar before queueing up their prisoners.

They floated through the docking boom, then followed an ensign to the enlisted mess and a makeshift triage area. Laramie saw troopers from the other platoons floating among torn pressure sleeves and melted ARC vests. Two corpsmen were taking vitals and dispensed painkillers, while one of the engineering crew was yelling that Epione was ready for the next procedure. A bitter taste entered Laramie's mouth as she watched a trooper haul a bloody crewwoman away. The spacer was missing her lower leg, the tourniquet around the stump barely holding back the blood flow.

Laramie wondered who would lead the medical effort. The AI was meant to assist, not lead. Doctor Kenta's murder still felt raw, especially at the hands of men who were supposed to be fellow RESIT troopers. Another senseless death of a person whose help they really could have used right about now.

Wyatt floated through the microgravity directly in front of Laramie. He suddenly reached for a grab bar and stopped. She ungracefully smacked right into his back.

"Otto!" he said.

She had to crane around Wyatt's head to see the Fast Attack skipper floating with his crew. Amazing. First a fight with *Razor,* now sparring with a destroyer. She didn't understand how Otto was still alive.

The commander flashed them both a smile. "My favorite ground team. Good to see you both."

"Good to see you, too. How did ...? We saw *Sawtooth*, the wreckage."

"Timing's everything." He raised an eyebrow. "Especially with the eject button."

"I'm sorry."

Otto shrugged. "We got our licks in. Tried our best to give the team a chance." Otto glanced around the mess. "What's left of the team, anyway."

"Copy that."

The Fast Attack skipper glanced to their left. "Your platoon leader wants you."

They turned to see Chappelle motioning them over. Laramie gave Otto a nod as she moved to follow. She still thought he was certifiably crazy, but at least he was on their side.

Chappelle has already launched into a list of tasks with Wyatt by the time Laramie caught up. "I've got orders to take Drexel for interrogation. You take care of what's left of our team. Get the platoon through triage, make sure our priority cases get attention. Korbett and Fuji are going to be two of them."

Wyatt nodded. "Aye. But you should have an escort to the bridge if you're taking an enemy combatant."

"Yeah, okay." Chappelle turned his head toward Laramie. "McCoy. Grab Drexel and come with me."

"Aye, sir."

They separated from the rest and retrieved Drexel. Laramie maneuvered him through the zero-gravity corridors on the way to the bridge. The path proved surprisingly clear of damage, with just one detour around a broken powered hatch to get there. The only real obstacle came from the troopers guarding the hatch.

Two battered troopers aimed their Vectors at them as they approached. "Halt."

"Captain Chappelle, reporting to the skipper as ordered. She wants to have a chat with this one." Chappelle jerked his head toward Drexel.

The head guard went silent as he conversed on the comm. "You can go through, but weapons stay out here."

Laramie noticed that neither trooper lowered his Vector. She moved with extra care as she placed her weapons in the nearby storage locker. All three of them received an additional pat-down before they were allowed to proceed.

Kazimira was waiting for them on the bridge. "My ready room. Now."

A minute later, they were hovering inside a small cabin with one desk and four adults. It would have been plenty crowded with just the desk.

Kazimira turned toward their prisoner. Laramie could see barely contained fury in the captain's eyes.

"So. It *was* you," she said.

Drexel studied her for a moment. "Good to see you, Kate."

"No, we're not doing that. Explain what just happened out there."

"We were dispatched to keep you away from Bering Gate. Not an order I ever expected to get, to tell the truth." He frowned. "Why are you here?"

"I'm asking the questions. All you need to worry about is the answering."

Drexel let out a little snort. "Spare me. There's only one reason we're even talking, and you know it."

"And what would that be?"

His eyes narrowed. *"Because I threw the fight."*

Laramie blinked. What?

That sounded crazy. Her platoon had forced its way aboard their vessel, for God's sake. They had waded through gunfire and floating body parts. There was no conflict that could be more real. What was this guy talking about?

"You expect me to believe that?" Kazimira asked.

"Yes."

Drexel took on a superior expression, a professor teaching class. "How many of our laser shots were just off the mark, Kate? You know what computer targeting can do. And how many torpedoes did I land?"

"I have torpedo holes all over this vessel."

"But not from me." Drexel glanced at Laramie and studied her for a moment. "Why is your boarding party still alive? It's a good thing we had a compressor 'malfunction.' If we had been able to evac the cabin, it sure would have been harder to use grenades on those defensive positions."

A ball had formed in Laramie's stomach. She didn't believe this guy. She wanted to punch him in the face.

Chappelle apparently felt the same. "I lost eleven troopers boarding your spacecraft."

Drexel made as if to retort but then abruptly bit off his words. A look of pain crossed his eyes.

"My crew wasn't in on it. They were defending their vessel. It was just my bridge officers and I who made the decision." He glanced at Kazimira. "After your hail."

Captain Kazimira didn't look convinced, but her next words came out fractionally softer. "What's the story with the other destroyer?"

Drexel shook his head. "Their call sign is *Myrmidon*. And you've seen their combat performance now—more reason for me to keep up appearances. Even if my crew didn't turn on me, those bastards would blow me out of the sky if it was obvious I was disobeying orders."

Kazimira raised her voice. "Epione, get me the specifications on a RESIT destroyer named *Myrmidon*."

"There is no record of that vessel," the omnipresent, ethereal voice replied.

Drexel shook his head again. "You won't find them in any RESIT database. It's not a RESIT ship."

"That's impossible. RESIT's the only one with military-grade spacecraft."

Drexel's eyes filled with a pained expression. His voice dropped to a near whisper. "Why are you here, Kate? You shouldn't be here."

"Tell me why."

Drexel stared hard at her. Then, to Laramie's amazement, the scaffolding of command suddenly dropped away so dramatically that she thought he might collapse if he'd been standing in gravity. She reflexively tightened her grip on his arm as if to keep him from falling.

"It's out of control."

"Constriction?"

His voice became detached, like he was remembering something in a ledger he'd read a long time ago. "It's too contagious. First Juliet. Then the orbital depots. Freighters, the fleet, troopers coming down with it after simple inspections." His eyes defocused. "We can't stop it. The government—the *new* government—they've been trying quarantine. But everyone keeps getting it. *We* keep getting it."

He turned back to the skipper. "How do you stop an epidemic when you're also part of the problem?"

"You try to find a cure, Bill."

Drexel let out a dismissive sniff. "Don't you think they've been trying?"

"Yes, I know they have." The skipper's voice had lost the harsh edge. "We have one of Juliet's key scientists onboard. They're working on some leads right now."

"There have been a lot of leads," he said, his voice distant.

"We've got to try, Bill."

"Trying just means the researchers come down with it too. Even when the treatment centers are in space."

Kazimira hesitated. Laramie watched the captain's eyes narrow as a new thought entered her head.

"You destroyed *Alexander*."

Laramie watched as Drexel bowed his head, eyes closed. He nodded without looking up.

"Marwat had a veritable medical compound on that carrier. He was finding too many infected spacers. Juliet sure as hell didn't want them planetside, so he set up shop. But he got in over his head, Kate. He didn't have the capacity, he didn't appreciate what a contagious disease this is. He was releasing anyone with mild symptoms back to their vessels. He was breaking quarantine. We had orders to put an end to it before it spiraled out of control."

"You don't really believe that, do you?" Kazimira said.

Drexel blinked. "What is that supposed to mean?"

"We boarded *Alexander*, Bill. We have the logs. We have the bridge recorders. Marwat didn't release anyone. He received orders to euthanize them, orders from Juliet. He wouldn't do it. His teams were working on treatment right up until the end."

"He was letting them go, Kate."

"No, he wasn't." Kazimira floated closer to Drexel. "We have all the records. He refused orders to murder a bunch of refugees. He refused to replace humanitarian outreach with search-and-destroy missions. And the whole time, he did everything he could to keep it from spreading, at great risk to himself and his crew."

Drexel shook his head. "No. You're reading those logs wrong. There are missing details."

"You think Colonel Marwat wasn't explicit with details?"

Laramie was starting to feel uncomfortable. In Caustic Team, there were so many stories about Colonel Acevedo's focus over operations that troopers joked he eavesdropped on their neural stubs. She didn't know Marwat, but she had a hard time imagining he would be any different.

"Who sent *Myrmidon*?" Kazimira asked.

"Earth."

The air seemed to rush out of the room.

Laramie glanced at her platoon leader. Surely she had misheard. The intense stare coming back at her from Chappelle told her she hadn't.

Kazimira spoke carefully. "Earth sent them."

"Of course," Drexel said. "Can you find me another shipyard that can build military spacecraft? Not to mention one with those capabilities. I'm sure you noticed the upgraded capacitors."

"Yes. Two shots to our one."

Silence fell over them. Kazimira folded her arms and studied her prisoner. Chappelle's face was an enigma. Laramie kept glancing around the tiny room, her mind reeling, unable to process what she was hearing.

Drexel's eyes defocused again and he spoke in a distant voice. "Do you know how many spacecraft we blew to hell, Kate? Trying to stop the spread?"

"It's not important right now," Kazimira replied. "What matters is you pulled back today. You gave us a chance to help you."

Drexel didn't seem to hear. His seemed to be reading through some kind of mental inventory. "All those intercepts. So many to hunt down. So many lives."

"Bill."

"How many were based on lies, I wonder?"

"*Bill.*"

Drexel blinked. He looked up at the skipper.

"This fight is still going on," Kazimira said. "Help me. I need details—Dagger's operational capabilities, *Myrmidon*, mission orders. We can bring more resources into Alpha A. But I need your help to do it right."

"There is no way to do it right."

"Bill, snap out of it. You are a RESIT captain—"

"Did you have constricted aboard *Vigorous*?" Drexel said, interrupting.

"What?"

"When we were told to intercept you, they said you'd been exposed to constriction. A recon team had verified it. Is that true?"

Kazimira seemed to be weighing what to share. "There is that possibility, yes."

Drexel stared hard at her for a few moments. Then, seemingly satisfied, he nodded.

"Help us fight this, Bill," Kazimira said.

"I've done what I can. I wish it were more."

The skipper drew her lips tight. Laramie sensed anger returning, hidden behind the professional exterior.

"Captain Chappelle, escort Captain Drexel to the brig."

"Aye, ma'am."

Chappelle gave Laramie a nod and they each took one of the prisoner's elbows. As they headed toward the hatch, Laramie could feel the heat from the captain's gaze on the backs of their necks.

43

The next seventy-two hours proved to be some of the most exhausting in Laramie's career. Damage-control rotations and a shortage of able-bodied troopers meant lots of fatigue, and a stimulant diet made dangerous work even more so. The rest of her company struggled along with her. One trooper nearly ran out of oxygen when he got trapped behind a bulkhead that shifted under acceleration. Another work team exceeded their allowed radiation dose in the power plant room. By the time she collapsed in her own bunk, Laramie had no trouble falling asleep. She didn't even know where she was when her comm blared in her ear.

"Battle Squad, this is Wyatt. Report to Ready Room B in five minutes."

"Oh, LT," Laramie mumbled. "Why?"

A half-open eye revealed that no one else was in the enlisted berth. She seized the unexpected privacy to clean herself up and remove several layers of dried sweat. When she was done and moved toward the hatch, she caught sight of her ARC vest hanging crookedly in her locker. Three of its ablative pucks were missing and she hadn't even noticed.

Her feet carried her where she needed to go without any real conscious direction. When she walked into the ready room, Wyatt was leaning against the small podium at the front. Three people sat with their backs to her.

"Hey," Wyatt said. He nodded to her to have a seat.

She stumbled with weary steps toward the remnants of Battle Squad. Gavin and Rash gave her a nod as she sat. Chris's gaze seemed to linger.

Wyatt watched them for a moment before he said anything.

"I'm going to cut right to it, guys. Havoc Company got hammered in that last action. We lost Third Platoon completely, and sixty percent casualties across others, including ours." He hesitated, his eyes flitting to each one of them. "This is what's left of our squad."

Silence ruled the room. Just five of them now—no one killed, but Carlos, Kenny, and Finn were all badly hurt and out of the rotation. Laramie stole another glance at the others. Rash stared at the deck, his fingers tracing the orange ink of the tattoos on his arm. Gavin's eyes were locked on the LT. Chris seemed to notice her attention and watched her with a bland expression.

"I have a couple things to cover with you," Wyatt continued. "First, Beck's ordered a reshuffling of personnel to scrape what's left of our platoons together. First Platoon will remain under Captain Chappelle, but Chemo got decimated, so they'll be replaced by Echo. As for Battle, we're going to absorb Washington from Chemo, and

Landauer and Sims from Fury. Try to make them feel like part of the team. Our guys are all going to survive. A lot of others didn't."

"LT?" Laramie said. "You said *Sims* is getting folded into our squad? He's a lieutenant."

Wyatt held up his hand. "We'll talk about that in a minute."

"Okay." She felt uneasy. It sounded like she was about to be displaced as a fire team leader.

"Second thing," Wyatt continued. "It's pretty obvious our task force is now combat ineffective. Kazimira's made the decision to pull back to Proxima. We lost both the Fast Attack and the destroyer. *Vigorous* is barely holding together. Dagger is still in control of the system, and McManus still controls Juliet.

"Even though we can't perform direct action, Beck doesn't want to lose sight of the situation here. Our new platoons are going back to Juliet. This is going to be a covert observation mission. We will insert via Javelin and set up forward observation posts outside the main population centers. When Beck comes back with reinforcements, we'll need intel on the opposition's activities and on the spread of constriction."

Wyatt peered hard at Chris. "Surveillance is the primary objective. Not engagement. A bunch of troopers getting themselves killed is not conducive to that end. Understood?"

"Understood," Chris said, not quite convincingly.

Laramie felt compelled to answer for the squad. "LT, we got this. Once we get on the surface, we'll follow your lead and get it done the way you want."

A strange expression crossed Wyatt's face. "I'm not going," he said.

Laramie blinked. "What?"

"That was that last thing I needed to tell you all."

A knot started to ball up in Laramie's stomach. She didn't like how this was going at all.

"Major Beck wants me with him," Wyatt explained. "He needs to brief RESIT brass about the situation here, and he wants me to relate what we know about fighting constriction. He says along with Bell and Elton, I'm one of his primary experts on that matter."

"Then who's going to be leading our squad?" Gavin asked.

"Second Lieutenant Sims, reporting to Chappelle."

"LT," Laramie said, "with respect, Sims is green. I know he's an officer, but he doesn't have many ground missions under his belt."

"Chappelle does." He gave her a hard look. "And so do you. You'll need to help him."

She frowned.

Wyatt looked like he wanted to say more. He scanned the room, his eyes resting for a moment on each of his troopers. After a few moments he stood up from the podium and cleared his throat.

"You guys have been like family to me. Stay safe and good luck. Dismissed."

With that, Laramie watched her best friend and squad leader exit the room.

***

Jack Bell pulled open another storage locker and rummaged through the scattered contents. He couldn't find burn cream anywhere. The computer's inventory count said there should be more supply here in the med bay, but every locker he opened revealed a mess from desperate hands raiding it before him. No one had bothered to scan what they took in the rush to treat the wounded.

"Epione, there's none here," he said. He slammed the locker shut so hard, the door rebounded open.

An ethereal voice projected a calm that was almost annoying. "Inventory control says there are six units in Locker E—"

"Inventory is wrong, and I've got troopers going out of their mind in pain. Find me another store."

"Yes, Doctor Bell. One moment."

The truth was, the med bay was in shambles. Desperate corpsmen had trashed the place looking for supplies to treat the dozens of injured in the enlisted mess. And to top it off, a laser strike had severed the main power trunk, leaving every berth on this side of the spacecraft to run on emergency power only. Epione's arm wouldn't even unfold from the ceiling.

But Bell was a physician. He had chosen this profession because he wanted to save as many lives as possible. Even if it meant making some of the toughest choices imaginable. Even if it meant designing Firebreak.

You did what you had to do, Jack. Because of Firebreak, at least some will live.

He wanted to believe his own justifications. He needed to if he was going to live with himself.

"Doctor, there are six units of silver sulfadiazine in the secure locker located in the pharmacy," Epione said. "The concentration level may be higher than what you are looking for, but given the misplacement of—"

"That's fine."

Bell stepped through the hatch to the adjacent medical compartment. Scanning the room, he found the locker he was looking for on the far bulkhead. He started to walk toward it, but his feet felt heavy with reluctance.

Kenta died here.

An empty supply can in the center of the floor marked where his colleague had been murdered. A good woman. A dedicated woman. Dumped on the floor like the sterile wrappers and bits of trash that lay there now.

How had it gone down? Why? Chris Thompson claimed the scout crew saw Corporal Jameson and immediately conspired to kill him. If that were true, Bell could understand the fear, the panic. Anyone who had been on Juliet near an outbreak understood the danger. The burning sparks would either seize your mind in attack or slip into a siren call inviting you to rapture. Either meant the end, one way or another.

But Annika Hewitt somehow resisted both. So had Corporal Jameson. Whatever had happened to them had proven not to be contagious. Kenta hadn't been infected.

The Dagger spacers had shot her anyway.

Scowling, Bell forced himself across the compartment. Ignorant fools, those spacers. Kenta had a good mind. She knew how to use Epione, how to stabilize Annika, how to draw conclusions from the tests on Jameson. She might have been able to help find a cure. No, she *would* have found a cure. It was all gone now, thrown away like the dreams of all the other wasted lives.

He tugged on the pharmacy locker door and found it wouldn't budge.

"Epione, unlock the secure locker."

A metallic *clack* sounded behind the thin metal. Bell pushed the latch button to find an array of plastic vials lined up in a storage rack. He removed them one by one and filled the pockets of his physician smock.

Why hadn't Jameson been contagious? Why wasn't Annika?

That was still a mystery. Perhaps it would prove to be the biggest mystery.

Both had constriction. He was certain—the eyes, the mute voices. And, for lack of a better word, the quantum communication. Annika had used it to ward off the trooper in the hangar and again in the lab on Juliet. There was something there—something vital to understanding this threat, he knew it. Just as ancient researchers had stumbled on penicillin in their petri dishes, the recording he had made of this quantum interaction might prove to be the key in preventing the disease from annihilating life on Juliet.

Kenta won't be part of the discovery.

Such a waste. So much waste.

Bell blinked. He found himself standing in front of a large cylinder. The decompression chamber? Huh. He'd walked straight through the main med bay and into the other compartment. Now he was staring at the far bulkhead, his unfocused eyes transfixed by a flash of red reflecting near the floor.

He bent down and peered closer. Underneath a foldable patient bed, amid sterile wrappers and empty medication containers, a red light repeated a slow cadence, as if calling to him.

A personal tablet computer. The low-battery light crying for help.

Was it Kenta's?

A sudden urge filled him to see what her last thoughts might have been. What was she working on before she'd moved on into the beyond? Tracking lab tests? Thoughts of family? She knew they were going into a battle. Maybe she had dashed off an odd missive to a spouse, a daughter, a son?

He should do something to make sure nothing like that was lost. Kenta deserved better.

Bell got down on his knees and scooped the device from the deck. The size was wrong for an adult. This tablet was made for small hands, school-age hands. The momentary elation he'd felt suddenly vanished into the air like the vacuum of a hull breach.

He switched it on anyway. A written lesson plan appeared on the touchscreen. Nothing fancy, no diagrams or 3D holo models. It didn't even look like it was formatted for neural stubs. It was just a middle-grade history book that probably lost a kid's attention in less time than it took to turn the page.

He flipped through a couple of the pages, scanning through the text as if paying a last homage to the normalcy it once represented. He finished a paragraph on Duncan Piper, the captain of *Longshot*, the pioneering mission that brought mankind to Juliet. Everyone knew that story. A lifetime in a space capsule, tremendous isolation, mental strain turned to psychological trauma. All the preparation from the best mission planners hadn't been able to shore up the inherent frailty of the human mind. Piper's story was the epic tragedy of a man gone insane. His tragedy had informed every subsequent spaceflight.

This tablet belonged to Calista. Finn's daughter. Bell remembered her visiting Annika, goofing around and gushing thanks that her friend had survived. God, that was weeks ago. She obviously hadn't been interested enough in her studies to notice her missing tablet.

But in a testament to power conservation, the battery had hung on all that time.

You can hold on too, Jack.

He had work to do. He had injured troopers writhing in pain from radiation burns and laser fire. But Bell knew his meticulousness bordered on obsessive-compulsive, so he wasn't surprised to find himself swiping tabs to save lessons and close bookmarks on the tablet. It just wouldn't do to leave everything open in active memory to consume whatever was left of the battery.

He kept swiping until he came to a simple notepad that had a series of phrases written in multiple lines.

SCHOOLWORK.

THAT'S NOT WHY!

HISTORY.

THAT'S NOT OUR PLANET.

WE'RE LEARNING HOW DUNCAN PIPER DISCOVERED JULIET.

BUT CAPTAIN PIPER FLEW HERE.

HE MUST HAVE BEEN OLD.

WOW.

I CAN'T REMEMBER.

WHAT DID THEY DO BEFORE?

THEY BUILT BABY ROBOTS?

SOMETIMES I FEEL LIKE A BABY ROBOT.

Bell scowled. More child nonsense, he supposed. This level of notetaking wouldn't earn a passing grade in any class he knew of. He raised his finger to swipe one last time.

A distant thought made him hesitate. What was it? Something ... maybe something Sergeant Thompson said to the girls while sitting in the med bay?

He suppressed a chuckle. If Thompson said it, it had to have been something juvenile.

No, that wasn't it. What was it?

His eyes went back to the tablet. He had already closed the lesson plan about Longshot. Only the notepad remained open. But he remembered some of the text that had covered the mission.

But Captain Piper flew here.

Yes, he did. And he killed his five crewmates. He went insane after sixty years cooped up in a can.

What did they do before? the tablet said.

Bell searched his memory. Scattershot. That was the name of the mission before Piper's. A flight of auto-surveyor probes.

They built baby robots.

Auto-surveyors were programmed to replicate themselves. Locate native resources, mine them, build copies. After achieving enough quantity, the probes would construct a communication node to transmit survey data back to Earth.

Sometimes I feel like a baby robot.

He frowned. Something was off. Just ... wrong. What?

Bell blinked. Thompson. He was standing next to Thompson's bed.

Calista hadn't come in here, had she?

No. As a visitor, she'd been limited to the main med bay.

But Annika hadn't.

His eyes read the words again.

Sometimes I feel like a baby robot.

Bell felt the frown stretch across his face.

"No. That's ... crazy."

The battery light abruptly cut off. Bell tried to swipe one last save, but his hands were shaking too badly.

44

"Slow down, Jack. I'm not following." Wyatt was beyond tired, and Bell had barged in while he was in the middle of transferring his command key over to Sims in the commlink directory.

"Of course," Bell said. The doctor stroked his chin, collecting himself, then moved around Wyatt's desk and sat against the edge. Wyatt winced at the invasion of his personal space but didn't have the will left to push back.

The doctor turned to him. "Constriction. What if we're wrong about it being a disease?"

"Doctor, I'm—"

"Are you familiar von Neumann probes? No— of course not, let me ... they're self-replicating spacecraft. Cheap. Simple. Instead of one expensive probe, you send out a bunch of simpler devices, so all your eggs aren't in one basket. They reach a destination, mine local resources from moons, asteroids, whatever. Then they build copies of themselves. And you get this expanding net of probes able to search in a far more efficient manner than a single entity."

Bell paused as if he expected Wyatt to have some major aha moment.

Wyatt stared back dumbly.

The doctor cleared his throat and continued. "We used this schema to scout Alpha Centauri. Project Scattershot. That's how we knew Juliet would be habitable before we committed a live crew. Small spacecraft, high speed, inserted into the system. Worked beautifully. The probes built enough of themselves to size up Juliet and send their report back to Earth. By the time Longshot was funded, we knew there would be pay dirt that would support life at the end."

"And what does this have to do with constriction?"

"The same pattern." Bell was working his hands together like he did when he got excited. "Scattershot was just a physical version of the model.   But suppose you weren't interested in exploring lifeless systems. What if you only cared to collect data if you found life? Forget mining iron and silicates. You could use biologics as your raw materials.   Just hijack the physiological functions of a lifeform and you don't have to build anything. You just ... repurpose."

Wyatt looked longingly at his holo monitor. "Jack, I'm tired.   I have six more credential transfers I've got to finish before—"

"Maybe I'm not being clear.   Compare constriction with Scattershot.   The replication rates are similar. We haven't been able to stop the contagion, but it has slowed.   We assume the slowdown is from Firebreak. What if it's because the probe count has achieved critical mass? That's exactly how Scattershot was designed.   Once it had enough probes to form an amplified data transmission back to Earth, the mission parameters changed away from replication and more toward exploration."

Wyatt struggled to keep up. He wanted to finish his work and catch some sleep. Even if he was lucky, he was probably only looking at four or five hours before he was back up again. But he knew Bell, and he knew he wouldn't get a dismissal unless he tried. "Let me get this straight. You think constriction is some kind of probe?"

"Maybe," Bell said, sighing. "I don't know. But just think about this for a moment. Look at what constricted people do in their ... downtime. They lie prone in those little circles with their heads together. That doesn't make any sense for a disease, does it?"

"No, but—"

"And if there's some kind of quantum interaction occurring, something like we've seen with Annika Hewitt, perhaps they're transmitting reports somewhere? Maybe not even just transmitting. What if they're receiving? Firmware updates. New instructions that helped them adapt." Bell's face darkened. "Perhaps like how to use a laser cutter and cut into a main power trunk? A way to remove a potential threat?"

Wyatt shook his head. He heard the words, but they weren't making sense. Bell was babbling.

"There's even an error rate, Lieutenant," Bell said. "Scattershot was building probes in the field, not a factory. Some had problems. They wouldn't behave right—they'd mine the wrong materials, they couldn't connect to the bot network. They had orphans." He lifted his chin and peered directly at Wyatt. "*We* have orphans. Annika Hewitt. Corporal Jameson."

The doctor fell silent in apparent satisfaction that he had made his case.

Wyatt leaned back and looked at the doctor. He felt like his eyes were made of lead.

"Kazimira has us pulling out of the system, Jack," he said. "We're headed to Proxima. And then you, and I, are going to spend the next couple weeks debriefing the top brass on opposing force strength and the state of the planet surface. Are you really going to walk in there and lay some half-baked scientific babble on the table? You know what we call that in RESIT?"

"What?"

"A turd."

Bell blinked. He crossed his arms and drew a deep breath. "Yeah. I have thought about that, actually."

"And?" Wyatt said, trying his best not to yawn.

"Well, we'll need proof."

"And where's that going to come from?"

"I think our best bet is *Longshot*."

Wyatt frowned. "Come again?"

"*Longshot*. Piper's spacecraft."

"The actual spacecraft," Wyatt said, incredulous.

"That's right." Bell leaned forward. "Quite a historic vessel, that vanguard of humanity's expansion. Very strange that it was lost. Very strange that, even with all of RESIT's surveillance and recon capabilities, some ancient junker of a spacecraft has been missing all this time."

Wyatt sighed. This had to be a joke.

"Doctor, come on. Space is big. Spacecraft disappear. Piper went to the zoo, so if he killed his entire crew, who knows what the hell he did with his ship? He probably drove it right into Alpha A. The man went batshit crazy."

A grave expression fell over Doctor Jack Bell's face.

"We're talking about constriction."

Wyatt cocked his head. Huh?

Bell lowered his voice to a whisper. "I don't think Piper went crazy, Lieutenant. In fact, he might have been the only sane person left.

"And that's why we have to find out what happened to him."

ABOUT THE AUTHOR

Jonathan Isaacs never thought he'd be a writer.

In college, he studied to be an engineer. But after years of his wife telling the screaming children to "use their words" (which comes naturally to neither toddlers nor engineers), he too decided to give it a go. Now what he says even occasionally makes sense.

Isaacs now works as a technology executive in Texas, where his hobbies include poking fun at other technology executives.

Check him out on his website at http://jpisaacsauthor.com/ for the latest noise he's making around writing the next book.

You can find him on Facebook at: http://www.facebook.com/jpisaacsauthor.

Follow him on Twitter at @jpisaacsauthor.

Or if you want a late-night conversation, drop him a line at jpisaacsauthor@gmail.com because he works in the technology industry, doesn't sleep, and is actually a robot.

ALSO BY JONATHAN PAUL ISAACS

Printed in Great Britain
by Amazon